# What Reviewers Say About Boli

**Kim Baldwin**

"*Force of Nature* is filled with nonstop, fast paced action. Tornadoes, raging fire blazes, heroic and daring rescues…Baldwin does a fine job of describing the fast-paced scenes and inspiring the reader to keep on turning the pages." – L-word.com Literature

**Rose Beecham**

"…her characters seem fully capable of walking away from the particulars of whodunit and engaging the reader in other aspects of their lives." – *Lambda Book Report*

**Georgia Beers**

"Beers weaves a tale of yearning, love, lust, and conflict resolution. She has constructed a believable plot, with strong characters in a charming setting." – *JustAboutWrite*

**Ronica Black**

"*Wild Abandon* tells how these two women come to realize that 'life was too precious to be ruled by…fears, by…demons.' While these two women struggle with their issues, there is some very, very hot sex. If you enjoy complex characters and passionate sex scenes, you'll love *Wild Abandon*." – *MegaScene*

**Gun Brooke**

"*Course of Action* is a romance…populated with a host of captivating and amiable characters. The glimpses into the lifestyles of the rich and beautiful people are rather like guilty pleasures…a most satisfying and entertaining reading experience." – *Midwest Book Review*

**Cate Culpepper**

"…an exceptional storyteller who has taken on a very difficult subject …and turned it into a spellbinding novel. As an author, she understands well that fiction can teach us our own history." – *JustAboutWrite*

**Jane Fletcher**

"*The Exile and the Sorcerer* is a mesmerizing read, a tour-de-force packed with adventure, ordeals, complex twists and turns, and the internal introspection of appealing characters." – *Midwest Book Review*

**JD Glass**

"*Punk Like Me*…is different. It is engaging. It is life-affirming. Frankly, it is genius. This is a rare book in that it has a soul; one that is laid bare for all to see." – *JustAboutWrite*

**Grace Lennox**

"*Chance* is refreshing…Every nuance is powerful and succinct. *Chance* is not a novel about the music industry; it is about a woman discovering herself as she muddles through all the trappings of fame." – *Midwest Book Review*

**Lee Lynch**

"Lynch, with a dozen novels to her credit dating back to the early days of Naiad Press, has earned her stripes as a writerly elder. She was contributing stories to the lesbian magazine *The Ladder* four decades ago. But this latest is sublimely in tune with the times." – *Q-Syndicate*

**JLee Meyer**

"*Forever Found*…neatly combines hot sex scenes, humor, engaging characters, and an exciting story." – *MegaScene*

**Radclyffe**

"…well-plotted…lovely romance…I couldn't turn the pages fast enough!" – Ann Bannon, author of *The Beebo Brinker Chronicles*

**Susan Smith**

"This disparate duo's lush rush of a romance - which incorporates reincarnation, a grounded transman and his peppy daughter, and the dark moods of a troubled witch - pays wonderful homage to Leslie Feinberg's classic gender-bending novel, *Stone Butch Blues*." – *Q-Syndicate*

**Ali Vali**

"Rich in character portrayal, *The Devil Inside* by Ali Vali is an unusual, unpredictable, and thought-provoking love story that will have the reader questioning the definition of right and wrong long after she finishes the book." – *JustAboutWrite*

# Rising Storm

*by*

JLee Meyer

2007

**RISING STORM**



ISBN-10: 1-933110-86-4
ISBN-13: 978-1-933110-86-8

This Trade Paperback Original Is Published By
Bold Strokes Books, Inc.,
New York, USA

First Edition: August 2007.



---

**Credits**
Editors: Shelley Thrasher, and Stacia Seaman
Production Design: Stacia Seaman
Cover Design By Sheri (GRAPHICARTIST2020@HOTMAIL.COM)

## By the Author

Forever Found

First Instinct

# Acknowledgments

I have been blessed with many teachers along the way:

Shelley Thrasher steadfastly kept after me until I did it right.

Jennifer Knight told me what to cut to make it better, and she was spot on.

Sheri, of course, continues to dazzle with her cover art.

Stacia Seaman was always right there to answer technical problems or give friendly advice.

Radclyffe continues to set the bar and lead this wonderful community of authors, staff, and volunteers.

## Dedication

For Cheryl—I became a part of your soft world twenty years ago. You make all things possible.

# CHAPTER ONE

Conn Stryker strode into the cabin surrounded by redwoods and phoned Colonel Maggie Cunningham, her liaison to a world she had chosen years before and now wanted to leave. Ten years of cloak-and-dagger was enough. Then there was Leigh.

"Hi, Maggie. I'm checking in. Any news?"

"Yeah. The Highway 1 incident was reported as a one-vehicle accident. In fact, Caltrans is probably out there now trying to pull the truck wreckage out of the water. We've already cleaned up the accident site. It looked like quite a struggle took place. Jess said that your aunt Jen's house was pretty messed up, too. How's Ms. Grove?"

Conn felt her throat tighten at the mention of Leigh. She had never wanted Leigh associated with her other world. She'd almost gotten her killed in her effort to protect her.

"She's asleep. It's been a helluva few days."

"I realize—"

"Do you know if they're still after us? We stopped halfway up the coast for supplies. If Dieter or his thugs come looking, the teenage boy who rang us up will remember Leigh. She's hard to forget." Conn slapped her forehead as soon as she made the comment. She knew Maggie wouldn't miss it.

After a brief hesitation, Maggie quipped, "So is a six-foot beauty with auburn hair."

Silent, Conn barely registered the words, her heart and mind at war. She wanted Leigh for the rest of her life, but she knew their relationship could be a death sentence for Leigh and that she should end it while she still had enough determination.

Maggie moved on smoothly. "Our last intel reported Dieter and the woman we think is his lieutenant, Georgia Johnson, have crossed into Canada. But with 3,500 miles of border, that might not mean much. I don't feel good about this, Conn. The people in charge of Dieter base their lives on revenge. They won't forget that a woman discovered their stock scheme and set the feds on them. If nothing else, Dieter will lose his job, and probably his life, if he doesn't seek retribution. Until we know more, we really should put Ms. Grove in a safe house. I know she refused yesterday, but think about it."

The thought of separating from Leigh so soon made Conn queasy. "We discussed it, Maggie. I told her…who I am. She wants to stay with me."

Was she being selfish? The memory of the previous night made her ache with desire. Perhaps their love for each other had clouded logic. She didn't really have a choice. As much as Conn wanted her to stay, Leigh needed to be safe, and Conn had to make the logical decision.

"I'll call you back, Maggie. Thanks for the advice."

She flipped the phone closed, leaned her forehead against the cool windowpane, and stared bleakly into the distance.

Leigh materialized by her side, slid into Conn's arms and held her close, then kissed her lightly on the ear.

The kiss sent a shock wave through Conn. *Dear God. Just tell her. Before you lose your senses.*

"I…I just talked to Maggie again. They don't know who, if anyone, might still be pursuing us, Leigh, but you need to be in a safe house until we have more details." She knew her tone didn't match her words, but she couldn't help it.

Leigh's face registered surprise and hurt. "I thought we'd discussed this, Conn. I won't be separated from you again."

"But you have no idea what these people can do."

Leigh's eyes narrowed and she moved away, folding her arms and staring intently at Conn. "I beg your pardon? I know *exactly* what these people can do. They tried to do it to me several times."

Conn fumbled for words. "No, I mean, I have to keep you safe, Leigh! If anything happened to you…" Her throat refused to let the words come out, but finally she managed to confess, "I don't think I could survive that."

Her words seemed to only steel Leigh's resolve. "No."

"Listen, Leigh. That kid that waited on us in the convenience store yesterday will remember you. All it would take is one slightly underfunctioning goon to trace us to this area. I don't want to take any chances. I think—"

Leigh raised a hand. "Don't do this to me, to us. I'm safe when I'm with you, not someone else." She seemed to notice Conn's running suit and boots for the first time. "Have you been outside?"

Conn could only nod. The color of Leigh's eyes rendered her mute. They ranged from teal to indigo, but now they were gunmetal.

"Do you love me, Conn?" Leigh's voice was husky, her expression focused.

Conn was helpless to tell anything but the truth. "More than anything in my life. More than my life."

Leigh slid her arms around Conn's neck, and Conn reflexively embraced her as she forced herself to say, "The risk is more than—"

Leigh put a finger on Conn's lips and gently shushed her, her eyes bright with tears. "It's more risky to be separated again. My heart can't take it. I won't do it."

They kissed softly at first, but their passion was overwhelming, making Conn weak with need.

Leigh took her hand and led her to the couch in front of the fire Conn had made when she came inside. "Now," was all she said before she slipped her shirt off her shoulders to reveal her beautiful full breasts and a scorching invitation in her eyes. She untied the string holding up her sweatpants and they dropped to the floor. As she stepped out of them Conn reached for her, but she backed away. "Let me see you."

Leigh's body created a perfect storm in Conn, and within seconds, she stood naked before her, aware that her nipples were hard. Leigh's eyes on them only increased the ache.

Reclining on the sofa, Leigh opened herself to Conn. "Anything."

"All I want is you. All of you. Only you." Conn settled on top of Leigh and moaned in pleasure at the contact. Daylight revealed the flawless skin that she had touched all night, heightening her arousal. Their bodies undulated together as their kisses reflected the urgent need their words had created.

"Need you, Conn." Leigh sounded breathless.

As Conn slid her fingers inside, she gasped at how wet and open, how ready Leigh was. She stroked the delicate folds and found her center, hard and pulsing. Placing her thumb over Leigh's clitoris, she entered her and put her body weight behind her thrusts. "I want you to look in my eyes when you come. When…we…come." The words barely emerged. Her own body was already in overdrive.

She cried out as Leigh grazed her center and slipped inside, matching her strokes.

They held one another's gazes as they moved, and Conn existed in a place of reverence and awe as she experienced the type of love and trust she'd always longed for. She stilled, tight and expanded at once, then crashed through whatever had held her back in the past, not knowing if their union lasted forever or a second, but she was sure of one thing: they would stay together until Leigh told her to leave.

# CHAPTER TWO

The sun was high when Conn opened her eyes and looked down at Leigh sleeping in her arms. Hard to believe that less than forty-eight hours before, they had been running for their lives. Now here she was with the woman who had occupied her dreams for months. Without thinking, she kissed the head of blond hair that stuck out in all directions. After making love on the couch they had barely made it back to bed before lust claimed them again.

Leigh stirred, made a few small noises, and tightened her hold on Conn. Her eyes opened slowly. "Mornin'." She turned over and pushed back into Conn, spooning her.

When Conn responded in kind and they gently rocked together for a moment, the fire threatened to reignite.

Leigh turned to Conn and kissed her, then kissed her again. But when Conn pulled her on top of herself, she winced.

"What's wrong? Your shoulder?" Conn wouldn't have been surprised if Leigh's shoulder had stiffened. Some of their activities the night before had been athletic, not to mention the damage that had been inflicted on Leigh by the men who had chased them from San Francisco before Conn had rescued her.

Leigh kissed her lightly on the lips once more, then let her head drop into the crook of Conn's neck. After staying that way for a few minutes, she met her eyes.

"Let's just say I'm a little sore. It's been a long time since I've had sex of any kind, and I have never, *never* had two nights like that. I just don't think I can. I hope that's okay." She looked almost apologetic, though she quickly beamed. "But I could make love to *you* all day, no problem. As a matter of fact, I would treasure it."

Conn suspected her grin was slightly lopsided, but it was the best she could muster. "Well, now that you mention it, I'm in the same boat. To say it's been a while would be an understatement." She looked directly into Leigh's eyes. "But the desire is there, believe me."

Leigh moaned and rolled off her. "My God, you're going to kill me. Give me your hand." She placed it between her own legs.

Conn looked at her tenderly, then began to stroke her.

"I can't. Please." Leigh placed her hands over Conn's. "I just wanted you to know that my body reacts to you all by itself. Now, no more sexy looks or I'll never survive the day. And neither will you, by the way."

"Promises, promises."

"Let's find some very soft, loose things to wear, and I'll make breakfast. Maybe you could warm the place up. Without you as my blanket, I'm freezing."

Conn marveled at her extraordinary fortune to have Leigh return her affection. She was not only beautiful and intelligent, she was a passionate, caring lover. And she seemed to think Conn was, too. Leigh could have anyone, male or female, but had chosen Conn and repeatedly shown her how much her choice was a fact, not a possibility. Conn even dared to trust that choice. The idea quickly raised a red flag of self-protective caution in Conn, but she consciously chose to ignore the warning.

After she crawled out of bed, she found fresh warm-ups for both of them, then aimed for the thermostat and firewood. She smiled when she heard Leigh in the kitchen.

❖

Conn gazed at Leigh as they ate, slowly sweeping with her tongue for any errant crumbs, real or imagined, on her lips.

"Oh…my." Leigh couldn't take her eyes off Conn's mouth. She forced herself to take a sip of coffee, willing her body to calm down, but the tongue distracted her. As she watched Conn, her nipples began to ache, so she folded her arms and tried for a stern expression.

"I, ah, I don't know how to explain this, so this is the best I can do. I've never had a lover before, and you've opened a floodgate that I can't control. Please don't tease me right now." She unconsciously reached over and covered Conn's hand with her own, which felt like the most natural movement in the world.

Conn quietly studied their hands and nodded. "I apologize. I feel the same way about you. I just can't stop. It's so wonderful to care about someone and have her care about you, too. I'll be good." They sat quietly for a moment, Conn lost in their closeness.

"Leigh? You said you've never had a lover. You were engaged to Peter. Didn't you count him as a lover?" The thought of Leigh with anyone, man or woman, hurt Conn, but she had to ask.

Leigh looked away and seemed to consider the question. "I haven't thought much about it. He was my boyfriend, my boss, my fiancé. But I never thought of him as my lover. Ever." Her eyes drifted back to Conn's. "You're the only one."

Their hands parted as Conn sighed and sat back, still holding Leigh's gaze. "And now, *I'm* in trouble. I suppose it serves me right, but we'd better get out of the house or we're liable to hurt each other. Want to hang out in Mendocino, then go to a women's bar in Fort Bragg tonight?"

"That sounds like a plan."

"I'll clean the kitchen while you shower."

Leigh laughed, her eyes sparkling in the late morning light. "You think I need a shower? Well, you might be right. I don't want a pack of dogs to follow me around today."

❖

As Conn dried the kitchen counters a thought occurred to her. After tossing the wet dishtowel onto a pile of dirty clothes in the utility room, she walked back through the house to poke her head into the bathroom.

"Hey, Leigh. Did you know that, um, the—" The words died on her lips.

Leigh was naked, leaning over in the shower and apparently trying to figure out the nozzles and faucets. She raised her head when she heard Conn's voice and smiled. "Yes?"

"What? Oh! I came in here to…let's see." Thought was impossible.

"Oh yes, did you know that the shower also has a steam vent? I could, um, show you how it works." Her composure was rapidly dissolving. *Control yourself, Conn. You promised to be good.*

Leigh straightened up and smiled at Conn. "A steam vent? Oh, those are great. Sounds perfect. How does it work?" With a sexy smile she opened the glass door wide.

Conn hesitated but, enticed by Leigh's almost-palpable body heat, she stepped into the shower, still in her sweats. "See, two showerheads, one at each end, and the steam vent up in the ceiling. Press this button and turn the lever to regulate the steam. It's easy." *There, you did that without drooling. Good girl.*

Feeling at least honorable, she turned to find Leigh right behind her. She smiled deliciously and pulled her into a slow, deep kiss.

"Why are you still in sweats?"

"Because I…am…trying…to be…good."

Leigh grinned. "Show me how to turn on this shower over here." She backed away and indicated the one behind her.

Reaching around her, Conn pointed the head down so Leigh wouldn't freeze while the water warmed. The temperature of the room rose when Leigh leaned into her.

"Uh-huh. Now the steam vent."

Conn pushed the button in the ceiling of the shower and then adjusted the lever to a medium setting. Before she could drop her hands, Leigh had eased under Conn's sweatshirt and caressed her breasts, then pulled the shirt off in one motion and tossed it over the shower enclosure.

Conn swayed as Leigh ran her thumbs over her nipples. Already puckered from being so close to Leigh, they were now hard and erect. "But I thought that we—"

"Now the other showerhead. Here, let me." Leigh reached behind Conn, brushing her breasts against her body, then stood upright again, her arousal obvious, and placed her hands on Conn's sweatpants.

"Oops, these are getting wet." She pulled them down, kneeling with them, then urged Conn to step out of them and flung them on top of the sweatshirt. After she wrapped her arms around Conn's hips, she lightly kissed her pubic hair.

"My God, Leigh, I can't stand up."

Leigh quickly stood and leaned Conn against the wall between the two showerheads.

"Better?" She directed the hot water from both heads toward her, then squeezed shower gel into her hands and rubbed them together before lathering Conn's body.

Conn nodded and tried to breathe as steam enveloped them and she heard Leigh's husky voice in her ear. "I'll be gentle, don't worry. And, Conn? Sorry, but I really can't help myself."

The steam and water and lust made reality fade, and she let Leigh caress, suck, and kiss her, gently bringing her to a powerful orgasm within minutes. When she could gather her senses, she was sitting on the built-in bench in the stall, completely spent.

She watched Leigh smile and sing to herself as she soaped her own hair and body, pointedly avoiding the same area she'd just ravished on Conn. Managing to stand, Conn allowed Leigh to bump into her as she put the shampoo bottle down.

"Oh, hi. You okay?" Leigh continued to scrub her scalp as she grinned with her eyes closed. She looked beautiful.

"Yeah. Great, in fact. I was about to help you finish your shower. Let me get some gel."

"You know, Conn, I'm not sure I could—"

Conn gently slid a hand between Leigh's legs and slipped through the swelling she knew was there. "You can't walk around like this all day. And if you don't let me, I'll tease you every minute. Understand?"

Leigh gasped as Conn went inside her. "Okay. Whatever…oh… yes."

Conn lowered her onto the bench, then spread Leigh's legs, knelt, and found her center with her mouth, kneading with her tongue and thumb until Leigh cried out in surrender.

They finally gazed at each other, tepid water streaming over them.

"You know," Leigh managed, "you were right. I wouldn't have made it all day, not after making love to you. Just promise me we don't have to take the motorcycle for a few days. Really."

Conn helped her up. "You got that right."

They finished their shower without too many more distractions.

❖

Leigh carefully picked the loosest pair of jeans she had brought with her. The weeks she and Conn had been apart and the stress she'd been under had taken a few pounds off, so most of her clothes would qualify as loose.

When she looked up, Conn stood there in black jeans, shining black boots, and a periwinkle and black sweater.

"You. Are. Gorgeous."

Conn rolled her eyes and turned pink. "I swear I almost said, 'Aw, shucks.' I must be losing it."

"Are we ready to go? I've got our jackets."

Conn pulled out a small gadget from her pack. Satisfied with the settings, she walked over to a table by the great room's sliding door and positioned it so that only a tiny part was visible between a silk plant and the lamp on the table.

"What *is* that thing? It's so little."

Conn looked up briefly. "Remember that motion detector I used at your apartment after someone had bugged it? Well, this is one step better. It's a digital camera with a security function. It'll take a picture of any movement it detects, and if the movement becomes more active, it'll take more pictures. I can download it onto the laptop and check to see if we've had any visitors."

She saw concern on Leigh's face. "Don't worry, sweetie. I'm a gadget freak, if you haven't noticed. It's new and I'm just trying it out. If we do get any pics, they'll probably be of inquisitive deer or raccoons. I want to know how it works in case we really do need it. The security around here is good because I designed it. This is just a toy."

"Do you think they're close?" Leigh's voice was just above a whisper.

"It's only been a short while, and we still have time before we need to be on alert. They may have decided we aren't worth it. I hope so. But from now on I want to be totally prepared. That's all. This is practice." Conn tried to sound casual.

But Leigh obviously wasn't fooled. "Oh, so that's why you strapped on your trusty skin-diving knife. To be prepared."

Busted. "You noticed. Yeah. You never know when some damned giant squid might leap out of the water and attack. And I'm taking the magic cell phone, too. I aim to take care of us, madam. Oh, and I'd better call before we leave and see if there's anything new on Dieter and Georgia."

The mention of their names deflated what had started as a playful conversation, and Conn didn't know how to restore their light mood. She knew how ruthless Dieter was, as was his co-conspirator and lover Georgia Johnson, who had been Peter's secretary. According to Leigh, Georgia was a calculating bitch, so Conn planned to be extra careful. She couldn't take any chances, not with Leigh.

After Conn phoned in their destination and discovered there was no word from Canada—Dieter and Georgia's last known location—Leigh hugged her, and Conn returned the hug fiercely.

"We should hear something soon. Let's call Paris later and see if we can connect with Aunt Jen. She'd like to hear from us, I'm sure. Maybe Marina is still there, too."

Aunt Jen had flown to Paris to rendezvous with her partner, Marina Kouros, who had taken a break from her assignment in Pakistan. As one of the world's most famous faces in broadcast journalism, Marina often had to meet Jen in faraway places so they could be together, but that had never interfered with their devotion to each other or Conn. Knowing how close Aunt Jen and Leigh had become, Conn was hoping to distract Leigh from the terror Dieter's name evoked.

Finally leaning away from their embrace, Leigh regarded her steadily. "I'd love to talk to them. Conn, I can deal with anything as long as I have you. Don't ever sugarcoat the truth or try to protect me from it."

Conn glanced away, but Leigh's voice called her back. "Hey. Look at me. We stand a better chance together. You don't have to do this by yourself. You've got me now. Don't shut me out."

Unable to stop, Conn blurted, "I just don't know—"

"Hush." Leigh pulled Conn into a tight hug. "Don't go there. I'll say this as often as I need to. I'm a big girl and I make my own choices. I choose you. Now, let's leave before the day is over."

# Chapter Three

During their uneventful drive to Mendocino, Leigh savored the fresh air and company. The ever-present afternoon breeze off the ocean had picked up, and they put on their jackets as they walked to a linen shop.

Conn had told Leigh she needed to talk to Ally, a friend who worked there, but wouldn't say more than that. Though Leigh was curious, she was having fun, and by the time they got to the store, she and Conn were jostling each other and laughing.

After Conn introduced her to Ally, Leigh spent a long time chatting with the friendly young woman as they looked at the merchandise in the store. Immediately attracted to Ally's warmth and enthusiasm, Leigh was glad to meet one of Conn's friends, but couldn't help wondering if they had ever been involved.

Leigh felt her stomach tighten when Conn finally interrupted them, glanced around the room with a serious expression, and said, "Ally, I have a favor to ask."

"Sure, what do you need?" Ally hadn't hesitated, and she regarded Conn evenly with hazel eyes.

"If anyone asks about us, could you not give them any information? We'd appreciate it. And when you see us, let us know who was asking. We'll be around for a few more days."

"No problem. This town is pretty tightly knit. We consider you a townie, so no questions asked and no information given. I'll pass the word."

Just before they left, Conn stopped. "As a matter of fact, we plan to go to Sirens after dinner. If anything comes up, or you want to join us for a drink, we'll see you there."

Ally smiled. "Thanks, I might just do that."

They waved their good-byes.

As they strolled up the wooden sidewalk Leigh said, "You know, I'm grateful she agreed not to tell anyone we're in town, but what if we were serious felons?"

"Remember when I said this town is the pot capital of northern California?"

A light clicked on in Leigh's brain. "Oh, yeah. Got it. Although it might give her a start to know you're a fed. You are, right?"

"Of sorts." Conn continued walking, constantly scrutinizing their surroundings. "She knows I'm not a narc. If I was I could have busted people a long time ago."

They had slowed their pace and turned to each other. If Leigh had been oblivious to the weather before, now it ran through her like a knife and she shivered, zipping her jacket.

Conn put her arm in Leigh's and they started up the street again. "Come on, we need a latte to warm you up and a big cookie to get us through to dinner. Right?"

"Right!" Leigh's appreciation of Conn's talent for distraction deepened.

❖

After they picked up their cookies and coffee, they found a nearby bench with a view of the ocean and the street and sat, side by side, leaning against a weathered wooden building.

"Um, Leigh?"

Conn's tentative tone got Leigh's attention. "Yes."

"Do you mind that I invited Ally to the bar tonight? She seemed to really like you."

Slowly, Leigh replied, "Uh-huh. She likes you, too. She's nice." *And I hope you haven't slept with her.*

"Well, yeah, but not like that. She really hit it off with you. Do you…um…do you want to—?"

The conversation had just taken a 180-degree turn that left Leigh scrambling. "No. Not only no, but hell, no. Why would you ask that question, Conn?"

Now Conn was blushing, not meeting Leigh's eyes. She

leaned forward, apparently finding her boots fascinating. "I was just thinking."

Leigh stared at Conn, amazed. "Conn, take off your shades, sweetie, and look at me."

After Conn did as she requested, doubt and pain in her eyes, Leigh removed her own sunglasses and met her gaze. "I want only you."

Conn looked at her with uncertainty.

Sighing, Leigh said, "Look, I'm truly not the kind of person who dates a lot. When I did go out, most of the time I just wanted to be at home. I had fun, but the rest was a chore, one that I usually avoided. Was that because I was really gay? Perhaps. But most likely it was because I don't do casual dating that well."

She glanced around at the mostly deserted street. "You sure bring up these topics in weird places, but here's what's important. I love you. I want to be with only you. And I'm sure about it. And by the way, I was wondering if you'd ever been involved with Ally."

When Leigh saw first relief, then a mysterious expression in the eyes that so enraptured her, she turned shy and looked down. She hoped her honesty hadn't frightened Conn.

Conn gazed at Leigh and spoke clearly. "I love you, too. I want to be with only you, Leigh. Just you. I want us to last forever. Just so you know, Ally and I have always been just friends."

At that moment a dark car glided up to the curb in front of them, the passenger window lowering as it stopped.

Conn saw it first and roughly shoved Leigh behind her, but relaxed almost immediately. She released Leigh and stood, pulling her up with her.

Leigh's heart pounded with an adrenaline rush as she recognized Jess behind the wheel of Conn's dark blue Audi. Jess had been the chauffeur who had driven them around in San Francisco one night when they double-dated with Leigh's friend Pat and his date. She was also the one in charge of restoring Aunt Jen's house in Bolinas, after the men chasing Leigh had trashed it. If Jess realized she'd interrupted something, she graciously ignored it.

"Hey, you girls need a ride? A really nice ride?" Jess smiled lazily behind wraparound sunglasses, then removed them to reveal large, friendly brown eyes.

Leigh had never really had a chance to look at Jess. Both times they'd met, Leigh had been so distracted she'd paid little attention, and this encounter wasn't much better, having interrupted one of the more important conversations in her life. After she recognized Jess, she needed a moment to wits-gather.

Conn didn't seem to be doing much better. Her cheeks were flushed, but she had at least recognized the car and the driver before Leigh did. "Hey. I wondered if my chariot would show up. How are you, Jess? I expected you to call before I saw you next. Is everything okay?"

Jess got out of the car and stretched, then walked around its front end and up the few steps to where they stood. "Yeah. But we should probably talk. Where did you get that coffee? I'd kill for one right about now."

Conn motioned for her to follow. "Come on. I'll even buy you a cookie." Then she turned to Leigh and winked. "Be back in a minute. Don't forget our conversation."

Leigh gave her a look meant just for her and watched the two stroll down the wooden sidewalk. Jess was long and lanky, almost as tall as Conn, and moved with a grace and a light tread that she had probably developed by training in martial arts. She wore her dark brown hair behind her ears, and her olive complexion completed a handsome package.

She knew Conn considered Jess a friend as well as a colleague. Did she work for the same government agency? Probably. Leigh had previously assumed she was Conn's employee, but when they were at Jen's vandalized house just before they fled up the coast, Conn had said something about Jess bringing in a team. As Leigh sat on the bench, munching her chocolate chip cookie and sipping her latte, she wondered how long they had known each other, and how well.

"Leigh, stop it. It doesn't matter. Weren't you listening to what Conn just said? She and Ally are just friends. The same probably applies to Jess. She loves you. Yeah, but what if it's just physical? Maybe her definition and my definition aren't the same. I mean, look at Jess. Very attractive. What if—"

"Who are you talking to, hon?"

Leigh emerged from her monologue to see Conn a few feet away, clearly looking around for the other party to the conversation. A few seconds later, Jess arrived.

"Me? Oh, uh, no one. Just talking to myself. I do that sometimes."

Leigh smiled weakly and prayed her words hadn't been audible from that distance.

Conn gave her an amused look and they all sat on the bench, with Conn in the middle.

"How's the house?" Leigh did want an update but mostly wanted to divert attention from herself.

Jess sipped her latte. "It's coming along. We needed to replace some of the stuff to update it anyway. Your aunt's friend and some others are taking care of everything else. They're really accomplished craftspeople. When Jen and Marina get back, they'll be pleased."

*So she knows Jen and Marina on a first-name basis. Great.* Leigh fell into silence, but Conn didn't seem to notice.

"How are they?" Jess asked. "Has Marina returned to Pakistan yet? They'll need another week or so to make the house look good, Conn. You know, painting and such."

"I think Marina leaves for Karachi in a few days."

Jess's concern made Leigh like her, though in another way, it made her insecure. Then a thought occurred to her. "Do you have someone special, Jess?" She could feel Conn stiffen a bit beside her, but because her head was turned toward Jess, she didn't know if she'd just made a big mistake.

Jess kept her eyes on the ocean. "No. Not now. Not for a while. My partner…is dead."

Feeling like a complete ass, Leigh mumbled, "I'm so sorry. I didn't mean to pry."

Jess finally smiled at her, a sad smile. "Actually, I'm glad you did. It's been two years. No one asks, because they want to be polite and all. I just realized that it doesn't hurt as much anymore." She took a bite of cookie and chewed thoughtfully.

Leigh wasn't sure if the conversation was over or not.

"She was an FBI agent, killed in the line of duty. We always agreed that if something happened to one of us, the other would get on with her life, but I haven't."

Leigh leaned back against the building and watched the ocean's constant movement as it undulated toward the shore. She knew there was simply nothing to say.

Taking her sunglasses off, Leigh asked, "Would you join us for dinner tonight?"

"I'd like that," Jess said. "I actually haven't seen much of Ms.

Conn for a while. It would be nice to catch up, but I have to do some shopping first, and I need to find a place to stay tonight. I'd planned to exchange vehicles and drive back, though dinner sounds more fun, and I can pick up the motorcycle tomorrow."

Conn began to say something, but Leigh got there first. "Why don't you stay with us? Right, Conn? I'll make breakfast before you have to leave. Is that okay, hon?"

Taking her hand, Conn smiled and turned to her colleague, obviously aware that she was making her relationship public. "That would be great. How about it, Jess?"

Jess dropped her eyes to their hands. "That's okay. There are tons of places around here. I don't want to impose."

"No imposition. It's settled. Besides, you have to pick up the Ducati anyway. And trust me, Leigh's a fabulous cook."

Leigh gave her an affectionate shove, but loved hearing Conn brag about her to Jess.

"Well, in that case, I'd be honored. But first, do you know where I can buy a wedding present? My brother's getting married and I want to get them something, especially since I can't be there."

"As a matter of fact, there's a wonderful bed and linen store just down the street," Leigh quickly said. "Ask for Ally. I'm sure she can help you. She's very friendly and knows the inventory well. Tell her Leigh and Conn sent you. And if you meet anyone you want to invite to join us tonight, feel free. Right, Conn?"

Leigh looked into slightly befuddled blue eyes and willed her to silence.

Jess stared at them for a moment, then said, "Uh, right. Well, see you later."

As Leigh watched Jess amble down the street, Conn quietly asked, "Were you trying to fix her up with Ally?"

Keeping her eyes on Jess, Leigh nodded.

"I wouldn't have thought of that," Conn muttered. "You're good."

❖

They'd just settled at a table for four and ordered appetizers and a bottle of pinot noir when Jess walked in the door, grinning as she spotted them and saying to the waitress, “Someone’s joining us in about fifteen minutes.”

Trying not to look smug, Leigh asked whom she had invited.

Jess looked directly at Leigh. “A big biker chick I spent the afternoon with at a bar. Who do you think, Leigh?”

Leigh glanced at Conn, who seemed to be trying hard to keep a sip of water in her mouth and not all over the table. “You’re kidding, right?”

Jess folded her arms. “Yes, Leigh, I am. I invited Ally. It took me a few minutes to snap to the reason you steered me in her direction, but it was a very pleasant snap. She found the perfect gift for my brother and his fiancée, and then we talked for almost an hour, between customers. She’s charming and likes you guys a lot, so I invited her. And she asked me to a bar called Sirens after dinner. Do you know it?”

“We will after dinner,” Conn answered. “Hey, good for you, Jess. This could be fun.”

Jess laughed. “Well, Conn, I’ve never known you to socialize much or offer an opinion one way or the other about a woman, so I guess Leigh’s responsible for some of this new behavior.” She glanced at Leigh. “I like this woman more and more. Thanks, Leigh. It was a good idea.”

Leigh wondered if Conn had really never paid any attention to anyone socially. Dismissing her fears, she caught what she hoped was a look of contentment in Conn’s eyes as they all chatted amiably. She also fell a little more in love.

When Ally arrived, Jess poured her some wine and Conn raised her glass. “A toast. To friendship and love. May we always have both in abundance.”

As they all clinked and sipped, Conn’s expression of delight and love, meant just for her, made Leigh silently thank her for changing her life completely.

## CHAPTER FOUR

After dinner, they followed Jess and Ally, in Conn's Audi, to the bar in Fort Bragg. It was in an industrial part of town, with a small, unpaved, and deeply rutted gravel parking lot, and the bar was notable only for its darkened windows and barely noticeable neon sign announcing Sirens. It was a miracle they'd found it. Of the few other vehicles in the lot, most were old trucks.

Inside they found a long bar, tiny tables, a few booths, and three pool tables; toward the back were a small wooden dance floor and a jukebox. After they got drinks at the bar, Leigh and Conn strolled over to the jukebox while Jess and Ally went to claim one of the open booths.

"You know, I could get used this." Leigh smiled up at Conn, one arm around her waist.

"Me, too." Conn kissed her lightly on the lips. "Feels almost like real folks, huh? Being openly affectionate with the person you love. What a concept."

Leigh's eyes sparkled. "Wait. Say that last part again."

"What a concept?"

"No, no. The one before that."

"Being openly affectionate with the one you love?"

Leigh pulled Conn down and whispered in her ear. "Yeah. That one. 'The one you love.' Keep saying it and don't forget it. Because the one you love feels that way, too. Get it?"

Between the sound of Leigh's voice so close and the words she'd spoken, Conn thought she now knew the meaning of the word "nirvana." Whatever bliss was, this couldn't be far from it. She nodded, speechless.

After they picked a string of songs and headed back to the table, Conn realized that Jess had probably observed their interaction, but decided she didn't care.

As it turned out, Jess seemed much more interested in Ally than in them. The two were deep in conversation and seemed surprised to see Leigh and Conn back at the table so soon. Jess had an expression on her face that Conn hadn't seen in a long time. She seemed alive, enjoying herself. Conn looked at Leigh, who winked at her, evidently having picked up the same thing.

Leigh tugged on her arm and leaned toward Ally and Jess. "We're going to play some pool. Join us if you want." She took Conn's hand and they aimed for the pool tables, all of which were busy, so they watched and sipped on their club sodas.

As Conn leaned against the wall with Leigh in front, wrapped in her arms, she could smell the subtle scent of ginger on her hair and skin. She was practically vibrating, she was so happy. No. Wait. She *was* vibrating. *What the hell?*

Her pocket was vibrating. Straightening abruptly, she said, "Come on," and they hurried over to Jess and Ally. "Jess, the alarm on the Audi went off. Let's—"

Jess was up before she finished her sentence and they headed for the door.

Leigh turned to Ally. "I think we're supposed to stay here. Want to?"

"Hell, no."

Outside, Conn saw a mountain of a human being sprawled facedown on the hood of the car. Asleep, unconscious, or dead, she couldn't tell. Surrounding the car and the figure stood three very tall, very muscular women.

"Hey!" Conn yelled. "That's my car!"

Before she could step any farther forward, she heard the distinctive sound of a shell being pumped into the chamber of a shotgun. The sound came from Conn's left and behind her. She froze, and Jess, still coming out of the door, bumped into her.

The three women who had been studying the car turned and glared at Conn and Jess, then spread out and started in their direction.

Conn and Jess slowly met them halfway, Conn thinking to distance them from the bar to have more options for defense. "Look, I don't want trouble. I just want to know why that person is on the hood of my car."

One of the women, clad completely in denim and wearing heavy work boots and a black Stetson, spoke. "That's as far as she got. You got a problem with that?"

Ally and Leigh had been right behind Jess, and Ally said, "Shit. Where's Robin?"

All movement stopped, and a voice came from where the sound of the shotgun had been. "Right here, darlin'."

"Robin, call off the troops. These are friends of mine." Then Ally glanced at Conn's car. "And get Tuck off the damned car. What's she doing there, anyway?"

The three women surrounding Conn and Jess looked a little confused and hesitated, apparently waiting for orders.

"Oh. Okay, then. Relax, girls. They're friends. Go help Tuck."

The three tall women shifted into more friendly postures and again started studying the problem on the hood of the car. Conn let out a sigh of relief and thought to join them until she heard footsteps.

A very short, thin woman with long black hair and large dark eyes, a strong nose, and full, sensual lips that curved in an insolent smile strode out of the darkness and into the solitary light that shone on the parking lot. With the shotgun broken open and resting in the crook of her arm, she sauntered over to Ally and kissed her lightly on the lips. Conn felt Jess stiffen slightly at her elbow. The woman then walked over to Conn and stuck out her hand, which Conn took. They looked at each other, calculating.

"Sorry about the car. Tuck sometimes has a bit too much to drink, way too early in the day. We've been looking for her. My name's Robin. Who are you?"

"Conn Stryker. I'll go help them." She started to move, but stopped when she saw Robin turn in Leigh's direction.

"And who might this be?"

Conn could feel the smile on Robin's lips. She knew exactly to whom she was referring. Wheeling around, she saw Robin amble over to where Leigh stood.

Ally stepped in front of Leigh and narrowed her eyes at Robin. "This is Leigh Grove. She and Conn are together. As in *together*."

Robin and Ally stared at each other for a moment before Robin's gaze drifted to Leigh. "Is that true?"

"Yes. Big-time." Leigh noticed Conn's body relax before she turned her attention back to the car.

"Well, can't blame a girl for trying. Right, Ally?"

The obvious familiarity between them made Leigh glance at Jess, the light dimming that had been in her eyes a few moments before.

Ally growled at Robin. "Well, since you asked, I'd like you to meet *my* date, Jess Smith. Jess, this is Robin Cruz. Lifelong friend and *former* lover." As Ally spoke, she took Jess's hand.

Jess looked at her, then at their entwined fingers, and smiled before she offered to shake with Robin.

Robin shrugged and seemed to accept the truce. She and Jess seemed to size each other up for a moment, then both stalked toward the car, where a major removal project was underway.

Leigh and Ally watched the group for a moment, then Leigh moved to Ally's side and quietly said, "Thank you. That could have been a large problem. You seem to know how to handle Robin well."

Ally shook her head. "Years of practice. She was my first lover, when we were in high school."

"So what happened? Why did you break up?"

Ally looked at her, seeming to gauge her trustworthiness. Finally, she said, "We were both kids and we grew in different directions. I went to college while she stayed and established herself here. And she's always had an eye for the ladies, as you might have noticed. The breakup was painful, but we each found a dear friend in the other after the hurt went away. We love each other, but never like that again."

They watched as some of the women gently raised Tuck from the hood of the car and carried her to the back of one of the trucks, where they settled her in with a couple of blankets. The three who had done the heavy lifting were sweating by the time the job was done. Conn, Jess, and Robin had evidently supervised, because they looked fine.

Leigh moved closer. "Hey, thank everyone for helping. Let us buy a round of drinks. Come on!"

After checking with Robin, the women started joking with each other as they headed toward the front door. The three "supervisors" followed suit, and as they walked by Leigh, Conn draped her arm possessively around her shoulders.

Ally slid her arm around Jess's waist on one side and took Robin by the hand on her other side for the short distance to the door. Leigh had to admire the way she'd defused a potentially dicey situation.

Out of the corner of her eye she checked on Jess, who was smiling again. Maybe not as much as before, but at least she was smiling. Leigh saw that Conn was watching, too, her eyes protective and wary.

When the others went into the bar, Leigh put her hand on Conn's stomach to stop her and pulled her into the shadows. "How's the car?"

"Fine. How are you?"

"Well, other than feeling like a prize porterhouse steak, just ducky." She filled Conn in on what Ally had told her about Robin.

"I have to hand it to Ally. She handled that woman and Jess perfectly." Conn looked at the door for a moment, biting her lip, then blurted, "Robin sure was interested in you. She's pretty, in a small, scrawny, illegal, dangerous way. Um, by the way, did you mean that about 'big-time'?"

Leigh slid her arms around Conn's neck and nuzzled her throat. "Oh, yeah."

They hugged each other for a few moments, enjoying the quiet.

"Besides, there's nothing porterhouse about you. You're definitely filet mignon."

Leigh groaned. "Thanks, Bubba. Let's go in and see if any brawls have broken out yet."

❖

About an hour into what turned out to be a good time, Tuck showed up at the front door, looking tired and hungover but ready to join the festivities. Robin evidently filled her in on her unfortunate napping location, and she found her way over to Conn to apologize. She was so sincere and cracked so many funny jokes that it was impossible to be angry, and soon she was sitting at the table chatting with Leigh and Ally while Jess and Conn walked over to feed the jukebox.

As they stared at the numbers and song titles Conn ventured, "So, how's it going with Ally?"

"She, ah, she invited me back to her place tonight."

Even in the minimal light cast by the jukebox Conn could see Jess grin and blush, so she tried to keep her voice neutral. "Oh. Are you going?"

"Well, I don't know. I should get back in the morning. Got to tend to the house and all."

Conn punched in a few song numbers and searched desperately

for something to say. She wished Leigh were there beside her, because she would know what to tell Jess. She took a stab at it. “Why don’t you take the truck and, if all goes well, the two of you meet us tomorrow for brunch at the house around eleven. Maybe take her for a spin on the bike before you leave. We can talk to Maggie and see what’s happening. You haven’t had a day off since, uh, well, in a long time.”

Jess hesitated. “What if it all goes to hell?”

“Well, then, you come for brunch alone and take the bike back down the coast.”

Jess was still, staring at the jukebox.

Conn took a breath and hoped she didn’t screw it up. “You know, Jess, Ellie would want you to get back into life. You even told Leigh that this afternoon. If you love someone, you want the best for her. She’d want you to have some tenderness in your life, even if only for one night. You’re not a nun, you know.”

“Perhaps you’re right.” Jess sighed. “I’ll see if the invitation’s still there and accept it. I, uh, hope I don’t disappoint her. I’m way beyond rusty.”

“Hah. Trust me. You’ll be lucky if you don’t kill each other.”

When Jess looked startled, Conn realized she’d just given away a lot more than she should have. She looked down at the floor and felt her cheeks warm with embarrassment.

Sweetly, Jess said, “Don’t worry about it. The way I feel right now, she might need a restraining order.”

Conn snorted and gave her a good-natured elbow, and when they turned toward the table they discovered all eyes were on them, Tuck having returned to her friends. Jess ducked her head and muttered, “Here goes.”

Jess asked Ally to dance, and Conn extended her hand to Leigh. Leigh stood but glided into her arms and kissed her firmly.

“Let’s go home,” Conn whispered in her ear. “I want to make love.”

Leigh tightened her hold on Conn and gazed into her eyes. “Me, too.” Then her brow furrowed and she added, “Oh, dear. What about Jess?”

Conn gave her a sly smile. “Seems Ms. Jess has been invited home by Ms. Ally. And she’s going. If it works, they’ll both come by tomorrow for brunch and then, who knows?”

Leigh seemed delighted that her matchmaking had been

successful. Jess and Ally were on the dance floor wrapped in each other's arms, so she walked over to say good night and confirm a time for the next day.

As they were leaving they said good-bye to their new acquaintances, including Robin, who abruptly grabbed Conn by the arm. "Is that woman good enough for Ally?" Her expression wasn't friendly.

"I was going to ask you that question about Ally."

They glared at each other for a moment, then Robin nodded slightly and released Conn's arm.

When they were finally settled in the Audi, Conn put the seat heaters on high and pulled out of the lot. "Well, that was intense. You and Tuck seemed to hit it off. What's her story?"

Leigh, reveling in the comfort of the heated bucket seats after the chill outside, closed her eyes. "Tuck is a defrocked nun, or excommunicated or whatever they're called. She said she discovered she liked women and booze more than serving the priests like a slave. Personally, I wonder if one didn't follow the other—her guilt over the love of women drove her to drink. Who knows?"

She shrugged. "Anyway, Robin grows medical pot and gives it away to those who need it and can't afford it. Ally said that somehow Tuck found her way to Robin and joined the crew, then gave herself the new first name of Friday. Maybe as in 'Friday's child is full of woe.' But, according to Ally, she tends to the spiritual needs of the group. You know, a shoulder to cry on, a kind ear to listen. She's a nurse, so she takes care of most of the bumps and bruises in the group, and probably more. They all seem to love her and look out for her, but obviously she still has a few issues around alcohol."

She was about to say something else when she heard Conn snort, and she opened her eyes to see her start to laugh. "What? What's so funny?"

Conn glanced over at her. "I just got it! Robin and her band of thieves. And Friday Tuck. Friar Tuck! What a trip! I feel like I've been indulging in some of Robin's wacky tobacky."

Leigh stared at her, then slapped her forehead. "Of course! Whoa, I must be slowing down. I should've gotten that."

Conn took her hand. "Don't feel bad. You've had a few things on your plate recently."

A comfortable silence fell between them until Conn had found the road back to the cabin. Finally Leigh sighed and said, "I feel like my life has just started. The colors are more vibrant, the people more interesting, and my emotions are so vivid. It's wonderful." As they sped along the highway, she cracked the window and listened to the sound of the waves crashing against the rocks. "Because of you."

Conn squeezed her hand. "Don't give me that much credit. You're just being who you are."

"Perhaps. But you're the only person who wants me to be who I am. Thank you."

As they broke the plane of the entrance to the house, the outside lights flashed on. Conn caught movement in her peripheral vision and saw a doe and some yearlings freeze in the light. The deer watched for a few seconds as the garage door slid up, then resumed their grazing.

The deer had been there a while if the lights had turned off, so it was probably safe around the perimeter. Exhaling, she pulled into the garage, then pressed the button to close the garage door. Glancing at the control panel by the door, she saw only green lights, which told her the house security hadn't been breached. As she unbuckled her seat belt and started to get out of the car, Leigh tapped her on the shoulder.

"Yeah?"

Leigh hesitated. "You should know something."

Conn felt an instant knot in her stomach. "What is it? Is something wrong?"

"Just that I'm falling more in love with you every moment. If that feels like too much, you need to tell me now because I'm fast reaching the point of no return."

As Conn locked eyes with Leigh, she could hear alarms sounding everywhere in her body. The rational part of her brain told her it was too soon; luckily, the other parts weren't listening.

She moved the Audi's steering wheel up as far as it would go and reclined the seat to maximum. Then she released Leigh's seat belt before lowering Leigh's seat and gently pulling her on top. "Why would you want to return?"

Their kisses started gently, but both women were soon on fire and they fumbled with buttons and zippers, finding soft flesh to stroke and satisfy. Conn opened the fly of Leigh's jeans and touched her stomach with the palm of her hand, letting her fingers slide down under the silk panties to her swollen center.

Leigh felt her body rise to Conn and explode within minutes, and her orgasm only intensified her need to satisfy her lover. She rolled slightly to one side, enough to reach down and go inside her, stroking and loving her to a strong climax. It took a while for their breathing to return to normal, and Leigh stayed inside Conn, almost dozing.

Conn's voice in her ear brought her around. "My God. They just keep getting better. Are you sure you've never been with a woman? Because, honey, you are *very* talented."

A lazy smile tickled Leigh's lips as she nuzzled and kissed Conn's neck and throat. "I've been wanting to do that all day. And I aim to please." She moved the fingers inside Conn just slightly. "Would you like to know more of my fantasies?"

"Djaah! Well, yes and no. Yes, I want to know all of your fantasies, and no, not at this very moment. As much fun as it was to do it in the car, and, trust me, that was a first for me, I can think of a much softer place to play. But I can't figure a way to get there with your hand where it is. Gently, my love."

They slowly disengaged and buttoned and zipped enough to get out of the car and inside the house. As soon as the door closed, they were all over each other again until the alarm began to beep. Conn pulled away and glanced at the pad.

"Shit," she panted. "I have to punch in the code within thirty seconds. Ah, what is the code? Now let's see…"

Leigh leaned on the utility sink while Conn struggled with several combinations, swearing each time one didn't work. Finally, the right numbers went in and the green light came on.

Conn let out a big breath. "I've never forgotten the code before. I think I just learned the meaning of the word 'besotted.' My vocabulary is growing."

Leigh smiled in the dark and took her hand. "Come on, time for a vocabulary lesson."

When sleep finally claimed her several hours later, she and Conn lay in a jumble of sheets and blankets, snuggled together against the cold.

## CHAPTER FIVE

Wrapped in Leigh's arms, vaguely stirring, Conn nuzzled Leigh, tasting her skin. "Mmm. Smooth and salty. Been working out?" Her voice was gravelly from sleep.

Leigh stretched against her. "You could say that. What time is it?"

Conn tried to focus on the clock. "9:30. It's early. Let's fool around."

Leigh cracked her eyelids and smiled slightly. "Silly me. I thought that's what we did all night. Still, it *is* a new day, and there are a few nooks and crannies that I haven't explored. Like right…there."

Conn groaned with pleasure.

After they'd kissed deeply and Conn buried her face in Leigh's chest, Leigh sighed. "I just hope Jess and Ally had half the fun we did last night. After we got home."

Conn lifted her head long enough to mumble, "I suppose we can ask them at brunch."

One. Two. They sat up and stared at each other. "Brunch!" Simultaneously they inventoried the room.

"Ohmygod. The house is a mess, we have to shower, and I have to cook *something*!"

"Jess is supposed to take the Ducati," Conn yelped. "It's covered in mud!"

Quickly they abandoned the bed and did a version of a fire drill for cats. After thirty minutes the house was at least presentable and Leigh was in the shower while Conn was outside, backing the motorcycle out for its bath. While scrubbing it, she checked for any developments on

Dieter, keeping the conversation with Maggie brief and vague, except for one item of business.

By the time the bike was clean, Leigh was in the kitchen while Conn hit the shower at full speed. When the old truck pulled into the driveway, thankfully fifteen minutes late, they were cutting and chopping and only slightly breathless.

The garage door was still open so Jess could bring the truck in when she took the bike, which Conn had left outside to dry. After Ally and Jess climbed out of the truck, Ally walked over to admire the motorcycle, reaching for Jess's hand, and Jess followed her, wrapping her arms around her.

From their vantage point at the kitchen window, Leigh grinned at Conn. "Come on, looks like things are going well. Let's go greet our first guests." Then Leigh nudged her. "I like the sound of that: our first guests. Let's go, darling."

Conn took a second to enjoy just how good those words felt.

Their welcoming hugs were mixed with awkwardness, and Conn realized that in the light of day their lack of familiarity with each other was more pronounced. They all stood around the motorcycle with Leigh and Ally making admiring noises about it, and when it looked like Leigh was stuck for small talk, Conn decided she should take the lead and got right to the point. "So, are you staying for a few days or taking the bike and going back?" She thought she got a look from Leigh and hoped she hadn't said the wrong thing. This socializing stuff wasn't easy.

Jess studied the ground and turned a bit pink. "Well, uh, I'm going to try and stay for a few days. I didn't really have time to check in because we were running a little, um, late this morning. I'll do it later, after brunch. But I did promise Ally a ride on the bike. Right, Ally?"

Ally beamed at Jess. "Right. You can't go back until absolutely necessary."

Clearing her throat, Conn grinned at Jess. "Ah, well, I just happened to have chatted with Maggie and requested your presence for two more days. She gave the okay."

Seeing the look of confusion on Ally's face, she added, "Maggie is our…boss."

Ally jumped into Jess's arms. "Yippee!"

They both looked happy, and Conn got a very approving look from Leigh. Conn was inordinately pleased.

As Conn and Leigh started into the house, Leigh called over her shoulder, "You lovebirds come on in now. Food's about ready." Conn walked up behind her and scooted her along, making Leigh giggle, and they laughed as they entered through the garage, Jess and Ally following.

Once inside, Conn noticed Jess and Ally eyeing each other and snickering. "What's so funny?" She hoped her shirt wasn't on inside out.

"Well, we were just wondering how easy it is to drive the Audi with the seats fully reclined," Jess said. "How did you manage?" She gazed at her with wide eyes.

Conn shot a look to Leigh for help but found her completely intent on the frittata she was making, her back shaking slightly. She felt heat start to work its way up her face. "Oh. Ah, it seems we didn't quite make it into the house last night before an…important…discussion took place. That car is a damned fine place to discuss urgent matters, too."

Ally seemed to take pity and chimed in. "Well, if it makes a difference, the truck is *not* the place to have a 'discussion.' The seats don't recline." Her eyes were dancing as she placed an arm around Jess's waist.

Laughter broke the earlier awkwardness, and during the rest of the meal Conn was aware of their growing friendship.

Jess and Conn claimed cleanup detail while Ally and Leigh went outside to walk around the property and search for the motorcycle helmets. Conn hadn't had time to clean them, so Leigh and Ally carefully began to wash the mud off.

"Wow," Ally said, "these are a mess. How was the ride up, Leigh?"

Because Leigh didn't know how much to say, she tried to keep it vague. "A bit on the dicey side, actually. A loser at this little grocery store we stopped at tried to follow us. It was raining and Conn had to do some intense maneuvering to—to get away from him. Luckily, she's really good on the bike. I just closed my eyes and hung on for dear life. By the time we got to the house she had to practically lift me off the thing. It was a long, long day."

After they'd cleaned in silence for a while, Leigh asked, "Have you ridden motorcycles before?"

Ally smiled. "Oh, yeah. Robin has a Harley. We were quite the rebels without a clue for a few years. I've never been on a Ducati, though. This thing looks hot! Have you guys ridden it since you've been up here?"

"No. For several reasons, really. It's noticeable and we didn't want to attract attention, and, um, we were both a little sore from the, uh, ride up and everything." She was polishing the enamel off the helmet by the time she finished the sentence.

"Oh. Ooh! I hadn't thought of that. That could be a problem. I think I'll suggest just a short ride today." It was Ally's turn to polish intently.

She never asked about the divot that one of the helmets had in it, the divot placed there by a bullet. Leigh wondered about that.

After cleaning the helmets they walked through the thick duff from the tall conifers dotting the land, the long branches of the majestic trees creating a filtered effect from the sun. The air was clean and pure, mixed with a scent of pine and redwood that was distinctly northern California.

On the way back to the house, Ally opened the truck door and pulled out a local newspaper. "I thought you might like to read up on the latest around here. See if there's anything to do that interests you."

They returned to the house just as Jess and Conn finished bringing in more wood for the fireplace and wood closet beside it. Jess suggested they take the bike out for their ride, and when Ally informed her it would be a short one, the look of relief on Jess's face was almost comical.

Conn and Leigh walked the women out, waved as they left, then returned inside and took their coffee and the paper in by the fire. Leigh used Conn's lap as a pillow while she perused the paper and read some articles out loud to Conn, but most of the time she just read to herself. After about ten minutes Conn was dozing, her head lolling on the back of the couch.

Suddenly Leigh sat bolt upright, waking Conn with a start. "Wha…?" She struggled to orient herself as the urgent tone of Leigh's voice put her on alert.

"Listen to this. 'Yesterday evening a teenage boy was found beaten and unconscious behind the convenience store where he worked in Two Forks, on Highway 1. Jerry Dale was taken to the local hospital in critical condition. His mother, who owns the store, hadn't noticed anything unusual other than a stranger asking her son a lot of questions a few hours before. Police are investigating.'"

A sick feeling settled into Conn's stomach. "Sounds like that place we stopped on the way up. Shit. They'll be looking for the bike. Where's my cell phone?"

They both jumped up while Conn dug out her phone and tried to reach Jess. Leigh ran outside.

Conn scowled at the cell. "Crap. Nothing. I don't even know if she has her phone with her."

Behind her she heard Leigh's voice.

"She doesn't."

She turned to see a cell phone in Leigh's hand.

"It was in the truck."

"Damn it! Stay here, I'm going to look for them." She had already found her Glock and binoculars in her duffel and started for the door.

Leigh stood in her way, the keys to the Audi in her hand. "The hell you say. I'm coming with you."

Conn grabbed the keys from her. "Okay. Let's go."

After reaching Highway 1 in record time, they headed north, Leigh scanning with the binoculars for the bike. They drove for three miles. Nothing.

"I don't like it," Leigh said. "Ally didn't want a long ride, and neither did Jess. We should have seen them by now."

The feeling in Conn's stomach had reached her throat. "We're turning around. Ditch the binoculars and watch for tire marks and any sign of a break in the safety rails, especially around corners."

Reversing their path, they drove slowly, watching the highway for tire marks. The road was treacherous, with blind curves and steep terrain. Normally Leigh wouldn't have even looked. The height made her feet sweat. Now she ignored that sensation as she searched for any sign of the bike and their friends.

A mile farther down the road they saw it—a single skid mark and a gap in the railing. No other vehicles around. Conn abruptly pulled across the highway to a turnout cut into the hillside, they jumped out, and Conn popped the trunk, pulling out a coil of heavy rope and a red duffel. She gave her phone and the rope to Leigh, and they raced over to the break in the rail.

Looking down, they could see two inert forms and debris from the bike. The first figure, smaller and still wearing a helmet, had to be Ally. The second was much farther away, on the edge of a bigger drop to the ocean, looking like a large rag doll splayed on the rocks. The bike wasn't there.

Grimly, Conn said, "Come on." She took two steps and stopped, facing Leigh. "I have a little training in emergency stuff. Let me take the lead." She waited for Leigh to nod before continuing.

They carefully made their way down the hill and found Ally curled on her side. Conn examined her cursorily for obvious injury and checked her pulse. When she found only cuts, scrapes, and abrasions, she gently lifted Ally's head and helmet, using about as much pressure as she'd need to lift a six-pack, to prevent Ally's neck from further possible injury, and they carefully rolled her as one unit onto her back. Leigh raised the visor to make sure she was breathing easily and kept talking to Ally in a soothing voice.

Conn said, "Leigh, squeeze her shoulder and call her name several times. Use a strong voice, but don't startle her."

After a few repetitions Ally's eyes fluttered open and she coughed, then started to struggle. They held her and called her name until she could focus on Leigh. "Leigh! What are you—Jess! Where's Jessie?"

"Ally, you have to be still. We don't know if your spine is hurt."

The urgency in Leigh's tone must have registered because Ally stilled for a moment. "Let me see, let me see. I can feel everything, wiggle my toes." She grabbed Leigh's hand. "I'm fine, I'm a doctor's kid. Go help Jess."

Conn looked at Leigh and was pretty sure she understood her exasperation at the chance Ally had just taken. "Keep her as still as possible," she said and nodded slightly in Jess's direction, then left them to go to her.

"We can see her, Ally. Conn will reach her any minute. Please stay quiet. Let's not take chances, okay?"

Ally ignored her and tried to sit up, Leigh supporting her as much as she could. She seemed bruised but not broken, but she did need help removing her helmet.

"I've got to get to Jess. Someone came up on us from behind and shoved us off the highway. It all happened so fast!"

"Stay put. Conn will be right back and then we'll decide what to do. Can you remember anything about the car?" Leigh asked, trying to distract her by focusing her attention elsewhere. Conn was almost there. She said a silent prayer for Jess and for both of them to not fall off the precarious perch where Jess had landed.

"It seemed like an American car, I think a metallic blue. Everything happened so fast. Its front end should have some damage, too, maybe some black paint or something. Is that Jess? What's taking so long?"

Conn was now rapidly climbing and soon reached them. "We need help. Her leg is definitely broken and she might have internal injuries. She's out, but I think the helmet saved her life before it flew off to God knows where. Ally, how do I contact the fire department search-and-rescue unit? We need a backboard and maybe a Med-Evac helicopter."

Ally placed the call, accurately describing their location and need. After she hung up, she said, "I'll call my father. He's the doctor for the unit."

Leigh vaguely remembered Ally saying that Robin cleared who got medical pot with her father. Now it made sense.

When Ally heard her father's voice, she started crying and handed the phone to Conn, who assured him his daughter was okay and filled him in, giving him the directions she'd heard Ally use with the fire department.

"Got it. See you soon." She ended the call and tossed the phone to Leigh. "He's on his way. As soon as Jess is taken care of, I'm going to look for the prick who did this. Maybe you should stay with Ally."

Ally had composed herself. "Give me the phone again. I'll have him rounded up by the time you get to Mendocino."

The look in her eyes told Conn she meant it.

Within ten minutes the volunteer rescue unit was there, Ally's father on its heels. Conn was amazed, considering the narrow, twisting road they had to travel.

Using ropes and a backboard, they were able to gingerly slide the still-unconscious Jess away from the edge of the cliff. She had minimal external bleeding, probably thanks to the leather pants and jacket she'd been wearing. They then immobilized her broken leg, strapped on a cervical collar, loaded her into a basket stretcher, and carried her to the waiting ambulance. There they fit a supplemental oxygen mask on her face and whisked her away. Conn knew Jess might possibly have internal injuries, but she chose not to share that information. Ally rode to the hospital with her father, who had promptly placed a cervical collar to match Jess's on his protesting daughter.

After the excitement died down, Leigh noticed Conn talking to a woman whom they'd met the night before and who was also a member of the rescue team. She gave her a business card and they shook hands before the fire truck departed, then Conn walked to the Audi where Leigh was already sitting.

"What was that all about?"

Conn smiled briefly. "I was asking if they knew a way to get the bike hauled up and out of there and the hillside cleaned up. Seems Robin and her Merry Wenches just happen to have a tow service with a flatbed truck. For a reasonable fee they'll haul it up and take it to their—are you ready—shop, where they'll either restore it or junk it and let me know the cost."

She shook her head. "I guess Ally wasn't kidding when she said Robin had other businesses. The woman is a real entrepreneur." Conn put her hand on Leigh's shoulder. "I'm going to have to stop trying to tell you where you should be. I apologize. I'm so glad you're right here beside me."

Leigh took her hand and gently kissed her fingertips. "Me, too. Let's go see if Robin's had any luck finding the prick."

Conn angled the car onto the highway and drove north.

# CHAPTER SIX

As they pulled up next to an ancient station wagon in front of Ally's linen shop, Leigh recognized another of the women from the bar sitting behind the wheel, demolishing a large ice cream cone. She smiled, tipped her black cowboy hat, then started the car and pulled out. They followed.

A short distance out of town they headed inland and up into a densely wooded area with roads that got successively more narrow. Not exactly "county maintained," either. Finally they reached a small clearing where the truck stopped and the driver got out and ambled back to them.

"Hi. Park it here. You'll ride with me, blindfolded. Not that you ever *could* find your way back, but we can't take chances. You understand."

Conn was actually relieved she didn't have to put her car, designed for speed and agility rather than camping, through any more two-foot-deep chuckholes. And she very well understood the need for secrecy. She thought her trainers could actually learn from this outfit. Glancing over to see a look of concern on Leigh's face, she winked and smiled, then got out of the car to follow. Leigh was right behind her. The sun was heavier in the western sky, casting everything around them in deep shadows.

They accepted the blindfolds and were bounced around for probably fifteen minutes before they stopped and the driver told them they could remove them. They blinked as they saw only another rusty vehicle in front of a small shed in a clearing. The lone window of the shed was curtained, with a faint light behind it. Conn idly wondered what the real compound looked like.

When they got out of the truck and stretched their legs, Robin emerged from the shed.

"How's Ally? And your friend?" She was all business.

Conn took the lead. "She's got some scrapes and bruises, but Jess is more serious. They took her to the hospital, and Ally went there with her father. But I'm guessing you already knew that. Maybe we should ask *you* how they are."

A look of what might have been appreciation crept into Robin's eyes. "They'll survive. Jess has a broken leg, but the break's clean. A concussion and some broken ribs, too. So far they think she's escaped internal bleeding, but they're watching her. She'll need time to mend. According to Ally she's taking her home when they release her. And I hope that's okay, because Ally's a very single-minded woman."

Conn was considering how to handle that situation with Maggie at headquarters when a scream from inside the shed interrupted her thoughts. "I gather you found the guy who did this. Any luck with who paid him and why?"

Robin stared at her intently. "He needed a little attitude adjustment. We found the car with fresh front-end damage and snagged him as he was walking out of a restaurant. Just as unconcerned as could be. Then he swore a lot and called us names I really don't appreciate. Hence the adjustment. I'm just getting ready to question him. You want to join me?"

Conn started for the shed. "Yeah."

Robin put a firm hand on her arm and stopped her. "First, I need some answers. Did this joker want Jess and Ally? Or you two?"

Conn glanced at Leigh and then admitted, "That asshole was supposed to find us, not them. That's why I need to question him."

Robin studied Conn for a few seconds. "Good enough for now." Then she turned her attention to Leigh. "Tuck is coming to pick you up and take you to the main compound. She said she wants to show you around. Conn and I'll be up directly."

Just then a huge Chevy Suburban rolled up, and Tuck slid the window down and smiled at them.

Conn spoke quietly to Leigh. "Please. It'll be better if you go with Tuck. We'll be along in a bit."

Leigh glared at Robin. "See you *both* soon." Kissing Conn lightly on the lips, she climbed into the SUV, which drove off down a dirt road Conn hadn't noticed before.

Robin rocked back on her heels, hands in her jeans pockets, and smiled as she watched the big vehicle disappear in the dust. "A real spitfire, that one. You are one lucky woman, Ms. Stryker. Or should I call you Dr. Stryker? Either way, you're one lucky woman."

Conn wasn't surprised that Robin had done her homework. She just didn't know if she felt better or worse about it. She looked at the shed. "I know how lucky I am, and I intend to keep it that way. Let's go have a talk."

❖

Tuck and Leigh rode in silence for another ten minutes. Tuck hadn't asked her to put on a blindfold, but since they drove primarily through trees and undergrowth, and it was getting even darker, she hardly needed one.

When they finally pulled into a clearing, Leigh was amazed to see a small town. The buildings were from another era but, on closer inspection, refurbished. "Was this a real town at one time?"

Tuck smiled. "Yup. A gold-mining town. Been abandoned for years before Robin bought the property and we started rehabbing it. We have a mess hall and a damn fine cook. As you can see, I sure as hell like the food around here."

Tuck pointed to one of the outbuildings. "That's our tech hub. Solar collectors and backup generators produce most of our electricity, even though we occasionally tap in to borrow some. We're off the grid as much as possible. We're also state of the art as far as technology goes. Quite a trip, huh?"

Leigh looked around in wonder when they stopped at a barnlike building. The town was impressive.

"Ally said you were a nurse. Do you have an infirmary?"

"Of sorts. If it's more than stitches or setting a simple fracture, I call Doc, Ally's dad. He's been our doctor ever since Robin and Ally were together."

"Is there a…church? I mean, are you pagan, Catholic, nothing, something?"

Tuck smiled at her. "I guess the answer is yes. We have a chapel of sorts. More like a quiet place so people can do what gives their hearts peace. Are you asking if I still consider myself a Catholic?"

"I guess so." Leigh was fascinated.

"I'm a Tibetan Buddhist. That's a very long story, one we won't go into now. I try to take care of the spiritual needs of our community no matter what their beliefs. Kind of a chaplain."

Tuck's eyes lit up as she said, "Want to see the kitchen and meet the cook?"

Leigh noticed Tuck was almost bouncing on her toes with enthusiasm. "How much longer do you think Robin and Conn will be?"

"Hard to say. Let's go meet Martha."

They walked into the building, which was actually more like a hall. Various tables were placed around, and toward the back was a cafeteria setup, with a full, professional kitchen behind that. The aroma of bread baking and some sort of food cooking reached Leigh, and her stomach reminded her she hadn't eaten since brunch. They heard pots and pans being slammed around, and in the midst of everything, a tiny woman with flame red hair was laughing and talking to several helpers.

When Tuck bellowed "Martha!" the woman turned around, gave Tuck a huge grin, and waved. She put a pan aside and wiped her hands on her apron as she approached them.

"I want you to meet Leigh," Tuck said. "I'm showing her around while Robin and her partner have a meeting."

Martha's friendly green eyes appraised Leigh as they shook hands. "Hey, good to meet you. Tuck, you be nice to her. She's so skinny she might blow away in a strong breeze. How about a thick slice of bread just out of the oven and some butter and homemade jam? I'll make some tea, too."

Tuck grinned and Leigh started to salivate. "Thank you. Sounds great."

Everything was melt-in-your-mouth delicious. Leigh hadn't realized how hungry she was, and once she was full, Tuck demolished the rest with gusto.

Martha grinned. "Now. see there? A woman who knows what she likes. Most of the time." While something personal passed between her and Tuck, Leigh politely ignored them and admired the spotless kitchen.

The sound of heavy footfalls interrupted the conversation as one of the crew who had been with Robin strolled in. "Hey, Mar. We need a couple of bags of ice. Robin and her friend got a little banged up." The women didn't appear concerned, and Martha went over to the icemaker and started assembling several small bags.

Leigh was instantly on her feet. "Where are they? Are they okay?"

The woman took the ice and shrugged. "Yeah. Are you Leigh? Your friend ordered me to find you and bring you over." She seemed amused more than offended. "Follow me. Hey, Tuck! Would you bring some grub for everyone? Five of us. Thanks." She glanced at Leigh and casually said, "Come on. I'll take you to them."

They walked across the dusty street, which was unmarred by tire treads and the smell of gasoline, over to the two-story main house. The compound was sparsely lit with small yellow globes placed over doors, and some lights shone behind curtains. Conn and Robin were on the veranda that surrounded the house, Conn seated in a glider, absently moving back and forth while she quietly spoke.

As Leigh scaled the last of the stairs, Conn smiled and patted the seat next to her. Leigh sat, took her hand, and felt Conn flinch. Her knuckles were bruised and swollen, and the woman who had walked Leigh over handed one of the bags to Conn and one to Robin.

"What happened?"

Conn settled the bag onto her hand and sighed, and Robin did the same. Then they chuckled at the same time.

Leigh was getting upset over the offhand behavior and lack of information.

"Remember that attitude problem we were having?" Robin finally said. "Well, it started all over again when the guy spotted Conn and realized he'd hit the wrong people. He called her a few names, which, by the way, she said she'd heard before."

She leaned forward, eyes dancing. "But he made the mistake of saying something really nasty about you, and boom! Broken nose. The idiot. Anyway, he steered clear of that subject from then on."

Leigh sat back in the glider, shoulder and arm welded to Conn, and put her hand on her beautiful protector's thigh and squeezed. "How did your hand get hurt, Robin?"

Conn answered for her. "That happened just before we were getting ready to package him up to take to the sheriff. Guess he just couldn't help himself. He had to make a remark about Ally, and Robin gave him a right cross that sent a few teeth flying. Between that and the other informational techniques we needed to apply to get what we wanted, he was begging to be in the loving arms of the law."

Leigh had been watching Robin as Conn spoke and noticed her gaze slide away when the part about defending Ally came up. *Interesting.* "So, after all this, did you find out who hired him?"

Conn's frustrated sigh confirmed what she feared. "He's just a hired gun. He beat up the kid to get information. After the jerk phoned that in, he was told to look for the bike and kill whoever was on it. Evidently the descriptions of us were pretty accurate, because he *did* realize his mistake when he saw me. He didn't get a good look at who was on the bike, just aimed for it."

"Do you know if they've found the house?"

"They told him to look for the bike and someone else would handle the rest, whatever that means. I'm going to have to contact Maggie and fill her in. Then we're packing the car and leaving. Tonight. I know a safe place where we can stay for a few days while we work things out."

Robin spoke up. "You can stay here. Believe me, no one comes here without permission."

Conn shook her head. "Thanks for the offer, but we can't. We aren't sure what we're dealing with here. What started out as simple fraud may have much deeper implications."

She looked at Leigh and covered her hand with the one that still had the ice resting on it. "I can't try to reach my contact from here. This location could be compromised."

Robin smiled proudly. "We have pretty sophisticated scrambling equipment."

"Not this sophisticated. Trust me."

"Feds?" Robin's smile disappeared and the coldness in her eyes was unsettling.

"Yes."

"Then give me one good reason why I should let you leave this place alive."

## CHAPTER SEVEN

Conn sat perfectly still, Leigh's hand frozen on her thigh, and never broke eye contact.

"I'm not connected to DEA, and I'm not interested in turning you in. It wouldn't be in our best interests. It's invaluable to have a place to go that absolutely no one can connect to us. And you'll have a contact inside, if you ever need it. It's all I can offer."

Robin sat back in the rocker, but she still wasn't smiling. "This place is secluded enough to not attract attention. Anybody that knows about it doesn't talk. It's a refuge."

"Understood. And appreciated."

Robin turned to Leigh. "You?" There was nothing flirtatious in her demeanor.

"Absolutely."

Complete stillness surrounded them.

"Let's have something to eat and then you can go."

❖

As they were getting ready to leave, Robin gave them a number to call for emergencies only, adding that they should contact Ally for anything else. They all shook hands, Robin lingering just a bit too long with Leigh for Conn's taste, but she chose to ignore it.

She was grateful they were getting out unscathed because she'd seen what Robin had done to the man they "interviewed." Efficiently and without mercy, she had extracted everything he knew, and Conn had no doubt that Robin would kill to protect her lair and those she loved. Conn suspected she had done all of this for Ally and wondered if Ally realized what a friend she had.

"Hey, where are you? Tuck's waiting." Leigh tugged gently on her arm, moving her toward the car.

"Hmm? Oh, sorry. Come on, let's get out of here."

The ride to their car was sans blindfold. Passing the shed, Conn noted it was deserted. Robin had said they would hand the man over to the sheriff, but she wasn't willing to bet on that and wasn't going to check on it either.

Back at the Audi they said good-bye, Leigh and Tuck hugging, and watched until the truck's taillights disappeared down the dusty road. Then Conn shone a small flashlight over her car to see if it had been tampered with in any way. The coat of road dust on it would have revealed at least a trace of mucking around, so the inspection was fairly easy.

After they found their way back to town, they located the hospital to check on Jess, who was in a private room, asleep. Her leg was in a cast and she looked pretty banged up. Beside her sat Ally, who smiled and motioned for them to come in.

Conn spoke quietly. "How is she?"

"She'll survive. My dad said her being in such good shape probably saved both of us. She was able to angle the hit so we took less damage than the bike. I flew off on impact, but she stayed, and it rolled and dragged her. It was lucky that she cleared the bike before it went over the cliff. She saved my life."

Leigh glanced at Jess, then Ally. "How are you, Ally?"

"Just a few cuts and bruises. I'm starting to get sore and will probably need three aspirin to get out of bed tomorrow, but I'm okay. How did you make out with the guy who hit us?"

"He was a hired gun who mistook you two for us," Conn explained. "So it's time for us to get out of here. When are they going to release Jess?"

"The sooner the better." The groggy voice came from the direction of the bed. "I hate hospitals."

Jess was trying to smile at them through slitted eyelids and a swollen face. Her lips looked painfully dry, and Ally gave her a few sips of water through a straw.

Then she bent and kissed her on the forehead and stood up, gently placing a hand on her arm. "Welcome back, Jess. We've missed you."

Conn and Leigh joined Ally beside the bed. "Yeah. You've got to stop trying to do tricks on the bike, Jess." Conn tsked. "Just to impress a girl."

Jess took Ally's hand. "But what a girl. Are you okay?"

"I'm fine, now. Dad says you'll be good as new in about six weeks. The break was clean, and your ribs are badly bruised, but not broken. And luckily you have a very hard head."

"Shit. Did they get the asshole that hit us?"

Conn stepped closer to the bed. "You can thank Ally for that one. She called Robin, and they had him rounded up by the time Leigh and I arrived. He was after us and couldn't tell the difference. I'm sorry, Jess. We didn't know until after you left that there might be a problem. We came looking for you and found the accident."

"Bastard. Don't feel bad. I was supposed to take the bike anyway. If it'd happened somewhere else I'd probably be dead by now. I'm just sorry Ally had to be involved."

Ally squeezed Jess's hand. "Don't say that. I'm not sorry at all. You're even coming home with me so you can recuperate. I'm taking two weeks off from work. By the way, isn't Maggie your boss?"

Jess and Conn stared at each other. "Holy shit!"

"I gotta make a call." Conn abruptly left the room.

As Leigh watched her lover's retreating back, Ally asked, "What was that all about?"

Jess had suddenly and, Leigh thought, conveniently drifted to sleep. Leigh shrugged noncommittally. "I don't know."

Ally continued, "A woman with a no-nonsense voice called for Jess and drilled me with questions. She wanted to know where Conn—she called her Dr. Stryker—was, too."

Leigh sidestepped the issue. "I guess they needed to contact her." She had no idea how Maggie had found them there.

While they waited for Conn to return, Leigh asked how Ally would be able to take the time off from work.

Ally grinned. "Well, the family owns the shop. Dad took care of that for me. He said I'd earned the vacation. I think he knew I'd take it anyway."

From the bed and with swollen lips, Jess mumbled, "Some vacation."

Just then Conn hustled in the door. "Okay. Jess, you're cleared to stay with Ally for at least two weeks. Evidently Ally already talked to

Maggie about this. But you have to be in contact through your laptop and phone."

Leigh and Ally high-fived each other.

"Leigh, we have to go. I'm sure they're looking for the house. Ally, come with us and you can take the truck and Jess's gear. We'll follow you to the highway. If anyone's watching, they'll come after us, not you."

"Wait," Jess said. "I'll protect Ally." She was struggling to stay awake and her speech was slurring.

From the doorway, Robin's voice made them turn around. "We'll provide an escort. That way you can be on your way to wherever, and Ally will have company on the way back."

Jess relaxed her head on the pillow. "Thanks, owe you one."

Robin looked at Ally and quietly said, "You damn sure do."

❖

As they stood in the kitchen watching out the window, the trucks disappeared into the night, and Conn took Leigh in her arms and kissed her. Softly at first, then with passion.

Coming up for air, Leigh gasped, "Phew. I needed that! This day has been too long. Do we have time to, uh, explore that train of thought more thoroughly?"

Conn grinned at her, but it faded quickly. "Not until we're safely out of here. Every minute counts. Let's pack and go."

Leigh studied Conn's face. "Is there something you're not telling me? I thought the place was clear."

"Later. Let's just get out of here."

Leigh stood her ground. "What is it?" She wasn't asking.

Conn let out a breath. "When I called Maggie, she said Dieter and Georgia were spotted in San Francisco. You know they've already killed Peter Cheney, and now they know approximately where we are. These people are serious, Leigh. They see us as obstacles to achieving their ends, and they don't like obstacles."

"My God. Let's get the hell out of here."

Conn fell a little deeper in love.

Leigh went to the bedroom and gathered their personal belongings while Conn packed her tech gear, then set the security system to silently signal her and others if a breach occurred. After throwing a few provisions from the kitchen into a bag, they were backing out of the garage within fifteen minutes. They discovered that Robin and crew had waited at the end of the road, guarding the place, and waved, signaling all clear. Then they drove in separate directions.

They headed down the coast, then east, cutting over to Interstate 80 to take them to their destination. As she drove, Conn reached under the dash and pressed a hidden button. The GPS screen activated, but it didn't look anything like the screen Leigh had seen Robin fiddle with when they'd driven down earlier. It was dark, but when Conn pressed a button some ghostly figures that appeared to be vehicles flitted on and off the screen.

"What on earth is that?"

A smile crossed Conn's beautifully planed face, and she kept her eyes on the road. "Oh, just another of my gadgets. It's a camera, switched to infrared readings. It's watching to see if we're being followed."

Leigh studied the screen, then looked behind them. She could only make out headlights. When she looked back at the screen, she could tell the size of the vehicle, sometimes more. Conn pressed another button and zoomed in on the vehicle directly behind them.

"*It's* watching? Don't you mean it lets *us* watch?"

Conn's smile grew. "No, it's watching. It analyzes the vehicles and notes distance and length of time they're behind us, make, model, etc. And it registers if we've seen it before. It sounds an alert if one of the vehicles seems to pay too much attention to us. Then we can decide what to do."

"You mean like press another hidden button and fire a rocket?"

"I haven't quite perfected that technology. But soon."

"You, my dear, are a piece of work. Thank you for taking such good care of us."

Conn lost the smile and concentrated on the road. "I'm not so sure about that. You were almost killed, and so were Ally and Jess. We have a ways to go before we're out of this."

Leigh squeezed Conn's shoulder. "We're together. That's a pretty strong combination. Now, talk me through how this thing works and what to look out for. I want to be able to use it. By the way, where are we going?"

The smile returned. "South Lake Tahoe. To a little lesbian

hideaway that anyone who tries to follow us would have a very hard time finding, let alone getting into. After I talked to Maggie I called the owners. We're still a couple of hours away."

"Did Maggie say exactly how Peter died? The poor man. He was guilty of arrogance and greed, but he didn't deserve being murdered for being in a stock scheme."

Conn didn't sugarcoat her answer. "Someone shot him in the face point blank before they shoved him into a closet in his office."

Leigh was quiet for a moment. Her hand tightened on Conn reflexively, and she finally registered the grief that she had been too preoccupied to feel until now.

"I know it must be hard for you. It's okay to cry, sweetie. I understand."

Then Leigh *was* crying. Between sobs she managed to get out, "No, you don't understand. I was *engaged* to him, for God's sake. But when you told me about his death back at Jen's house I didn't feel anything more than if I'd heard someone I knew in passing had died horribly. Now, when I think about anything, *anything* happening to you, I'm terrified." She almost choked on the last sentence, and her tears kept flowing.

Conn pulled to the side of the road, clicked them out of their seat belts, and lifted Leigh into her arms, holding her as she cried. They clung to each other.

When the tears had subsided into deep, ragged sighs, Conn crooned, "Leigh, I'm here and I'm fine. We've been through a lot. *You've* been through a lot. I'm not going anywhere."

Leigh raised her head from where it had been burrowed in her neck, and Conn kissed the eyes that were wet with tears for her. She also kissed her lips, then pulled back a bit. "Now we'd better get going. Much as I would like a repeat of our last 'discussion' in the car, this isn't the place. We'll be safe soon. Promise."

Leigh kissed her deeply, then sat up and looked at her. "How much farther?"

❖

Three hours later they came to a stoplight at the crossroads that took them along the lake road. Opening her sleepy eyes to see some stores and shops whiz by, Leigh realized it was late. While she was sleeping Conn must have turned on her seat heater, because although it looked cold outside, she was cozy. She checked the car's outside thermostat and saw it was in the thirties, then noticed a light dusting of snow on the ground.

Not far down the highway Conn turned the car again, away from the lake, and drove into a dark, quiet residential neighborhood. A few more turns and they were headed down a narrow road that seemed to dead-end in a large wooden fence. Conn jumped out and punched in a code to the right of the gate, her feet crunching on the snow and pine duff underneath. As the gate laboriously slid aside, she got back in and slowly drove through the gate, which closed behind them.

Floodlights were mounted high in some of the tall pine trees on the property where Conn stopped the Audi and started to get out, leaving the headlights on. "Don't be afraid," she quietly said to Leigh.

After closing the car door, she walked about three yards in front of the car and whistled softly. Leigh watched in fascination, unable to budge, as something pale and ghostly moved toward Conn. The apparition was pure white, with four legs, and at first she thought it was a large dog, maybe a German shepherd. But the legs were too long, and the body and head weren't right. The animal stopped perhaps fifteen feet from Conn, and Leigh could hear Conn talking to the apparition, but couldn't hear the words.

She looked at the face of the animal, illuminated in the headlights. A wolf. Suddenly it broke into a run and lunged at Conn, taking her to the ground. She lay there, motionless, the wolf standing over her. Then he opened his jaws, placed them over Conn's face, and clamped down.

## Chapter Eight

Paralyzed, Leigh stared, trying to scream, and watched in horror as the animal released his hold on her lover's face and nudged her with his snout. No blood. Conn reached up and pushed on the wolf's powerful chest, and the animal responded by clamping down on her arm. Gently. Conn laughed, then they wrestled on the ground, quietly growling at each other.

Leigh heard her name being called and, holding her breath, tentatively opened the door.

Conn scrambled to her feet and brushed herself off. "Come stand beside me. I want you to meet a friend."

Leigh closed her eyes and murmured, "Trust. Trust." As she forced her legs and body to do as she was told, Conn took her hand and held it, palm down, for the wolf to sniff.

"Lobo, this is Leigh. She is very important and very good. She is our pack. Leigh, meet Lobo. He runs this place."

Lobo sniffed, then gently clamped his huge jaws on her arm, which he quickly released, then sat down.

A friendly voice came from outside the glare of the headlights. "Welcome to Sally's Place. I see you've met the welcoming committee."

A short, sturdily built woman with curly brown hair appeared, hugged Conn, and shook Leigh's hand during introductions, then stood beside Lobo, scratching his ears. Conn slid her arm around Leigh's waist.

"Your cabin's ready, Conn. Just pull in over there and we can talk in the morning. Glad to see you brought someone this time. I'll have to tell your fan club you're off the market. Remember to keep your door locked, otherwise Lobo will figure a way to join you. See you tomorrow, and nice meeting you, Leigh."

As the woman strode out of the light she called Lobo, who seemed undecided, but slowly followed with his tail wagging. Conn pulled in front of a cabin with a porch light glowing, and they unloaded their gear.

As they were taking bags and luggage in, Leigh said, "You scared me to death. I thought you were going to be eaten by a ghost. What's with the noshing on people?"

"That's the way wolves greet each other and play," Conn explained. "They use their mouths. That nosh meant he's accepted you as part of his pack. He's a lap wolf, too. I daresay he's the only male a lot of the women who come here will let within ten feet of them."

"He's magnificent."

Conn nuzzled the back of her neck, then bit down with a low growl. "You're magnificent."

Laughing, Leigh pivoted in her arms. "So that's where you learned that. Does that mean I'm a member of your pack?"

"Oh, yeah. Official charter member. Secret handshake and all. Want me to initiate you?" She nipped Leigh's throat again, then licked, and Leigh felt a growing warmth in her belly. She needed Conn.

"Yes. But not until we're both a bit cleaner. You're covered in wolf spit and pine needles, and I'm a grimy mess. Is the shower big enough for two?"

Conn's eyes twinkled. "Alas, it's barely big enough for one. You get in first and I'll finish unloading the car. The initiation begins in twenty minutes!"

Leigh saluted her. "Aye aye, Captain. Engage." They rump-bumped each other and got to work.

Twenty minutes later they snuggled together under an electric blanket, but Leigh clicked it off. "I'll be warm with you wrapped around me. What about you?"

"Leigh, you can warm me up just looking at me across a room."

They kissed deeply, exploring each other until Leigh surrendered to the urgency of the day, the need to touch. Just feeling skin on skin brought her to the brink of release, and she found Conn's swollen clit and held her, motionless, for a moment before entering and steadily stroking her in rhythm with her body.

Conn gasped and spread her legs wider, inviting her closer, deeper.

Moving a leg over Conn's thigh, Leigh pressed down, her wetness coating the skin beneath it. Conn's response heightened her arousal.

"Deeper, go deeper. Hurry. Please."

Leigh went deeper, using her thumb to press and rub Conn's clitoris. As Conn started to release, moving against Leigh's hand and body, Leigh rode the motion and pulled her hand up as the muscles inside her lover contracted around her fingers.

Conn groaned, calling Leigh's name. After a few moments her breathing became quieter, but she was still moving. "My God. I've never, I didn't know—"

"Shh. Don't talk. Rest. You were unbelievable. Amazing. Wonderful. Thank you."

"Thank me?" Conn finally opened her eyes slightly. "I do believe I should be thanking *you*, my love."

Leigh smiled in the dark and kissed the neck just below her lips. Her body reflexively moved against Conn's pelvis, but she consciously stilled it, wanting Conn to enjoy her orgasm as long as possible. "Thank you for allowing me to love you. For giving yourself to me. When you let me pleasure you, I'm in a heaven I've never known."

They were quiet for a few moments, and Conn thought about what Leigh had said. Registering Leigh's continued arousal, she knew her partner was denying her own need, so she slowly pushed her pelvis into Leigh, who groaned in response.

Conn stroked Leigh's back, gently rocking with her, then slid her hands down over Leigh's firm buttocks and parted her legs so that they rested on either side of Conn's hips. Thanking all the powers that be for long arms and fingers, Conn first touched, then slid into, the wetness waiting for her.

"Oh, God! Oh, my G—"

Conn continued the motion as Leigh's eyes rolled back and she grabbed Conn's shoulders, arching her upper torso away as her pelvis ground repeatedly.

Then Conn moved her other hand between their bodies and put steady pressure on Leigh's clitoris. She came almost immediately, crying out her name, calling her Constantina as she collapsed on top of her.

After their breathing calmed, Conn rolled Leigh to her side so they could spoon. Leigh was like a rag doll, and Conn wasn't much better. Just before she drifted off she realized that she had never liked her given name before Leigh had spoken it in passion. From now on, she would feel differently.

❖

When Leigh opened her eyes to the faint morning light that crept through the drawn curtains, the warmth surrounding her didn't seem right. Then she heard a low voice coming from the other room. Turning over, she realized Conn wasn't there, but the electric blanket was on.

"Conn?" The name came out more like a squawk. Leigh stretched and moved her legs to try and wake up, sure she hadn't budged one millimeter after falling asleep.

She heard Conn say, "Okay, as soon as possible. It's your only priority, so pull in whatever resources you need. Hold on, I know she'd want to say hello."

Dressed in fleece warm-ups, Conn appeared in the doorway wearing her enigmatic smile. She walked to the bed, eyes locked on Leigh's, with a lot more in them than good morning. Leigh sleepily tried to respond, but guessed she was minimally successful.

Finally Conn seemed to remember she was holding a cell phone, which she handed to Leigh, letting her fingers linger. "Um, here. Someone wants to say hi."

Leigh broke eye contact to look at the phone and had to clear her throat before she could find her voice. "He…hello?"

The voice at the other end sounded familiar. "So, having a good time?"

"Patrick? Is that you? Where are you?"

"In D.C., working my tush off for my new boss, while you're off playing around with her. It's a lot better here than in Boston. And where might you be, my pretty?"

Looking at the tousled sheets, Leigh suddenly recalled the night before and felt warm. "Well, um, I'm in California at an undisclosed location. How's that?"

"Uh-huh. Are you having fun?"

"Well, other than almost getting killed and being hunted, I'd have to say yes."

Pat's tone changed immediately. "Oh, honey. I've been so worried about you. Conn gave me emergency clearance so I can get updates. I knew you were with Conn and was sure you'd be safe. Are you? Safe and okay?"

Leigh found herself unable to stop from blurting, "Patty, I'm so in love! I've never felt this way about anyone. As frightening as some of the things have been, I've never been happier. She's wonderful!"

Immediately Pat sounded guarded. "Well, that's good to hear. Yeah, really good. Okay, I hope to see you soon."

"You're not alone. Is this conversation being recorded?" Leigh was suddenly wide-awake and her stomach clenched.

"No, I'm not and I don't know. But better to be safe. I really am glad, Leigh. The other person, too?"

"I think so."

"I think yes, very much so. Well, I have to get back to work, see you soon, hon. Be careful. Bye."

Leigh looked at the phone as she folded it, then placed it on the nightstand. Hearing a cough from the doorway, she looked up and saw Conn holding two steaming cups of tea. In fact, she seemed to be studying the tea. Leigh knew she'd overheard the conversation, and her stomach knot tightened. What if the conversation was recorded? What if Conn didn't want her private life mixed with business? Silly, of *course* she didn't want them mixed. What was she thinking?

She breathed deeply to try to calm her anxiety. "Good morning."

When Conn put the cups down, Leigh noticed her hands tremble slightly and wondered if she was angry at Leigh for blurting out her love over the almost certainly recorded phone conversation. She should have realized Conn would want discretion.

"Are you…" Conn seemed guarded.

"Pregnant? Probably, after last night." It was the first thing that popped into her head.

Conn's mouth opened, then closed. She looked like she was sucking air.

Leigh grinned, then met her lover's eyes evenly. "In love with you? Yes. How often do I need to say it?"

"Are you sure?"

Her voice was soft, but those eyes— "I've never been more sure of anything in my life. Ever."

Propped up on her elbows, Leigh became aware that her breasts were bare just as Conn pulled the sheet up over them and sat down on the bed.

"Conn, I need to know what you really feel. You keep asking if I'm sure, and I keep telling you. Are you having second thoughts? Is that why you keep asking *me*? Have you decided that it's just great sex and that's it for you? Tell me from your heart."

She felt her face heat as Conn studied her. Conn might have a hard time putting her thoughts into words, but she'd always been honest with Leigh. It was too late to pray for the answer she wanted.

"That's why I covered your breasts." Conn kissed her gently on her lips. "I didn't want you to think that sex had anything to do with my words. It's why I asked you if you were sure. I…I am in love with you. Truly, madly, deeply in love. I want you always. I've never said that to anyone, and I doubt I would ever say it to anyone but you again. And, Leigh? I'm scared spitless." She stared at her hands, clasped tightly together in her lap.

Leigh covered them with her own. "Those are the most beautiful words I've ever heard. I'm scared, too. Of a number of things, but not about us. As long as I have you, I can get through anything. C'mere."

As she pulled Conn into a strong embrace, the covers fell down again and Conn's hand brushed the side of her breast. Her breath caught, and she rolled Conn over her body and onto the bed, so she was outside the covers next to her.

"So, great sex had nothing to do with it?" Leigh whispered.

They looked into each other's eyes, and Leigh unzipped the fleece top, sliding her hand inside to feel Conn's full breast. She cupped it and teased the nipple to make it harder, then covered it with her mouth as she finished unzipping the jacket. Pushing the material aside, she worked on the other one.

"Well, maybe, just a…a little."

Conn gasped and moaned as Leigh moved on top of her, kissing her lips and neck, then sat up and pulled the rest of Conn's clothing off.

"I want to know you in the biblical sense," Leigh said, her voice husky. "To taste you."

"I'm not sure that tasting," Conn panted, "was included in the bi—"

Leigh silenced her with her insistent mouth.

They kissed for a long time, exploring lips and mouths, ears and necks. Leigh gradually worked her way down Conn's body, licking and sucking, teasing with her tongue and lips. Using her knee to spread Conn's legs farther apart, Leigh settled between them.

Conn's auburn curls were already soaked with desire, and as Leigh parted her, she could see the swollen lips and clitoris. "My God, you are so beautiful."

She stroked first with her fingers, then with her tongue. Long, languid strokes, extracting pleas for more. Watching Conn react to her movements, she tasted, smelled, and savored the changes as Conn neared her release. She slowed her pace, then started again, harder and faster.

Finally, she heard, "Leigh. Now!"

As she rapidly worked her tongue and teeth to pleasure the bundle of nerves she held in her mouth, Conn's body arched up, perfectly still, trembling, then she started to roll and buck as the orgasms hit her. Leigh held on, continuing until Conn begged her to stop, then gently released her, covered them both, and lay beside her until Conn's breathing returned to normal.

"Was that biblical enough for you?"

Leigh snorted. "That went way beyond biblical."

After a few moments of holding each other, Conn mumbled, "I know I've said this, but my God, woman, are you sure you've never done this before? That was unbelievable."

"Actually, I *have* done this before." Leigh grinned. "With a woman with whom I'm hopelessly in love. It's just…now I'm getting to know her body and she trusts me more. And I'm a dedicated student."

Rolling onto her side, Leigh propped her head on her hand. "She knows I love her and will always keep her safe. I'll never hurt her and I'll never leave her. So you see, it's really—"

Conn silenced her with kisses. Leigh's fears of moments before faded.

❖

Hunger and an incessant whining and pawing at the front door of their cabin finally got them out of the bedroom. Leigh ducked into the shower, muttering something about not facing a hundred-pound male wolf in her current condition, while Conn managed to locate her fleece and start a fire in the fireplace, then turned up the thermostat and put some water on to boil. Reluctantly, she washed her hands and face to eliminate some of the more obvious traces of their lovemaking before dealing with Lobo.

As soon as she opened the door, the white wolf bounded in and jumped on the sofa, settling down immediately. He seemed content to stay there.

"Good morning to you, too, Lobo. Make yourself at home."

After picking up a newspaper from the front doorstep, Conn sat down beside him to read, and he lounged all over her, chomping and noshing, rolling and wiggling.

From the doorway Leigh toweled her hair dry as she watched them. "Are you sure I shouldn't be jealous?"

"Nah. Lobo doesn't have romantic intentions. He's my bro. He's like a fag hag. I don't know what that's called. A dyke dick? Dyke hag? Dyke dog?"

Leigh laughed as she picked up her cup of tea in the kitchen, then sat on the love seat adjacent to the sofa. "So we have an adopted son."

"Looks that way, doesn't it?"

Every time Conn heard Leigh use the word "we" she felt her heart open a little more, but wondered if she would ever be able to use the term as easily as Leigh did. How long before she could trust that she, indeed, had found someone who wouldn't betray or leave her? Leigh had never lied to her, never done anything resembling the games some women wanted to play.

Yet Conn had really trusted only two people in her life, her aunt Jen and Jen's partner Marina. Those two had been her support and love since she was a kid and had never let her down. Thinking that someone else could love her, love her like Marina loved Jen, seemed too much to ask, like a fantasy that was always just out of reach.

"Conn? Where were you? You left the room."

"Wha—oh. Oh, nowhere. I was just daydreaming." She busied herself with Lobo.

Leigh watched her avoid the question and let it go. She saw the clouds gather momentarily in Conn's eyes, but they disappeared when they came back to her. *Some day, my love, you will know what I know. There couldn't be another you in my life. I'll give you all the time you need to realize that I'll never let you go.*

"Let me repeat my question. Is that what we are? Dykes? I've always heard that used as a slur. Like the N-word. Pat has had people say he was a Jap and mean it in a hateful way. It even happened in college—well, you get the idea."

Momentarily confused, Conn wondered where Leigh's question had come from. Then she realized that though she'd had plenty of time to think about her sexual orientation, Leigh had just entered a new world. Perhaps in the end Leigh would decide that she didn't want to be considered a dyke. Would this issue be the one that made Leigh decide against her?

The question only added to her morose thoughts. It confirmed her suspicion that she wasn't worthy of a forever love like her aunt and Marina had. She shuddered a bit, but she took a deep breath and tried to center herself. She had to be honest.

"We're two women in love. That would make us lesbians. Some women live their whole lives with another woman and never use the word. They have no other friends or couples similar to themselves and don't allow themselves any public display of affection for fear of reprisal. Unfortunately, they have no sense that they aren't the only ones, and—I can't leave this one out—they have a deep sense of shame and self-loathing."

Fearing the worst, she watched Leigh carefully for any reaction, but saw only rapt attention.

"'Dyke' is a term we could use to describe someone we think is lesbian, too. But we'd use it when we're with other lesbians. Like African Americans use the N-word with each other to joke with each other. Does that help?"

"So I'm a lesbian? The moment we made love I'm a lesbian?"

*Oh, shit.* "Well, some people would say that. But a lot of women are curious and have an affair with a woman, then go back to men because it's safer and easier. And some explore and find that they simply prefer men. Others say that if they hadn't met their husband, they would be with a woman. Jen and Marina taught me that love is where you find it." She glanced at Lobo. "True love, anyway."

She watched Leigh as she seemed to consider the words.

*Okay, here goes. Nothing but the truth. If she doesn't want me, I'll just have to learn to live without her, without anyone.*

"Leigh? You need to know that I'm a lesbian. I've always been attracted to women. Not that I've done that much about it, but that's who I am."

Leigh gazed solemnly out into space. Even Lobo watched her

expectantly. "A lesbian. Who would have thought? My mother is going to have a cow."

Conn almost choked on her own saliva. "What? Is that all? Your mother's going to have a cow?"

"Well, obviously I need time to think about all the ramifications." Leigh smiled. "But if they wanted to call me a two-toed sloth, that would be okay. As long as I'm with you, I don't care."

Leigh sat on the coffee table in front of Conn, gently took her chin, and turned it to face her. "Let me say that again. As long as I have you, I…don't…care. Got it?"

Conn nodded slightly, knowing tears were threatening to spill down her face, but somehow not embarrassed. "Got it."

Leigh seemed to steel herself, then said, "By the way, was my conversation with Pat recorded or overheard by others? Because if it was, a certain number of people are well aware of my feelings for you."

Conn had recovered enough to smile at her ruefully. "It was recorded, although personal parts are supposed to be deleted. I wouldn't bet on it, though. There's been so much speculation about me that it's probably already posted on the company intranet."

After a pause Leigh said, "Well, you didn't confirm how you felt about me. If it makes you uncomfortable I could be just another of your love-struck admirers."

Conn looked at her steadily. *She'd do that for me.* "Not a snowball's chance in hell. As a matter of fact, I'm considering taking out a full-page ad in the *Wall Street Journal*."

Leigh gave her a for-her-eyes-only smile and kissed her solidly on the lips. "Good. Now show our son the door so you can get ready. I'm starved!"

# CHAPTER NINE

Leigh opened the front door and smelled the pine-scented air. After trying to absorb every atom of the crystal-clear sky and the slight breeze that whooshed through tall conifers, she turned to go back inside and noticed a folded note on the door. It had “Stryker” written on it, so she kept it folded and took it inside.

Leigh handed the note to Conn, who was brushing her thick auburn curls, and pulled her into a fierce kiss. When they parted, Conn’s eyes questioned her.

“Just in case the party’s over.” Leigh nodded toward the note.

Conn opened it and read out loud, “‘Call Maggie stat.’ Well. When we talked at the hospital I told her we were coming here.” She examined the note. “It came in after my call to Pat. He’s supposed to be my contact unless news comes in.” Then she checked her phone. “Damn. I missed a call. As good as this phone is, it doesn’t always work up in the mountains.”

She smiled reassuringly. “Hey, maybe they’ve caught Dieter and Georgia.”

Conn went into the bedroom, where they seemed to have a better connection, and a few minutes later she was deep in conversation, so Leigh left her alone.

She cleaned the kitchen, straightened the living room, then brought more firewood in from the front porch. Nervous, she conjured up all sorts of horrible scenarios and was relieved when Conn finally finished her call.

Conn’s face was unreadable as she approached and wrapped her arms around Leigh’s waist. “We’re okay. It was an update and a reminder that we have to be reachable. I'll keep the phone with me. Come on, let's go eat and I'll explain." She kissed her on the forehead, and they stayed in each other's arms briefly, then silently walked to the car.

After ordering fresh organic food at a café overlooking Lake Tahoe, they quietly regarded each other over coffee, and Leigh ran a finger around the rim of her cup. "Where do you want to begin?"

"Peter's business is shut down, and not just for the funeral. The feds came in and took all the records, but it looks like Georgia and Dieter grabbed what they could and split. From what Pat has found so far, they were setting Peter up to take the fall after they had artificially inflated some select stocks and sold them before the shit hit the fan."

Leigh nodded and Conn paused before she continued. "Peter must have finally realized what was happening and confronted them. He probably had no idea who he was dealing with. If he had, he might have turned himself in just to save his own life. But I'm speculating, Leigh. We'll probably never know for sure. He was, after all, executed professionally."

"By the man who tried to kill us." The certainty of it made her queasy. "Was Peter tortured before he was shot?"

"Yes, but how did you—?"

"Because that's what he promised me. Long and slow." She stared at the table. "Long and slow."

New, powerful feelings almost overwhelmed Conn: fear for Leigh's life, rage that anyone would threaten her, and the need to protect her. And she was certain these emotions endangered both of them; after all, she had always been so effective because she had no fear. She had to calm down and think, but she craved to kill him again, this time with her bare hands instead of her knife.

"Conn? Are you okay?"

"I, yeah, I just can't—"

Leigh covered her hand. "He's dead, Conn. We're safe, thanks to you. Do you know who he was?"

The distraction of talking and the reassurance of Leigh's touch helped Conn return to the moment. "Yes. He was German, named Gunter Schmidt and nicknamed Hatch. He was for hire and was tied to several terrorist organizations."

Just then Leigh spotted the waitress coming down the aisle with their food and withdrew her hand, but not before seeing that the server had noticed and smiled.

"Conn? Our food's here. We both need a break, so let's not discuss this until we're out of here, okay?"

Conn nodded and sat back while the waitress put their food down. "Oh, Maggie spoke to Jen. She's fine—in Paris and visiting old friends. Marina flew back to Karachi two days ago. When we get some pictures I can e-mail them to her, and we'll call later."

Leigh smiled, delighted to change the subject.

After driving down the road that circled Lake Tahoe, they turned left, away from the lake, and headed up and into the woods. Locating a parking spot, they took a light backpack and a few bottles of water and followed a trail to some beautiful vistas of the lake. Signs of fall were transforming the mountains; the leaves were turning and the air felt crisp.

After a half hour or so Conn diverted them away from the hiking trail and up a narrow deer trail where no human footprints were visible. When they reached the top of it she showed Leigh her favorite spot, a huge boulder, easily twice as tall as Conn. With some scrambling and a hand up from Conn, they were on top of the world.

Leigh held her arms out and did a full 360-degree turn. "My gods and goddesses. I've never seen anything like this. How did you find it?"

Conn sat and leaned against some rocks, watching Leigh. "I've hiked these trails for years, and one day I just decided to follow the deer. I come here to think, alone. I've never shown it to anyone else."

Dropping to her knees in front of Conn, Leigh said, "Thank you. Thank you for sharing your secret spot with me. I'll keep the secret. It will always be yours."

"It's ours now. Always ours."

Leigh smiled with every fiber of her being. "You know, of course, that I just fell in love with you again."

Conn regarded her shyly. "And I, you."

Lying on the light blanket that Conn had brought in the backpack, they held each other and listened to the sounds of the forest and the animals. The birds and squirrels seemed to have forgotten that they were there, and they heard deer pass by below.

When Leigh opened her eyes next, the sun was sinking lower in the sky and the air was cooler. She gently nudged Conn awake and they gathered up their gear, Conn helping Leigh down from the boulder.

As they walked quietly down the trail, at one particular vista Conn stopped to take a few more photographs. Then she fiddled with the camera's timer so they could both get in the picture. They had no shots of them together, and she definitely wanted some.

Behind them a female voice asked, "Want me to take it for you?"

"Oh, thank you!" Leigh immediately said. "That would be great."

Conn grinned at Leigh and handed the woman the camera. She was pointing to the shutter and was about to explain which button to press when the woman spoke again.

"Strike? Conn Stryker?"

Conn looked up into familiar eyes, but couldn't quite place the face.

"It's Andy. Andrea Jensen. From Stanford. How are you?"

The tumblers fell into place for Conn. The only woman who had stood up for her when the mess with Gwen had happened. They'd stayed in touch for a while, but hadn't seen each other since Conn had left for D.C.

"Andy? Damn! It's been years! I can't believe it!" They hugged a bit awkwardly, since Conn never had been a hugger.

Conn suddenly remembered Leigh. "Oh! I'm sorry. My manners are awful. Andy, this is Leigh Grove. Leigh, this is Andrea Jensen, an old friend from undergrad at Stanford."

"Please call me Andy." She enthusiastically shook Leigh's hand. "My friends all do. Now let me get that picture I offered to take. How does this one work?"

As Conn showed her the features, she added, "Oh boy, this is nice. I guess you still like all the gadgets. Leigh, you look like a model."

While Andy played with the camera, previewing the pictures as they appeared on the back of it, Conn playfully pinched Leigh's backside and Leigh yelped, "Constantina Stryker! Quit that!"

Andy looked up. "Constantina? I thought only your aunt was allowed to call you that."

"You remember that?" Conn was astounded.

"I remember a lot of things. I'm not sure you thought so, but you were a most remarkable person even back then. Okay, huddle up."

Leigh and Conn posed side by side, Conn draping her arm carelessly over Leigh's shoulders.

Andy took a shot, then said, "This is fun. Let me take some more. Come on, ham it up!"

They started mugging and jostling each other, with Andy clicking away. At one point they got lost in each other's eyes. *Click.*

"That's better. Conn, get behind Leigh and put your arms around her waist."

She did and the contact made her smile. *Click.*

"Got it. Made for each other." Andy looked over the camera and said, "You are, aren't you? Made for each other?"

They pulled back so they could regard each other. *Click.*

"In every way," Conn said. *Click.* She felt Leigh gently squeeze her arm.

Andy smiled. "Good, because you make an amazing couple. I'm really happy for you, Conn."

Conn relaxed. *Click.*

"Thanks, Andy." Conn thought the grin they exchanged signaled a new level of friendship.

Later, when they walked down to the car, Andy and Conn chatting the whole way, Leigh impulsively asked her to join them for dinner and Andy agreed, suggesting a place on the lake not far from their cabin.

Just before they were on their way Andy turned to Conn. "Say, have you heard from Gwen?"

Conn tensed. "No. Should I have?"

"Well, she's gone through two husbands and took them for as much as she could. She has a house up here, hard-won in one of the divorce settlements. All of the members of the old crew are aware of your success, Conn. I'm surprised she hasn't tried to make you number three."

"The chances of that are slim and none." Conn smiled tightly, appalled at the thought. "Besides, isn't she straight?"

"Let's just say sexual preference isn't her motivating factor. See you two at seven. I'll make the reservation and I'm bringing a friend, if that's okay."

"Good!" Leigh interjected. "We'll see you then. Come on, honey."

Hearing the word "honey" eased Conn's tension. She started the car and they waved as they passed Andy.

Leigh and Conn rode silently for a while, Conn mulling over pleasant thoughts about Andy and unpleasant ones about Gwen.

"Tell me about Andy. When did you meet?"

"What? Oh, uh, my freshman year. She was in my dorm, and we were in a study group together. She was always really nice to me, especially since I was the only freshman and the rest were older. Well, at the time I thought they were a lot older."

"How old were you when you started college?"

"Sixteen. I never really identified with high school. It seemed so, I don't know, silly. That, and I couldn't wait to get out of town and be on my own. I wanted to be close to Jen and Marina, which was always where I was happiest, so I applied for early admission to Stanford and got in."

"You were in a study group to help handle the college workload?"

Conn felt the corner of her mouth tick up. "Actually, I found most of the work, at least in the sciences, relatively easy. The woman Andy mentioned, Gwen Edwards, invited me to join the group because they were really struggling. I suppose I have a knack for explaining difficult concepts and was able to help them."

"Uh-huh. And be close to Gwen Edwards, too?"

Caught off guard, Conn almost stuttered. "No, I was just..." She stopped to consider what Leigh had just said. "Yeah. Be close to Gwen. She was nice to me, included me. You've probably gathered that I don't have a lot of close friends. I thought I'd found one, but I discovered the hard way that she was using me. I helped her with her grades and even pimped for her. Or, I should say, she pimped for me."

That comment seemed to get Leigh's full attention. "What?"

Conn felt her body tense as she remembered those painful days. "I, the budding lesbian virgin, had a huge crush on her, although I didn't realize then what was happening. She'd fix me up with all of these double dates with fraternity guys she wanted to impress, and I went so I could be close to her. I put up with their drooling and attempts at pawing just to be around Gwen."

Leigh could hear the self-blame in her voice.

"Every now and then I'd get fed up and refuse to go. Then she'd come to my room and flirt with me, tease me. A kiss, a touch, a promise.

And I always gave in. I found out later that her dating status had gone up because she offered the package. They were betting on who would be the one to nail me."

The hurt in Conn's voice made Leigh's heart ache.

"One day when I arrived early to the study group, I heard my name and stopped and listened in the hall. They were all laughing and joking about the crush I had on Gwen, and the only person who stood up for me was Andy. I quit the group that day and never spoke to Gwen or the others again, except for Andy. I decided to get the hell out of college the way I got the hell out of high school: early. By nineteen I was on my way to Boston. So that's the whole miserable story. Your girlfriend was a flop in college."

They'd stopped in front of the gate to Sally's, and when Conn started to get out, Leigh grasped her arm.

"My girlfriend was a lonely sixteen-year-old in a huge university. She was just looking for a friend. You were used, honey. There's no shame in that. How were you supposed to know? I understand what it feels like to be pimped out. Awful. I wish I'd been there. I would have settled her hash."

Conn's voice was rough with emotion. "You know, of course, that I just fell in love with you again."

Leigh smiled at Conn's repetition of her earlier words and completed their litany. "And I, you. Never stop saying it."

"Want to go 'discuss' things for a while?"

"No." Leigh ran her tongue lightly over her upper teeth. "I want to go fuck your brains out."

Conn sucked in some air. "Be right back." She ripped out of the car and speed-walked to the gate, punched in the code, and within seconds they were inside the cabin.

# CHAPTER TEN

Conn lay in the jumbled sheets, listening to the shower. She and Leigh were supposed to meet Andy and her friend in an hour, but Conn wasn't sure she had enough strength to crawl out of the bed.

She stretched and lay back, hands behind her head. "My, my. I always thought 'fuck your brains out' was just an expression. Now I are one."

They had barely made it into the cabin before ripping each other's clothes off and letting desire consume all thought, first on the couch and then on the bed. Just thinking about it made her body react again.

The covers slipped down and a warm mouth covered her breast, teasing her to attention. She groaned and opened her eyes to see Leigh gazing at her, tongue poised for another assault.

"Oh. You're awake. Just thought I would, um, play. A bit."

"Darling, if you play any more we won't make the restaurant. I promise."

Leigh looked at her solemnly. "And you always keep your promises."

"Yes, I do. So, are you hungry? Or are you…*hungry*!" She pulled Leigh down on top of her, and they wrestled for a few minutes, tickling and laughing.

"Okay, okay! Stop! I give up! I really think we should go meet Andy. And…I'm starved!" Leigh barely choked out the words.

After the tickling subsided and they held each other a moment, Conn sighed, "I'd better hit the shower. Maybe by the time I get out I'll be able to put a coherent sentence together."

She had just reached the doorway when she heard Leigh call her name.

"Yes?"

"You called me darling. That's the first time you've said it. I like it."

Conn leaned on the door frame. "I love you."

Leigh's eyes rolled back in her head and she flopped onto the bed. "Get in the shower, woman, or we won't be leaving for a long time."

Conn bowed. "Yes, ma'am."

As Leigh was getting dressed, she decided to prepare for their night out, just in case. She applied makeup, subtle and understated, for the first time since she'd quit her job. Finally, all those years as a model were coming in handy.

When Conn got out of the shower, Leigh was already in the other room, so she dressed quickly and smoothed on some mascara and lip gloss. As she walked into the living room she halted.

Leigh stood by the fireplace in dark blue jeans with snakeskin boots. Her plum-colored shirt was loosely tucked in over a stretchy white V-necked tee, but only buttoned near the waist. The tee revealed the softness of her breasts in a way that made Conn feel decidedly warm.

As their eyes met, the only thing she saw was the love in them for her. "We, um, had better get going. God, Leigh, you look amazing."

"Thank you. Wow. So do you." Conn had chosen black leather pants with a light blue shirt to accentuate her long, lean form and make her appear dangerous. Her tan made her blue eyes stand out.

They arrived at the restaurant only a few minutes late and were shown to their table, where Andy and her guest stood to greet them, shaking hands across the table.

Conn registered that the new woman, introduced as Sarah Ashland, looked vaguely familiar. In fact, the name was even more familiar than the face. She was small and petite, with white-blond hair and pale blue eyes, and looked at Conn as though she knew her.

"You don't remember me, do you?" Sarah was smiling.

"No. I can't place where we've met, except it seems like a long time ago. My apologies."

"None needed. I was three years behind you at Stanford, although I think we're close to the same age. You were a discussion group leader in one of my freshman classes. Of course, by that time you were a senior."

Conn nodded.

"Didn't you ever notice how, as a group, we were incredibly stupid? We passed notes to each other suggesting questions to ask you after class, just to keep you there."

The words took Conn back to her senior year, when she was a teaching assistant for a freshman physics class. Professor Weiser had joked about needing eye candy to keep the students awake, and he used Conn as often as he could.

"That was on purpose? I kept complaining that I'd never seen such an incompetent group of people. During lectures your faces looked like you were getting it, but the number of redundant questions during the discussions…"

Sarah and Andy laughed, and Andy added, "When Sarah first told me about her freshman crush on a TA, then described her, I didn't need the name. Conn, you have no idea the fantasies you evoked during your undergraduate years."

Conn blushed, and the innocence of her reaction endeared her to Leigh, who let her knee touch Conn's under the table. Conn returned the pressure.

"Well, that explains a lot. I thought I was a lousy teacher. But my student evaluations came back with extraordinarily high ratings. I couldn't figure it out."

Just then the waiter arrived and they asked for a bottle of zinfandel. They busied themselves with the menu, but by the time their wine was served and they'd ordered, Leigh's curiosity was burning.

"Are you two together?" The smiles from both of them encouraged her next question. "Since college?"

"Well, we met in college, but didn't pay much attention to each other," Andy said. "Then a year ago we were reintroduced and the rest, as the saying goes, is herstory."

"So, who reintroduced you?"

Suddenly both women looked uncomfortable. Embarrassed.

Leigh sat up straighter. "Did I say something wrong?" She glanced at Conn, who looked as nonplussed as Leigh felt.

"No, of course not," Sarah answered. "It's just that, well, uh, my sister introduced us. My *half* sister really. We're not close. But that's who introduced us." Her voice trailed off to nothing at the end, and she glanced pleadingly at Andy.

Andy took a breath and smiled grimly. "Her half sister is Gwen. That's how I know what she's up to these days. As much as we try to avoid her, family obligations keep rearing their ugly heads. So now you know. I hope you'll still speak to us."

Leigh was quiet as she watched Conn's eyes turn cold and her jaw tighten for a moment. Leigh squeezed her thigh under the table, and Conn sighed.

"If people held me responsible for my family members, it would be an unjust world. Andy, you were the only one who stood up for me. Sarah? We can't pick our relatives, just our friends. Let's toast to new friends and old. It's good to be with you both."

Andy and Sarah looked so relieved Leigh thought the wineglasses might shatter from the enthusiasm of the toast.

Their dinner came and they concentrated on it until coffee and dessert had been served. Sarah, who had been stealing quite a few glances at Leigh during the meal, finally asked, "You look so familiar. Have you ever modeled? Been on the cover of a few magazines?"

Leigh looked at Conn, who just raised her eyebrows. Her face warming, she answered, "Yes. I paid my way through college doing it. It's been a few years, but every now and then people with really good memories connect all the dots."

Sarah beamed. "What a treat to meet you! Connecting the dots is easy because you were my favorite model, and I believe you made most of the covers for a while. I'm so glad that you're with Conn. I'm really happy for both of you."

They toasted again, then Sarah asked, "How did you meet?"

Leigh didn't know quite what to say, so she turned to Conn. "I've never heard you tell this. You take it."

"We actually met through my aunt Jen," Conn said smoothly. "Leigh was her financial advisor and they became friends. She was engaged at the time and had sought out Jen for advice when, um, when they were breaking up. We met a short time later and one thing led to another. So here we are."

*Well, that was vague*. Leigh gave her a look, and Conn just smiled innocently.

Sarah didn't seem to mind. "When did you realize you were in love?"

Leigh jumped in. “Realizing and admitting are two different things. As I look back, I fell in love with her the moment I laid eyes on her. But, of course, I thought I was straight at the time. That delayed things for a while.”

The easy conversation went on, and they decided to continue the evening at a nearby bar. Andy knew the way, so Conn followed them.

On the way, Leigh looked over at her lover’s strong profile. “I really like those two. I can’t tell you what a treat it is to hear stories about you from people who’ve known you. You’re such a good person, Conn. I’m so proud to be with you.”

She could tell her compliments made Conn blush. “Honey, you’d better get used to me telling you how I feel. Good and bad, we’ll be talking about it.”

Conn glanced at her. “I know. I love it when you say those things. No one except Jen and Marina have ever—anyway, no one that counted. When you say them I think they might just have a bit of truth in them. And I want us to talk. It’s not something I’m accustomed to, but it feels easy with you.”

They pulled into a crowded parking lot, and Andy and Sarah found a place first, then waved and went in while Conn searched for a slot. Once they found one they sat for a moment.

“Watching you duck around the modeling thing was charming, you know,” Conn said. “I’ve met a few models and thought there was nothing below the pretty surface. You don’t take that part of your life too seriously, and I admire that.”

Then a ferocious grin popped onto her face. “That being said, my girl is a cover girl, my girl is a model!” Her head was thrown back and her chest puffed out as she kept chanting the sentence. Leigh was begging her to stop as they got out of the car and headed to the door of the bar.

As they walked in, Leigh spotted the restroom and gave Conn a quick kiss, pointing to the sign as she headed in that direction.

Conn stood, hands in her back pockets, scanning the room for Andy and Sarah, oblivious to the stares of the people in the bar. She felt softness at her elbow and smiled as she turned, expecting Leigh, but what she saw made her swallow her smile. Gwen Edwards was looking at her in a way that made Conn feel like a field mouse having just met a rattlesnake.

"Conn! It's so good to see you! It's been years! Did you know Andy's here? Come on. Let's go catch up. Andy's with my sister Sarah. They're over here." She grabbed Conn's hand and led her to where Andy and Sarah were sitting, looking decidedly twitchy.

Conn was suddenly an awkward sixteen-year-old, unable to resist whatever Gwen told her to do. She sat at the table as Gwen pulled up a chair next to her.

"You look great! I can't believe it's been so long since we've talked."

When Leigh came out of the bathroom and searched the room for Conn and their friends, she saw Andy first and started for the table. Another woman was sitting next to Conn, too close to Conn. Leigh stopped and studied the four people at the table. Andy and Sarah were sitting up stiffly and as far back in their chairs as they could. Conn looked almost catatonic, nowhere near her body.

The woman put her hand on Conn's arm, and Conn just stared at it like she didn't know what to do with it. *What the—uh-oh. Be careful what you wish for. I think I'm about to meet the infamous Gwen.*

Leigh took a few more seconds to size up the situation and decide on a plan, then surreptitiously positioned herself so she could see Gwen's face and watch the interaction at the table. Well, interaction wasn't quite the word. "Assault" came to mind.

Gwen was doing all the talking, and the others spoke only when spoken to. Her eyes were almost predatory, and it looked like Conn was dinner. Conn appeared so young and fragile sitting there, staring in the direction of the bathrooms.

*Enough. Time to rescue my honey.* Leigh shifted into a role she had been trained for since she was an infant by watching her mother, enduring debutante balls, and meeting all the right people. She added her experience as a model and produced enough star wattage to light the room, then transformed into Leigh Grove: Society Cover Girl. *People like Gwen love this shit. My mother would be so proud.*

Straightening up to her full height, she pulled the vee of her T-shirt down to reveal some additional cleavage and purposefully walked up to the table, eyes on Conn, who saw her coming and looked stunned. Leigh winked and rounded the table to stand behind her, possessively placing her hands on her shoulders. She slid them down her front, almost skimming the top of Conn's breasts. She hugged her and kissed her cheek, then pulled back to gaze into her surprised eyes.

"Sorry, I had to check on the shirt. Did I miss anything?"

She looked at Gwen as if noticing her for the first time and gave her a dazzling smile. Pure *Glamour*. When she glanced down at Gwen's hand on Conn's arm, Gwen removed it as though she'd been scalded.

Leigh stuck out her hand. "Hi. I'm Leigh. Conn's partner." As she leaned over to shake, she noticed Gwen quickly taking in her breasts and her figure. *Good.*

"I'm, um, Gwen Edwards. An old friend of Conn's. From Stanford." She seemed to be trying to regain control and emphasized the last word.

Leigh continued the smile. Two could play that game. "Ah, all these Stanford girls. An Easterner like me doesn't stand a chance."

Gwen seemed to gather courage from the remark. "Oh, what school did you go to?" she asked with a hint of smugness.

"Harvard. But only undergraduate. Wharton for my MBA. How about you? Where did you go to graduate school?"

Gwen's makeup seemed to smudge. "I, uh, didn't go to graduate school. I got married."

"To a man? That must have been fun. Can I buy anyone a drink?"

Leigh looked across the table and saw that Sarah was close to exploding and Andy had gone into a coughing fit. They both managed to shake their heads, but didn't look at her. Conn was speechless, her eyes perfectly round.

Gwen tried again. "You…you mentioned a shirt. What kind of shirt can you buy in a place like this?" Clearly derisive of the bar they were in, her eyes sweeping the patronage disparagingly, she angered Leigh, who crouched next to Conn.

"I put in a special order. It's for Conn." Using her hand to demonstrate where the writing would be, she explained, "It says, Warning: Private Property." Her hand swept across in front of Conn's breasts, then dropped to just below that for the next line. "Trespassers will be shot."

She gave Gwen another glowing smile. "Do you like it?"

Gwen suddenly stood up, nearly knocking the chair over. "Lovely. Well, I've got to be going. Nice seeing you again, Conn. Nice meeting you, uh, Leigh. Perhaps some other time. Bye!" She almost ran out of the bar.

Leigh stood up and dusted off her hands as she looked at the retreating figure. "Buh-bye."

Someone near the bar started clapping. Then a few more joined in, and soon the whole place was applauding and cheering. Evidently Gwen and her attitude had been in before.

As Leigh took a deep bow, she heard some strangling sounds behind her and turned back to the table to see Andy and Sarah gasping for air and pounding the table, tears streaming down their faces. Conn was still staring at the swinging door, grinning.

Leigh sauntered to the vacated chair and turned it backward, straddling it to sit, and looked around the table. "What?"

"Private property?" Conn managed. "Trespassers will be shot?"

Through narrowed eyelids Leigh said, "Yup. You got a problem with that, woman?"

"None at all, you big, strong, handsome *dyke*," Conn finally answered. "Is it okay if we dance, sweetie?"

"Dyke. I think I like it. Okay, let's dance. But remember, I lead."

Everyone at the table except Leigh groaned.

## CHAPTER ELEVEN

Panting and sweating, Leigh struggled to keep up with Conn as they ran a lakeside trail that started a few blocks from the cabin. Conn had been up early and had roused Leigh.

After Leigh's dismissal of Gwen, various patrons at the bar had insisted on buying her drinks, and Conn had sweetly held her head as she deposited the last few in the toilet.

Although Conn had stopped drinking a few hours before Leigh, both women woke up with hangovers. Conn swore the best cure was to sweat it out and drink a lot of water, but the only way she got Leigh to agree to come with her was to promise a huge, greasy breakfast after the run. Leigh's theory was grease and fat absorbed alcohol, but Conn wasn't so sure.

Telling Leigh they were heading toward the restaurant, she'd neglected to mention that it was three miles away, with a lot of ups and downs in between.

Once Leigh realized she'd been fooled, she tried to get close enough to strangle Conn, but the betrayer kept dancing out of reach.

"Now, honey, this is for your own good. We haven't been exercising like we should, and you'll thank me for it later."

Between huffs and puffs Leigh managed to scratch out, "Oh, I'll thank you, all right! I'm thinking of ways to thank you that involve great…bodily…harm! Slow down so I can thank you right now, sweetie."

"Great bodily harm, eh? Promises, promises, pookie dear. Not much farther now. Remember that great big breakfast you get to order. Anything your toxic little body desires. Keep going!"

Resisting the urge to stop and puke—again—Leigh kept her legs moving. She actually was feeling a little better, but wasn't about to admit it.

"Snookums? Exactly how far is 'not much farther'? I just want to pace myself, you know?"

Conn was effortlessly jogging backward now. "Oh, another mile or so. Just over that hill way off in the distance. Almost there, sweetiepieface." With an innocent smile she turned and jogged off.

Leigh looked at Conn's beautiful strong legs putting distance between them and would have screamed, but she didn't have the strength. Conn had managed to avoid drinking those last few rounds because she was the designated driver.

"Sheeez. Never again. That's what I get for being a *hero*!" She flung that comment in Conn's direction, but it didn't seem to have reached its destination since Conn had disappeared around a bend in the path. Because of the early hour, they hadn't seen another jogger, one more of Leigh's complaints. *What ungodly time is it?*

As she rounded the bend, two strong arms attached to a laughing partner pulled her off her feet and swung her around, then gently put her down. "You're my hero forever, darling. Don't ever forget that. Forever."

She kissed Leigh's forehead as she wheezed and clung to her. "Does this mean…I don't get to strangle you?" Leigh gasped.

"You can do whatever you want to me. I'm yours."

Between breaths Leigh huffed, "Okay. Strangling is out. Now let's go eat something. Lead on…my little kumquat."

Conn released her and ran down the path, yelling over her shoulder, "Yes, honey bun."

❖

After drinking copious amounts of water and taking some more aspirin, Leigh began to look forward to the huge breakfast she'd ordered, and even the rest of the day.

Back at their favorite breakfast café, she looked across the table at Conn, who was intently studying the message display of her cell phone.

"Will you marry me?" The words popped out of Leigh's mouth so unbidden, she almost glanced over her shoulder to see who was talking.

Conn's eyes stayed glued to the readout of the cell. "Hmm?"

*She didn't hear me. I could back out.* "Will you marry me?" *Evidently not.*

Seeming to tear herself away from the cell, Conn stopped halfway up to Leigh's face, staring into space. "What did you say?"

"Will…you…marry…me?" Leigh noticed that Conn's mouth was slightly open, though not quite agape. *That could be a good sign, maybe.*

"You do know we can't legally be married in California. That's going to be tied up in court for years."

Leigh's stomach knotted. *Is she saying no?* She sat up straight and tried again. "Will you marry me?"

Conn was perfectly still. Then she slowly closed her cell phone and put it down. Leaning across the table and gazing into Leigh's eyes, she said, "Yes. Anytime, anywhere, yes."

A quiet throat-clearing behind Conn made both of them jump. Their waitress from the day before stood there, holding their plates with tears in her eyes. After serving them, she hesitated, blushing.

"Congratulations! I'm so happy for you!" She hugged each of them, then hurried back to work.

Leigh shrugged. "Well, I guess that makes it official. We've announced it to our first friend."

❖

As they walked back to the cabin in silence, side by side, Conn stared at the ground. "Does this mean we're engaged?"

"Honey, I know I proposed, but I really don't know for sure. If we think in terms of tradition, yes, we're engaged. You've agreed to spend the rest of your life with me. How does that feel?" Leigh was trying to absorb it all herself.

They walked a bit farther. "Right. It feels right. Unless—"

"Unless what?" Leigh braced herself.

"Unless you want to have one of those open marriages. The kind where each person dates others, but says she'll always come home. I don't want that and would never want you to be with anyone else. Period. It would hurt too much."

Making Conn face her, Leigh said, "Why would I want to be with anyone else when I have you? I proposed because I want you just for me and me just for you for the rest of our lives. I'm in love with you, Conn. I'll say it to no one else but you. I'll *be* with no one else but you. Is that clear enough?"

A shy smile crossed Conn's face. "I don't know what to do now. What do you want to do now?"

Leigh narrowed her eyes and whispered, "Have you ever had a shower-stuffing party?"

Conn started grinning, and suddenly Leigh took off shouting, "Last one in is a rotten egg!"

They chased each other the rest of the way back to the cabin, jostling for the lead, both trying to get through the door at the same time. Leigh almost missed the note on the door addressed to both of them.

When she opened it, Conn was already in the bathroom turning the water on. Leigh stopped her from stripping out of her sweats. "The note says to turn on the news, any station. It's from Sally."

"Can you find the remote? I'll be out of the shower in five minutes."

Leigh scrounged around and finally accepted the fact that there probably was no remote. She switched on the small, ancient television that they'd ignored, not even sure if it worked. After a few moments of warm-up the picture appeared, only slightly blurry. It was an ad, so she started flipping channels, searching for Marina's network.

Suddenly Marina's face filled the entire screen.

"Conn? Come in here. It's something about Marina." The volume was so low she couldn't hear, so she searched for the volume control. "Marina's probably broken another impossible-to-get news story. She's amazing."

Conn joined her, a towel wrapped around her torso, ready for the shower. "Yup. That's Marina."

"Breaking news! Marina Kouros, award-winning journalist, and her cameraman, Jim Stone, have been kidnapped. They were in Pakistan working on assignment when unknown assailants attacked their car, shot and killed their driver, and abducted them. Nothing has been heard from them in over five hours. Local authorities are investigating."

By the time the reporter finished, Leigh had her arm around Conn's waist. Conn's body had turned to granite as soon as the first sentence was out, and her color wasn't much better.

"That's impossible! Marina's one of the most well-known and

respected journalists in the world. She's so popular with her audiences no one would dare to touch her!" Leigh's mind was awash with disbelief and concern for Conn.

"I'll get on the computer and phone Washington to find out what's going on," Conn said tersely. "Then I'd better…" She tried to pull away.

Leigh gently but firmly placed her hand on Conn's chest, over her heart. "Conn! Wait. You have to call Jen in Paris, see if she's heard the news. She needs you."

Conn seemed to see Leigh for the first time, and her eyes showed fear. "But I've got to do something!"

"Yes, of course! Let's call Jen and make sure she's okay. Then take your shower and devise a plan. We'll figure this out."

She watched tears form in Conn's eyes and held her tightly. "It's okay, baby, we'll get through this together. She'll be fine."

Conn held on tightly, her body shaking with fear and rage.

After they called Jen, they showered and Conn did what she could before settling down to wait for news. They were glued to the television screen for the rest of the day and into the night.

Leigh tried unsuccessfully to get Conn to eat. Later that evening Sally and Lobo brought over a spaghetti dinner, inviting them to the community room where the rest of the guests were watching on a big-screen monitor. Leigh thanked her, but said they didn't want to be around others right now.

Finally, around midnight, she turned the television off and forced Conn into bed, reminding her that the cell would be on and beside them. She stripped them both and climbed in beside Conn, pulling her into her arms and trying to warm her with her love and reassurances.

When Conn at last relaxed into sleep, Leigh lay awake, her heart aching for Conn and Jen, dreading what the price would be for Marina's freedom.

## Chapter Twelve

Leigh and Conn circled each other, balanced and crouched, each looking for a way to bring the other down. The area they'd cleared had traces of snow, and the grass beneath it was brown, the ground below almost frozen.

Leigh didn't like to feel like a mouse being played with. As she practiced patience, she looked for an opening. Conn had easily deflected her attempts to take her down, but Leigh herself had landed on the dirt several times, where Conn had almost gently placed her.

Conn was instructing her, telling her how to change her movements to protect herself, what to watch for, how to defend herself. Leigh was perspiring. She had removed her jacket and was down to light fleece pants and a tight-fitting sleeveless tee over her sports bra, but Conn had yet to break a sweat. Lobo lounged off to the side, his eyes on the action, or lack thereof.

They had attracted a small audience during the forty-five minutes they'd been at it. Leigh definitely felt like the rookie, which only irritated her more. But every time she lunged, she found herself flat on the ground. The hard ground.

"Leigh, think about what you're doing. You're supposed to be defending yourself, trying to get away, not attacking. Feel your feet. Think about what I've taught you. Do you want me to let you throw me so you don't feel so bad? Would an aggressor do that for you?"

Conn was merciless. Since they'd gone outside she'd seemed tense, pushing Leigh to learn and learn quickly. What had started as a playful suggestion, to practice some new skills, had become deadly serious. Leigh wondered if the audience had anything to do with it.

Conn had never seemed like a show-off. She shook off the hard landing and got up again.

*Okay. Breathe, ground yourself, and watch for an opening*. They circled each other, and suddenly Conn rushed at her. Leigh grasped the outstretched hand and pulled into the motion, and as Conn came closer she smoothly took her down to the ground, pinning her with her hand behind her back. The onlookers gave Leigh a small round of applause, probably out of sympathy. Still, it felt good, right up to the moment she relaxed for a millisecond and Conn bucked and sent her flying.

"Shit!" She lay there, gasping, until Lobo ambled over and nudged her, giving her a friendly chomp on the arm. A pity chomp.

"Okay, good. That's enough for today. Let's go get cleaned up." Conn walked back to the cabin, leaving Leigh to pick herself up, and the crowd quickly dispersed with a few kind, and several openly flirtatious, glances in her direction. Lobo was giving her a bath, probably trying to make her feel better.

Scratching his ears, Leigh said, "Thanks, son. You're the best," and looked up at Sally, who was smiling at them.

"He really likes you two." Sally gently called him to her side.

Leigh leaned back to catch her breath. "He's such a wonderful animal. Where did you find him?" She needed a distraction for a few minutes to cool her anger at Conn for her confusing behavior.

"Oddly enough, by the side of the road up near Mendocino. He was only a pup, and I think he'd been hit by a car. Looked like he'd been wandering for a while. We stopped, and as I opened the car door, he limped over and jumped in. We've had him ever since. He sure owns this place."

Leigh hoisted herself to her feet and gathered her sweater and jacket. She waved to Sally and Lobo and headed to the cabin, muttering, "And now to find out what *that* was all about." Conn had some explaining to do.

Once inside, Leigh found Conn sitting on the sofa, laptop balanced on her knees, staring at a piece of paper. The angry words she'd planned to hurl in Conn's direction died on her lips as Conn handed her the note. "'M. Priority 1600. Call 2000.' What does it mean?"

"It means the president is asking for or has approved whatever the meeting is about."

Leigh was speechless. "You mean the president of the United States?"

Conn smiled mirthlessly. "Yes. The very one."

"Have you ever gotten one of these before? From the president?"

"Not this president. But I've gotten two others." Conn's eyes drifted back to the computer screen.

"And you can't talk about them. Or won't."

"Yes."

The distance between them had grown during the conversation. Conn had suddenly shut down, become all business, but she had started the process outside.

Leigh studied the piece of paper. "When did you see this message?"

"When we went outside to practice." She kept tapping.

"Why didn't you come inside immediately and call?"

"The message says that I should call at eight o'clock tonight. Military time. When I talk to them, I'll find out where the meeting is. They aren't risking the information even on an encrypted computer. But my cell is better than any other out there. It will scramble our conversation."

Leigh sat down beside Conn on the sofa and watched her graceful hands fly over the keyboard. "Conn."

No response.

"Constantina Stryker."

Her hands stopped. Slowly she turned, her eyes unreadable.

Leigh grasped her arm firmly. She needed the contact. "I guess the party's over."

Conn's eyes stayed on hers. "Probably. Something has happened. I don't know what. It could be what we're involved in, could be anything. I'll know more after the meeting. Leigh, I…"

The raw pain in her eyes tore at Leigh. "Maybe it's about Marina. Maybe they have her and it's just an update."

"Perhaps. I've searched for more information about her, but haven't found any. They need something. As much as I want out of that part of my life, I'm still in it. I have to go, no matter what the request."

"Then I'll go with you."

"You know you can't."

"Can you at least tell me what the assignment is? How long you'll be gone?"

"If I can, I will."

"Am I a security risk? Why can't you tell me?"

"No. Actually, you have as high a clearance as Pat."

"Really?"

Conn sighed. "Maggie realized we were becoming more than friends and ran the check. I didn't realize the extent of it until she finished, and I didn't tell you because I didn't want to alarm you or insult you. By not telling you, I've probably done both." She looked down at Leigh's hand, still resting on her arm.

"When did you read the message?"

"A while ago."

Leigh scooted closer to Conn and hooked her arm through hers. "Well, that's good news, then. Since I have a high security clearance, you can tell me where you'll be going. Maybe I can help." She felt some of the tension in Conn ease.

"I'll ask if I can let you know. Depends on what it is. I'm just grateful they didn't arrive on our doorstep and take me away. If I'm not supposed to call until eight tonight, they've got some preparations that don't involve me. I'll stay as long as I can. I promise."

Leigh leaned her head on Conn's shoulder, fighting tears, her heart thudding with anxiety. Conn closed the laptop and set it on the coffee table, then swooped Leigh up, put her flat on the sofa, and lay down beside her.

"Leigh, whatever it is, I don't want you anywhere near it. I've been successful in the past because there was nothing to hold over my head—no husband, no lover, no child. I've been careful to stay separate from Jen and Marina. No one has been able to threaten me."

Leigh clung to Conn. "What about threatening you with your life?"

"Not good enough. Until—"

Leigh sat up, becoming strident with fear and anger. "What do you mean? You want me to sit and wait for you while you go out and play spy without any thought about us? What the hell do you think you're do—"

Conn roughly pulled her down and pinned her beneath her body, then covered her mouth with a hard, fierce kiss that their love turned into softness and understanding.

When they parted, her eyes were glistening. "I was *trying* to say, until now. Now I have so much at stake. I have someone I want desperately to come home to. You."

Leigh studied the woman she loved and finally commanded, "Let me up."

Conn released her and stood.

Leigh held out her hand, and when Conn took it she pulled her into the bedroom. "Take off your clothes. I want to see you."

Conn dutifully stripped, as did Leigh. As they stood facing each other, Leigh let her eyes burn down Conn's body and clearly saw the passion she evoked.

When Conn shyly tried to cover herself, Leigh pushed her hand away, moved directly to Conn's center, and easily slid inside. And when Conn's knees started to give way, Leigh helped her sit on the edge of the bed, her hand still inside Conn. She kissed her passionately, laying her down, then knelt in front of her, pushing her legs wide apart.

Conn moaned. "Oh, God, Leigh. Oh…my…"

Leigh thrust deep inside, stroking, feeling the tension change, memorizing the tastes, the smells, the feel on her tongue and hands. She watched as Conn responded to her, trusted her to keep her safe enough to lose control and give herself completely.

"Please, hurry! Now. Yes!"

Leigh plunged farther, sucking and holding her lover's swollen clit gently between her teeth, teasing and flicking, faster and harder. Conn came with a force and intensity Leigh hadn't seen before, but Leigh kept her fingers in motion and replaced her tongue with her thumb. She moved up Conn's body to hold her against her chest as the contractions continued, until Conn begged her to stop.

Leigh stayed inside Conn until she quieted, then slowly pulled out as Conn whimpered and collapsed, her arms weakly around Leigh. After settling them under the covers, Leigh held her lover to her as they dozed.

Conn finally stirred and gazed at Leigh, whose eyes were closed, but her lashes were wet with tears. As she kissed the tears, the salt of them brought her own. She lightly kissed Leigh's face: her cheeks, forehead, jaw. Tasting her own arousal, she followed the jawline over to Leigh's ear, tracing the shape of it with her tongue. Leigh's breathing hitched.

Continuing down her neck, she kissed and sucked along both collarbones, from the shoulder to the midline. Though Leigh kept her eyes closed, Conn felt her body heat up as she ran her tongue between

Leigh's breasts, gently caressing and licking the tender underside of each, reveling in the softness, the colors. As the nipples pebbled and became hard, waiting for her touch, she watched Leigh arch into her as she took one in her mouth. So sweet, so delicate, so incredibly erotic.

Her mouth on one breast, she covered the other with her hand, exhilarated by the soft sounds Leigh was making. Conn straddled one of Leigh's legs, pushing her thigh against Leigh's center. The blond curls were wet and slick, and she growled at the connection. Conn wanted all of Leigh—all of her passion, all of her love. She wanted to possess her as she had been possessed—no thought, no future, no past, no fear. Nothing but Leigh.

When Leigh came they both came, and both cried. The party was over.

## CHAPTER THIRTEEN

The tapping of the computer was the only sound in the room as Conn searched for some word on Marina. Leigh read and reread the same paragraph in a book she had picked off the shelves in the cabin, but it might as well have been upside down. Dressed in black, the women were ready to leave; Leigh had insisted on going with Conn, even if only to sit in the car.

"Nothing. Just rehash of old news."

"Does that mean something?"

Sighing, Conn said, "I don't have a good feeling about it. It's too quiet."

Leigh's stomach churned, and she threw the useless book on the table.

Conn checked her watch. "Time to call Maggie."

She closed down the laptop, connected to Maggie, and exchanged a few words. Less than a minute, beginning to end. Yet that minute could very well have determined their future.

"We're driving to Tahoe City, on the north shore, to a pier that's used to launch boats," Conn said. "The end of the pier in forty minutes. Let's go."

Silently they got in the car, which Conn had already loaded with night-vision binoculars and a digital camera with infrared lens attached. She wore her diving knife and carried a gun.

As Leigh watched her, feeling small and helpless and disliking the sensation, Conn removed something from the backpack behind Leigh's seat. She handed her a thin object, about six inches long, covered in black pearl, that Leigh studied and wondered what it was for.

Conn positioned it in Leigh's hand. "Press the rough part at the top. Carefully."

When she did, a polished steel blade solidly popped into place. "A switchblade. I've never seen one before. Aren't they illegal?"

Silence.

"Oh. Thanks." Leigh swallowed. Fear was evidently affecting her ability to make sense. Her body felt as cold as the steel she held.

"Keep it with you, and use it only in self-defense and to give yourself time to get away. Never let anyone see that you have it. Get familiar with it as we drive."

Leigh examined it more closely and noticed that the initials *CS* were set into the handle. "Was this a gift to you?"

"From a man I used to work with. He taught me how to use it before we went on another assignment together, one of those 1600 missions. It saved my life, but I couldn't save his."

"I'm so sorry, Conn."

"We both knew the risks. Anyway, now it's yours. I want you to have it." She kept her eyes on the road, obviously upset by the memory.

"Conn, you should keep it. You might need it to save your life again, and I want you back from whatever this is." The reality of the situation was sinking in. This was really happening; it wasn't some stupid movie. She *wished* it were some stupid movie.

Conn smiled sadly. "I'm telling Maggie this is my last one. I'll continue with my legitimate businesses and help gather information, but I'm out of the other side."

Leigh was grateful for Conn's decision, but had to ask. "Could you possibly refuse this one?"

"I don't know. I doubt it. They think I'm more valuable in my legitimate life now anyway, which means they call me if I'm the only one who can do a job. But this will be the last, regardless. Come on, we can't be late."

As Conn started the car, Leigh pulled her into a tight hug, then released her and sat back, facing the night. "Let's go."

Conn drove rapidly to the north shore of Lake Tahoe, speeding through the banks and curves with ease, and Leigh stayed busy monitoring the rear surveillance device and familiarizing herself with the switchblade, trying to contain her anxiety.

"Why do some cars show up red while others are green or yellow?"

"The red ones are repeat signatures. Green are new, yellow are also repeat, but within normal limits. Red means a vehicle's being seen too often or is approaching too rapidly. You have one?"

"Yes. Now what?" Though Leigh was alarmed, she tried to keep her voice even.

"Push this button. Then touch the screen on the red. The readout will identify where you've seen it before. It also gives probabilities of the danger level."

She glanced at the screen, saw one red, and touched it. "Older Volvo, light colored, seen two other times in the past twenty minutes. Probability: guarded."

"Keep an eye on it and see if you can use your side mirror to spot it."

Leigh busied herself watching the screen and side mirror, trying to match the readout with the headlights. As she picked it out and matched it in her side mirror, it turned off toward the lake. "It's gone."

"Okay. The device has registered it as a possible and will save the signature. If it appears again, anytime, it'll flash an alert. Good practice. We're almost there."

After studying the screen a bit longer, Leigh asked, "How accurate is it? Do you get any false positives?"

"Rarely." Conn shot an appreciative glance at her. "The only problem seems to be in bad weather. Heavy rain, snow, even really high winds can create a lot of static."

After they arrived in Tahoe City, Conn coasted down a long, unlit driveway and eased to the side of the road. There were no other cars or any buildings nearby. Evidently intended strictly for the guests and residents, the pier was visible across a field blanketed with a few inches of well-trodden snow. Conn was expected; an intruder would have a harder time. Conn trained the night binoculars on the dock and spotted a lone figure at the far end.

"Someone's standing at the end of the pier," Leigh whispered. "Is that Maggie?"

Noticing that Leigh was using the camera to sight with, Conn was again impressed with her resourcefulness. "Looks like her."

"What if someone has a rifle with one of these lenses?"

"I…am sure the area has been secured."

"So I shouldn't decide to just walk up to her and introduce myself."

"No! My God, Leigh, you could get shot!"

Leigh smiled. "Oh. Good to know. Will you bring her back to the car so we can meet? After all, she knows so much about me, and I don't even know what she looks like."

"I'm not sure that's a good—"

Leigh covered Conn's hand with her own. "She's sending the woman I love on a dangerous assignment. I want to look her in the eyes."

After a few seconds, "I'll ask." Conn silently exited the car.

Maggie turned and watched Conn as she approached.

"Life on the run seems to agree with you. You look well."

Conn felt her face warm and hoped Maggie couldn't see her reaction. "Thanks." She couldn't stop her gaze from drifting to the shore where Leigh sat in the locked car, probably watching through the infrared lens of the camera.

"Are you in love?"

Conn jerked her eyes back to Maggie so quickly, Maggie laughed.

She hesitated only a moment. "Yes."

"Does she return that love?"

"Yes." Conn felt her heart swell at her certainty of the truth of that word. After her days alone with Leigh, and especially after Leigh had so thoroughly put Gwen in her place, Conn felt more secure in their love than she'd ever dreamed possible.

Maggie slowly let out a breath. "Well. I should be upset, and I suppose on some level I am. I worry about the distraction. But I'm also happy for you, Conn. You've picked a winner. Honesty and courage are a good combination, if her past performance indicates what she's really like."

"Does that mean I can retire before this assignment?"

"Does retire mean what we talked about a few weeks ago in San Francisco?"

"No more covert ops. Just the software end."

Seconds ticked by slowly as Maggie seemed to consider. "The answer is yes." Conn held her breath. "But I'm afraid it will have to be after this mission."

"Why?"

"Because it involves people very close to you."

Conn's stomach ratcheted tighter, and a feeling of dread spread through her body.

"Marina," Maggie said simply.

"Where's Jen?"

"Still safe in Paris. We've put a guard on her and restricted her movements, and she's really pissed off."

"What happened?"

"You might want Leigh in on this, because it involves her, too. I'm betting she's in your car."

"Damn it, Maggie, she's a civilian! She can't be involved. You're not using her to get what you want."

"It's out of my hands, Conn. You know damned good and well that when she obtained that information from Peter Cheney's office—which she did for you, by the way—she unwittingly gave us the break we've been looking for in an international terrorism case. We were able to prevent them from scoring a huge—in the billions—amount of money in a stock scam that they were going to use to finance their operations. Look, it's cold and I don't want to say it twice. Things have been moving quickly. Let's go to your car and I'll tell you everything."

Numbly nodding in agreement, Conn listened while Maggie spoke quietly into a microphone in her sleeve and they started walking.

❖

Leigh had been watching, and when she saw them head toward the car she steeled herself to meet the mysterious Maggie.

But she wasn't prepared for the look on Conn's face or the fact that Maggie climbed into the backseat and said, "Ms. Grove, my name is Maggie Cunningham. I wish we were meeting under better circumstances." She pulled off a glove and offered her hand.

Automatically polite, Leigh shook it. "Please call me Leigh. I wish we were, too."

Maggie sat back heavily and Leigh touched Conn's sleeve. "Why don't we turn on the seat heaters? I'm sure Maggie's cold."

Leigh hoped that small act of normalcy would lessen the tension. It didn't do much for hers.

After Maggie explained what she'd told Conn, Leigh said, "Well, that's great, isn't it? About the stock scam?" She looked at Conn for confirmation, but Conn didn't respond.

"Yes, it is. The SEC and FBI were all celebrating. In fact, they'd like to buy you a drink. But here's the other shoe. Dieter and the Johnson woman, whom we haven't located, report to some much bigger fish. In the international world of terrorism, some very strange bedfellows emerge. Some profess religious reasons for trying to topple our government, some say ideologically we have to go, and some don't give a shit. They just want the money and power. Each thinks the others are idiots, but they've formed a loose little fraternity. They trade information, money, and bodies. A suicide bomber here, an assassination there, a stock scam to feed the machine. Bottom line, it's all about power, greed, and hate, even for us. We're better by degrees, but not all the time."

Maggie rubbed her face, as if trying to clear her mind, and spoke to Conn. "What's important to remember is that this fraternity is just that. Most of the members are men. The women, with a few glaring exceptions, are pawns and are on the periphery. Okay, enough of the lecture. Here's the situation. The two of you have created a storm, one that's taken on a life of its own. We fucked them and they want revenge. A woman screwed them over. Two women. You two. They've contacted Marina's news organization and offered a trade: you and Leigh for her. In Pakistan, in five days."

"What? Why would they want Leigh? She's not part of any effort to eliminate them. It was Dieter's damned fault he got caught. *My* group caught them. She's out of it! I'll go. We don't even know if Marina's still alive." Conn's jaw was rigid.

Leigh was aware that Maggie was watching her, watching them, and quietly said, "Let her finish, honey."

"We've confirmed Marina is alive, at least as of yesterday. And we think she *is* still alive because they want her as a bargaining chip. We know her photographer, Jim Stone, was executed."

Conn gasped. "Jim! Does Jen know?"

"No. The news agency hasn't released it yet."

"What happens if we trade?" Leigh asked.

"From our view, as soon as Marina is safe, we free you. We won't let them get away from us."

"And from their view? Would they shoot us immediately? Or do they prefer rape and torture?" Leigh couldn't erase the man who had hunted her from her mind. She knew who these people were.

"Forget it. You are not going anywhere near this. I'll go alone or no deal." Conn's face was stone.

Leigh's sharp tone surprised even her. "Answer my question. What would they do?" She was talking to Maggie, who returned the gaze steadily.

"To you? You're an infidel and you screwed them over. They'd go the rape-and-torture route before killing you. Probably in front of Conn."

Leigh swallowed the bile that threatened to rise in her throat and stared at Conn, who was now paler than the moonlight could possibly make her. "And Conn? What do you think they'd do to her?"

"She's the main prize. She's not as well known to the public as Marina, but her looks and a certain amount of fame within their world, coupled with the damage she's done to their operations over the years, make her valuable. They could sell her to the highest bidder, try to extract information from her to sell again, any number of things. In the end, if we can't pull her out in time, the same thing."

The car was quiet until Leigh finally said words she didn't think herself capable of uttering.

"I think the smartest way is Conn's way. I'll go if you want, but if you couldn't get to us, if something screws up, I would give them too much control over her. If the situation were reversed, I'd give them anything they wanted just to get them to leave her alone. I'm not trained, I'd slow her down." She was heartsick.

Conn whipped around to Maggie. "She's right and you know it, Maggie. Make the offer and make the plans. They'll take it. Just make sure you get Marina to safety before you come for me. I'll be ready to get the hell out of there." She shoved her hand between the seats to force Maggie to shake it and forestall any additional demands. Maggie took it.

"Okay. Sounds good. Operation Rising Storm is underway. You'll leave from Reno in three days. I'll pick you up and drive you there. Reminder: Dieter Reinhold and the Johnson woman are still out there.

Since they failed in their assignment, they're probably on the run from their employers. The only way they can get back in their good graces would be to bring them your heads. Even if you leave for Pakistan, they might still be looking for Leigh."

Conn was silent, but Leigh could see her jaw muscles working overtime.

Opening the back door, Maggie said, "Be careful. I'll call with the final arrangements, Conn. Leigh? We should take you into protective custody until we can return Conn to you."

"Let me think about that, Maggie. Will you keep me informed?" She wanted to talk with Conn before she committed to anything.

"Of course."

Leigh looked at her evenly. "Promise."

Maggie gave Conn a half-smile. "She's really something to come home to." Then, to Leigh, "I promise."

As Maggie opened the door, a vehicle suddenly appeared beside the Audi, and before she could climb into it, Leigh jumped out and walked over to her. They spoke briefly, then she was gone.

When Leigh returned, the quiet in the Audi was deafening. After a moment Leigh said, "Operation Rising Storm. Does the army name everything?"

Conn sighed. "I think the answer to that is yes."

Since Leigh wasn't offering to tell what she'd said to Maggie, Conn started the engine and pulled onto the road to return to the cottage. After a few moments, a small beep sounded three times, and they both glanced at the screen. The same vehicle that had been behind them before appeared again. The priority: alert.

"Okay, let's check it out." She heard Leigh check her seat belt.

Conn sped up slightly and changed lanes. The car was behind several others, but within a few seconds also changed lanes. Leigh pushed some additional buttons on the device.

"Older-model Volvo, light colored."

"Fuck." Conn was in no mood to play; she was ready to rumble.

The road narrowed to two lanes, and they watched as the red blip stayed a few cars away. When the highway widened for turn lanes in various towns around the lake, heading for the south shore, the blip changed with them, but kept its distance.

"He wants to know where we're staying."

Conn signaled a left turn and went into a Safeway parking lot. Since they hadn't yet been able to visually identify the vehicle, they watched the readout to be sure it was the same signature. After a few seconds a car turned and was confirmed. A gray Volvo with one male driving.

"Leigh, get out and go in the store. I'll come and get you in a few minutes."

"No way, Conn. I've only got you for three more days, and I'm sure not going to risk losing you to this asshole. Can't we just ditch him? Please?"

Conn started to argue, but the look on Leigh's face silenced her. Maybe this wasn't the night to be a hero. She winked at Leigh. "Come on, let's do just that."

❖

Dieter had just parked and turned off the engine when the blue car fired up and abruptly pulled out of the lot. He barely saw the direction they were taking.

*Scheisse!* When he realized they'd spotted him, his only thought was to catch them and dispose of them. *Stupid bitches.* If they hadn't killed Hatch he would have done it himself for letting them escape in the first place.

He gunned the engine and turned right, driving away from the main road and into dark, tree-lined streets, barely glimpsing the brake lights as the Audi turned left and disappeared around a corner. He followed, trying to close the distance between them.

He knew he was gaining on them. A few more turns and he'd be able to…nothing. *Where did they go?* He slowed and stopped, then killed the engine. Rolling down all the windows, he sat and listened, able to hear the distinctive whine of Stryker's automobile engine, but unable to see it. The sound was fading. They were moving without lights. Then nothing. They'd stopped.

"Close by, they have to be close by." He slid his guns under the seat of the car and pulled out a high-powered flashlight. It wouldn't do to have the police stop him for shining his light around and find weapons in the car.

He started the car and slowly and methodically crisscrossed the streets, windows still down, looking for the car or fresh tracks to show him where it was. He was freezing and angry. He couldn't even run the heater because of the noise. *Those whores are going to pay!* If he didn't get them, someone would get him. He had to kill them, take pictures of their naked, bullet-riddled bodies, and prove his worth again. He even had an instant camera with him. Couldn't take digital, too easily manipulated. Polaroid. That was how to do it.

He once again stopped the car and turned off the engine, letting the light play on the houses and garages. Suddenly a car started a few doors down from where he was. Lights flashed on and the car roared out of the driveway, turning toward him and blinding him with high-beam xenon lights, then sped past him before he could do anything but put his hand up to shield his eyes.

"Fuck!"

He threw the flashlight down on the seat and fumbled with the ignition, starting the car and trying to turn it around in the narrow street. He had chosen the older Volvo because it was virtually indestructible and forgettable; but nimble and quick, it wasn't. By the time he'd turned around there was nothing to follow, nowhere to go. He drove for a few blocks, stopped, and listened. The main highway was close. They could have easily made it there and disappeared.

Still, he sensed them near. He searched a few more minutes. Nothing. Deciding he and Georgia could return the next day to look for the car, he left. They'd search all day, every day, and every night. He turned on his headlights and slowly drove to the main highway. He could almost feel their eyes on him.

❖

As the Volvo crept by, Leigh and Conn watched from behind a wall. After flashing the high beams on him they'd quickly driven the few extra streets to Sally's, turned down the long driveway, and tucked the car behind a wall that was part of a city park, not having time to input the code to the fence and wait for it to open. Conn had killed the engine and they'd jumped out of the car. If he did find them, they weren't going to be sitting ducks.

They watched as the Volvo suddenly sped up and headed for the highway. Letting out a collective sigh, they leaned against the wall and slid down, settling firmly on the frozen ground.

"Do you do this often? You seem pretty good at it." Leigh tried to catch her breath.

"Actually, no. But I have training, and the car is designed for agility. Did you like the last few blocks without lights?" She could hear the grin in Conn's voice.

"Come to think of it, now that I can breathe again, weren't there any brake lights?"

"I can manually disable them. A little extra feature I added, just in case. This is the first time I've used it."

"Were you using the night binoculars?" Leigh had been so preoccupied with facing imminent death she hadn't noticed.

"Nah. Too clumsy. I just stuck my head out and felt my way along."

Leigh could now detect a touch of smugness in her voice.

"Well, aren't you just a macho super spy. Hey, thanks for not taking that guy on. I just couldn't bear it. The thought of—anyway, thanks." She took Conn's hand and pulled it close to kiss her fingertips.

"No problem. You were right. Did you get a look at him when the lights were on him? Dieter."

"I only saw him a few times at work, but I recognized him. I wonder where Georgia is?" Leigh continued to kiss the hand she was holding, turning it over to lightly brush the palm with the tip of her tongue.

Conn squirmed. "Ah, probably at home making dinner for her man. You know, we might want to get the car behind the fence and go inside. Just in case. Besides, my rear end is turning blue. How's yours?"

Leigh looked up and pulled Conn's face to hers, kissing her deeply. "In need of warming up. That kiss actually made a few degrees' difference. Shall we?"

"Oh, yeah. You get the gate, I'll get the car."

They spent the rest of the night warming up.

# Chapter Fourteen

"What the hell was that?" Cindy Regali, office manager at Sally's, looked up at the ceiling after she heard loud thumping cross from one side of the roof to the other.

"What?" Sally was studying the computer screen. "Oh. Probably either Conn Stryker or Leigh Grove. Conn asked if, since we don't have many guests for the next few days, they could have access to the place, including the roofs, closets, tool sheds, the works. She's basically renting the entire joint for three days."

"Why? And why the roof?"

Sally pulled her eyes away from the screen. "She said it was for training. Now, what kind of training? I don't have a clue. They haven't taken the car anywhere. I think they walk out through the woods to the store, because I've seen them coming back carrying bags. They've scared the living daylights out of the maids, me and Carol, and the staff. You've had a few days off, so don't be surprised if you open a door and one of them is standing there or they streak by like a rocket. If you think you see a shadow, it's them. They've been on the roofs, in the trees, out the windows, you name it. Then they spend hours doing that martial arts stuff."

Cindy grimaced. "You mean poor, beautiful Leigh is getting her butt kicked again?"

"Mostly. But she's getting the hang of it. Keeping up with Conn, hiding better, like that. It's taking Conn longer to find her."

"Hmm. Good for her. Although…being caught by that woman couldn't be all bad."

Sally smiled. "Why, Cindy Regali! You're married to a very nice man and have two kids. Shame on you!" She had to grin when Cindy blushed.

Stretching her back, Sally said, "Yeah. I've noticed a few times when the 'training' turned into making out and giggling. Be still my beating heart. Those two are crazy about each other. I'm really glad for Conn, and Leigh is so nice. They've given all us old dykes some pretty good fantasy material. Carol's not complaining."

Sally felt her own face warm and changed the subject. "But for the most part, they're serious about it. And they're good. About the only person they can't sneak up on is Lobo. He's gotten a huge kick out of following them around. They've had to lock him in here a few times because he knows where everyone is and gives it away."

Just then the door flew open and Leigh barged straight through the office and into the community room without a word. She was wearing a Lycra muscle tee and workout tights. Conn was ten seconds behind her, clad in only shorts and a sports bra, and bringing up the rear was a bounding white wolf. Silence followed, and Cindy and Sally scrambled to get up and peek in the community room.

They couldn't see Leigh, but Conn, a fine sheen of perspiration defining her lean muscles in the glow of the light, was searching, having told Lobo to sit in the middle of the room and stay. He was trying to be good but was whining and yawping, fidgeting in place.

Conn glanced at them just as Leigh opened the broom closet and pounced on her back. Absorbing the weight with bent legs, Conn flexed and reared, then deposited Leigh on the couch and pinned her there while she loomed over her.

For a few seconds the sexual tension between them was palpable. Sally held her breath as she watched Leigh apparently try to decide whether to play or be serious. She flashed a gorgeous smile and relaxed her muscles, and Conn did the same. Suddenly her knees rose and she catapulted her partner over her head and onto the floor. Bouncing up, she was gone before Conn could recover. Lobo trotted over and stood close to Conn, who sprang up, a rueful smile on her face.

"Having fun?" Sally leaned on the door frame and grinned at Conn, while Cindy just stood there.

"She's getting better, isn't she? Either that or I'm getting worse. She nails me with that smile every time. Oh, well, back to work." She nodded to them and disappeared out the other door, Lobo on her heels.

They returned to the office and plopped down in their chairs, and after at least a full minute Cindy commented, "Old dykes aren't the only ones. Bill's in for a pleasant surprise tonight."

❖

Leigh and Conn walked silently through the woods, carrying groceries. They had run, Leigh trying to elude her lover, the several miles to the store. She was getting better at stealth: stopping, listening, matching her footfalls to Conn's, using what sparse winter vegetation she could find for cover. The trees were tall and skinny, so they didn't offer much help. They had practiced at night also, which was more successful. One night Conn had given Leigh the night-vision monocular to use, and she'd actually almost made it to the store property before Conn tagged her.

It hadn't snowed since they'd arrived, so the only sound they made was the muffled crunching on the duff around the trees. They didn't follow the main trails that summer campers had made permanent. Instead they made their own way, using a slightly different path every time, taking turns circling back and checking to see if they were being followed on the return.

The day before, Conn had purchased a watch for Leigh in an outdoor supply store. It had night readout, compass, and several watch faces so that she could set the time for her location and for Conn's location, too. Leigh had been learning to use the compass during their forays into the woods, because Conn had made it crystal clear that she wanted her to be able to defend herself if anything went wrong.

Conn told Leigh that the intense preparation was overkill, a way to make her feel better about having to leave, and for the most part, Conn believed that what she said was true.

The silence they shared was peaceful. They were exhausted, but not sleepy, Conn suspected because of the adrenaline pumping hard through both of them. The only time they slept was after making love repeatedly, as though they could hold back time, imprint every cell of the other. They could sleep later, a time that Leigh had said she was dreading, and so was Conn.

Maggie had called and was picking her up the following evening at six p.m. sharp outside their favorite restaurant. Leigh planned to take the Audi after Conn left on her mission, drive to Mendocino, hook up with Jess and Ally, and stay at Robin's compound. Conn didn't want anyone to know where Leigh was, not even Maggie, in case of a leak. They still didn't know how Dieter had found them. She wanted Leigh off the grid until she could return to her. She wasn't thrilled to have Robin around Leigh, but she would be safe, which was all that mattered. Conn had no doubt that Robin could and would protect her.

The time flew by. Usually Conn was anxious to launch a mission, but this was different. She knew she had to focus and block all thoughts of Leigh from her mind once she was there, but until then, Leigh was her entire world. She reveled in her sight, smell, taste, the sound of her voice, the feel of her body as they made love. Each allowed the other to take her in any way: rough, soft, silent, or with cries of passion.

Back at the cabin they unloaded the food, enough for that night's dinner and the next day, when Conn was leaving. Leigh wanted to cook a favorite for her, and Conn had requested spaghetti. Knowing that if she plopped a mound of noodles on the plate and doused it with ketchup, Conn would love it, Leigh made a fresh salad and garlic sourdough bread while a meat sauce simmered on the stove. She put Conn in charge of opening the bottle of Sangiovese and setting the table.

She was stirring the sauce when she felt Conn's arms slip around her waist, pulling her into a hug. As she leaned into it, she felt a gentle kiss on her neck, and they stood quietly staring at the pot.

Finally, Leigh added some wine to the sauce and asked, "Have you talked to Jess or Ally?"

"Yes. Jess knows you're coming and what to do from there. I've programmed all their numbers on your cell, including Aunt Jen's new cell number while she's in Paris. By the way, Maggie has been asking what you're going to do. I've been vague, but she'll ask again, so I'm going to tell her you have a place and we've chosen to leave it at that. She won't be pleased, but she will have your cell phone number. Are you sure that's okay?"

Conn's face was next to hers, touching, and Leigh registered the warmth. "I think you're right. The only place I'm sure no one can find me is at Robin's. If Rising Storm goes according to plan, and it will, we should all be together within a week—Marina back with Jen, and you safe in my arms." She felt a gentle squeeze when she said the last.

"The only gray areas are me getting to Robin and you getting retrieved after the exchange. Yours is a helluva lot more dangerous than mine. Remember, I'll be in the chariot. We haven't seen that Volvo around, so I should be in the clear. I want you back in one piece. Just concentrate on that. I'll be fine."

The pasta was ready so they busied themselves with dinner, and Conn told Leigh it was the best spaghetti she had ever had. Leigh seemed content as they drank some wine and chitchatted about the day, though Conn had to struggle to keep up her end of the conversation.

"What is it?" Leigh regarded her evenly.

"What do you mean?"

"There's something you're not telling me. What is it?"

"Just because I'm quiet?"

Leigh put down her glass and took both of Conn's hands in hers. "Look, we may not have been together long, but we've been together well. I know something's up. Now, what are you not telling me?"

Conn had no choice but to confess. "I, um, I got an e-mail from Jen. She told me to not do this. She said she couldn't bear it if anything went wrong. She didn't know how she would make it without Marina, but she damned sure couldn't live with the misery of losing both of us. Or me."

Leigh watched Conn as she spoke. She was looking at her empty plate, not meeting her eyes.

"And you think that because she's given you an out, I'd try to stop you from going. That's why you haven't told me. Does that about sum it up?"

Conn simply nodded, staring at her half-filled wineglass.

Leigh released her hands. "When did you get the e-mail?" She spoke deliberately, neutrally.

Several seconds passed before Conn answered. "Yesterday."

Leigh just looked at her, fury building. "Why didn't you tell me, Conn? Don't you think your decisions involve me? My life? I *proposed* to you, for God's sake! You *accepted. I love you!* Don't you think I at least deserve to know something like that?"

"I just, I've never had to…I don't—"

Leigh suddenly stood up and slammed the table with her hand. "*Well, you do now!*" Then, just as suddenly, she sat down, the air gone out of her. Quietly, she repeated, "You do now."

"I'm sorry, Leigh. I would never want to—"

Leigh cut her off by standing again. "I need a few minutes here. Just give me a few minutes." She walked into the bedroom, closing the door quietly.

Conn sat at the table in shock, with no idea what to do. Automatically she cleared the table, washed the dishes, put things away, feeling helpless in a way she'd never before experienced.

Listening at the bedroom door, she heard Leigh's sobs. She started to knock, put her hands down, started to knock again, then finally tried the knob, praying it wasn't locked. The knob turned.

The room was dark, and Leigh was curled up on the bed, hugging herself. Conn lay down behind her, enveloping her with her own body, and could feel her lover shivering as she held her more closely. After a few minutes the shivering subsided. "Leigh, I'm so sorry. I've never had anyone else to consider before. I don't know how to do this. If you want me to stay, I will. I'd do anything for you, anything."

Leigh turned over and embraced her fiercely, tucking her head under Conn's chin. "I'm sorry, too, Conn. Ever since we met with Maggie, my fear has been growing. I've tried to keep things light, focus on the training, lose myself in making love, but it's always there. I don't know how to do this either. No one has ever meant so much to me. Though I try to stay in the present, I keep spinning out to 'what if something goes wrong?'"

Conn kissed Leigh's forehead and cheeks, tasting the salt of Leigh's tears mixed with her own. "When I got the message from Jen, I was torn for the first time in my life, Leigh. This situation could blow all of us apart. I hate the terrorists for that. If I go and everything works according to plan, I'm a hero. If I don't, we'll have each other and Jen will have us, but I'll always think I could have saved the one person in the world who means to Jen what you mean to me. My other mother. How could I live with that? How could *we* live with that?"

Leigh was quiet for a moment. "So you tried to solve the problem by yourself. Honey, not making me part of the decision drives a wedge between us. If I found out after the fact, no matter the outcome, I'd be more hurt than I am now, I can assure you."

Tears rolled down Conn's cheeks. "I don't know what to do! I want us to be a family so much it hurts. I've never thought about the future and never cared about anyone before. Tell me what to do, Leigh."

Leigh held her and let her cry. After some time, she said, "Don't you see, honey? I can't. Ultimately it has to be your decision, but you've got to let me be part of the process. *Please.*" They clung to each other in the dark.

"Conn, if I wasn't in your life and Jen had sent that message, what would you do?"

"I…would feel so grateful that she loved me like that. And I would go on the mission to try to get Marina back. Marina is a civilian, a pawn. I'm trained for this and I've signed on for it. At least for one more time."

Her words hung in the air between them.

"Then that's the decision. When you're there, make sure she gets out. I promise to be safe and wait for you. You have to promise to come back to me." Leigh was surprised her voice held a conviction she didn't really feel. She knew the *right* thing to do, but her heart wanted to turn tail and run away with Conn.

She felt soft lips brush her cheek. "I promise. I'll find you."

Conn held her for a minute longer. "Leigh? There's one more thing I need to tell you."

"What is it?" Leigh felt her stomach tighten.

"I, ah, just in case anything were to go wrong, I've made you executor and primary beneficiary in my will. Except for some money for Jen. The rest is yours."

"What? I don't want—"

Holding her tighter, Conn insisted, "Leigh, wait. Each time I, or any of us, go on one of these assignments, there's always a risk. It's procedure to have your ducks in a row in case something happens. I've always left everything to Jen, but now I have someone to leave it to who really, really matters. Whom I love. My own. You. It's only money and some stuff, but it's all I have. Please say you'll take it. Please."

Leigh was crying so hard that all she could do was nod. Conn turned the electric blanket on, lifted her and put her under the covers, and quickly shed her own clothes and climbed in beside her.

"Help me, darling," Leigh said. "Help me get these off."

Under the warmth of the blanket, together they worked her clothes off, then held each other and kissed—soft, sweet kisses that made the world recede. Their kisses gave way to passion, and they climaxed together. Sleep finally claimed them, and dawn came too soon.

❖

The morning passed in an instant. Although Conn nervously suggested one more training run, Leigh nixed the idea, saying that she wanted only to be near her, not trying to escape from her. She wasn't going to get that much better with one more round.

Leigh suggested making them a special breakfast, but her attempt was halfhearted, and neither of them was hungry. They took a walk and held hands, talked about the weather, and played with Lobo. He seemed to have picked up the tension and he, too, was more subdued.

As they lay together quietly, then began touching, Leigh whispered, "My heart is glowing, Conn. Just for you."

Conn paused as she looked into Leigh's eyes. "There's something, like a vibration, between our bodies."

Leigh separated from Conn just enough to see what seemed like a golden light between them, as if she were dreaming. "I've read about this in Persian poetry. I think it's called the soul's dance of love."

Conn breathed into Leigh's ear. "Love is the alchemy of the rising sun. A hundred thousand lightnings in a cloud, and within me the majesty of love spreads a sea drowning all the galaxies above."

Leigh was suspended in her lover's words. "Rumi. I can't believe you just quoted that poem. You are my galaxy, Conn. My stars, my sunrise, my sunset."

Conn looked full of ecstasy, drunk with passion, as she said, "When I kiss you we will be joined together in a new way, Leigh. This is the union of our spirits."

The kiss was so tender, so exquisite. Gaze to gaze, Leigh took Conn's hands. "Our soul marriage. Now we will always be together, even when apart."

As Leigh thought about it later, the physical was as intense as it always was, but the marriage of their spirits took her breath away. Time seemed to stop, and they truly found each other—not for the first time, she was sure.

They lay together afterward for a long time. Leigh finally kissed one eyelid, then the other, then the silky skin over her lover's heart. "First thought, last thought, always in my heart."

Conn did the same. "First thought, last thought, always in my heart."

They showered and got ready, packing the bags and the car, and said good-bye to Sally and, of course, Lobo, who howled mournfully as the gates closed behind them. Conn drove them to the restaurant, where they picked at dinner; Leigh thought she might be ill if she tried to swallow anything. She held Conn's hand under the table, and Conn looked just as miserable as Leigh felt.

At six o'clock a huge black SUV pulled into the parking lot and waited, lights on and engine running. Maggie exited and stood beside the vehicle, Leigh threw some money on the table, and she and Conn walked out. At the Audi, Conn retrieved a small duffel from the trunk, then pulled Leigh into a strong embrace and kiss, lingering on her lips.

"First thought, my darling. Stay safe. I love you."

Leigh wanted to brand Conn's heart with her words. "I'll be waiting. Hurry home to me. I love only you. Always in my heart."

Conn tore away and climbed in the back door after Maggie, who waved but wore a solemn expression. As the car turned toward Reno, snow began to fall, which Leigh thought matched her mood perfectly.

Sighing, Leigh climbed in the driver's seat of the Audi, pressed the switch to lock the doors, and checked the gauges before heading out.

"Damn."

She couldn't believe it. The car was almost out of gas. They'd been so busy doing everything else, they hadn't checked the most obvious. Though she considered stopping at a place on the way out of town, she knew how particular Conn was about her car, so she backtracked to the only station she knew of that sold the right brand of gasoline. She didn't mind. She had plenty of time, and this tiny gesture somehow made her feel closer to Conn.

At the station, she hopped out to fill the tank. The car was spotless because they had washed it the day before, spraying each other and freezing, Leigh whooping at the injustice of having to wash a car when it was so cold outside. The memory of the cold-fingered revenge she had exacted on her lover made her laugh as she pumped gas.

Removing the nozzle from the tank, she replaced the cap and closed the cover, feeling a slight shift in her sleeve. It was the switchblade, at once comforting and disturbing, reminding her of why she was going to

Robin's compound and of the dangers for both of them. Conn had also left the Glock, fitted into its place under the seat. Leigh hoped she'd have no reason to use it.

Inside the gas station's convenience store, she located some snacks for the long drive. Dr Pepper, bottled water, chips, candy bars—the basic food groups of caffeine, salt, fat, and sugar that had sustained her through college and graduate school, times when she was under stress and needed comfort food.

"Comfort food. Hell, by the time I see Conn again I'll probably be three hundred pounds and a mass of pimples."

The clerk rang up her purchases as she stared into the darkness. "Are you traveling tonight?" He grinned, and judging from his teeth, build, and complexion, Leigh suspected the food in the store was his main source of nutrition.

"Yes, I am. Do you know how much snow is expected?"

"Well, this one's kind of a surprise. I just heard it's pretty heavy comin' in." A battered old black-and-white television blinked behind him.

"Great." She had three hundred miles to go and wouldn't be there much before midnight with good weather. It was going to be a long drive.

With that cheerful thought and a Latin beat on her iPod blaring through the sound system, she pulled away from the station and turned toward Highway 50 and the San Francisco Bay Area.

Leigh drove and sang and drank water. The temperature was dropping, and it snowed harder as the elevation increased. She needed to crest the mountain before descending to sea level. The rear surveillance system was balky in the weather, and she almost swallowed her tongue when a warning buzz came on, then disappeared, then three, then static. Turning down the sound on the system because the white noise was driving her crazy, she practiced the downshifting patterns Conn had taught her for driving on winding roads and in bad weather. The Audi had a stabilizing system that kept it from sliding under most conditions, but she wasn't anxious to test it.

By the time she hit the peak, conditions were worse. Visibility was poor, and when the highway patrol stopped her, she had to talk her way out of the chain requirements, citing the car's all-wheel drive and large tires.

The patrolman said she was lucky, that they anticipated having to close the road within the next half hour. The weather continued to foul the rear detection system, so she turned it off until she was clear of the snow. When she tried it at a lower elevation, where the snow had turned to heavy rain and wind, the problem persisted, and she again turned it off. Now on full alert, she kept an eye on the rear and side mirrors, noting the few cars scattered on the wide highway behind her.

The forced exuberance she had felt at the beginning of the drive was evaporating. No matter how many songs she tried or how much channel changing she did, everything reminded her of Conn in some way. She turned the sound off.

"God, I never knew what falling in love could mean, Conn. You'd better hike your tush back here quickly—this is awful." Leigh teared up, and she found she was lecturing the car about being a grown-up and not being so needy. Then she felt ridiculous.

"Jeez, the woman's got me talking to myself."

Just then she noticed that she was about to sail past the exit she'd planned to take to cut over to Mendocino. "Shit! Fuck!" She braked hard, the car corrected a skid, and she skipped two lanes over to exit. Continuing to brake into a tight curve, she gained control and slowed even more to get her wits about her. Just then her cell phone started its tune and she jumped, startled.

She fumbled for the phone, dropping it twice before finally pushing the button to talk. "Hello?"

Even though the connection wasn't the best, the caller evidently detected the harried sound of her voice. "Hi there. Are you okay?"

"Oh, Conn! I love you and miss you so much!" The words tumbled out before Leigh could edit the whine out of them, and she mentally kicked herself.

"I miss you, too. It feels like weeks since I left. Where are you now?"

"Damn. I knew you would call just after I almost missed my turn to cut over to Cloverdale. It's raining like hell here, and that's slowing me down."

"Look, the road from Cloverdale to Highway 1 can be spooky during the day, let alone at night. When you get to 101 north, go through Guerneville instead. It's just past Santa Rosa. Take the Russian River exit to the coast. If you're too tired, you can stop there for the night. Go to the Lakewood resort and have dinner and chill. Just make sure no one's following, and you'll be fine. There's no rush. Have you called Ally and Jess yet?"

"Not yet. I wanted to be closer. The weather's crappy. I had to turn off the rear surveillance because of all the bells and static."

"What? You're breaking up, sweetie. I'll call you after we land and I know a little more. Hope you hear this. I love you! Bye!"

"Conn? I love you—" But the line was dead. "Too."

"Okay. Let's go to the Russian River." With her teeth, she opened a bag of potato chips, then popped a can of Dr Pepper and fired up the radio to try and find a weather report.

## CHAPTER FIFTEEN

The rain was letting up an hour later as Leigh pulled into a well-lit gas station in Guerneville. When she turned to put the nozzle in the tank, she caught something out of the corner of her eye and looked at the road, but it was empty. Several cars had gone by but were lost in the dark and distance. She felt unsettled, as well as hungry and cranky. The junk food had worn off, and her blood-sugar level must have been hitting new lows.

"When in doubt, ask a local."

She noticed the gas station attendant, a round woman with short, spiked salt-and-pepper hair, sitting inside and smiling at her, so Leigh walked over and returned the smile.

"Hi. I need the key to the restroom and a recommendation for a place to eat. My friend suggested the Lakewood. Would that be good?"

The woman's smile widened. "Yeah, it's pretty good. They have decent rooms, too. Even a bar with a dance floor. Do you dance?"

"Usually not without my friend. She's a good dancer." *There. I've answered her question.*

The attendant stuck out her hand and introduced herself as Deanna, the owner of the gas station. "There are a lot of good dancers over there. And you're going to get a lot of invitations. Tell me, are you and your friend serious?"

Just talking about Conn made her feel better. "Very."

"Does she look like you?"

"Oh, no. She's drop-dead gorgeous."

"Uh-huh. And you aren't." The woman was gently teasing, not flirting, and Leigh was glad to talk to someone, even if only for a minute.

"Not like her. Be right back."

As Leigh signed the credit slip, the attendant said, "Listen, my shift will be over in an hour. Mind if I mosey over and buy you a drink? By that time you might need a little help with the chicken hawks."

"Excuse me?"

"Chicken hawks. Ladies that are cruising. And you, my dear, would definitely qualify as a chicken."

Leigh laughed and felt herself blush. "Well, I have to get up the coast tonight. But if I'm still there, I'd be honored to buy *you* a drink. Thanks for being so helpful. I'm Leigh."

"Deal. See you if I see you."

They shook hands and Leigh left.

The lot was almost full when she got to the Lakewood Lodge, and because she really didn't want to park in the darkened area, she was relieved that they had a sort of valet parking. Pulling up to the front, she was greeted by an androgynous person easily Conn's height.

"Hi. I need to keep the car close and in sight. It's possible that I'm being followed. Will you watch it for me? I won't be more than an hour." She gave the attendant a fifty-dollar bill.

Big smile. "No problem. The ones following male or female?" The husky voice didn't give away the speaker's gender.

"Male, probably in a gray Volvo. Look, I'm not even sure I *am* being followed, but I need the car to be safe in case. Is that still okay?"

The attendant looked at Leigh. In the evening light, all Leigh could tell was that the eyes were dark colored and serious.

"Have you had problems with him before?"

"Definitely."

"Don't worry. I'll keep an eye on it. Besides, it dresses the place up. Nice car."

"Thanks. I'm Leigh, by the way." She stuck out her hand.

"Phil. Nice to meet you." The handshake was firm and friendly. As Leigh walked in the restaurant she wondered if it was Phil or Phyl.

❖

Leigh ate a hamburger and salad and drank an espresso to wake up. She did a mental inventory. Tired, frightened, and missing Conn more than she thought possible.

Deanna arrived just as she was paying her bill. "How much farther do you have to go?"

"Mendocino."

"Maybe you should stay here tonight. It'll take you another hour, at least, in this weather. Is someone expecting you?"

"Yes, but I need to call. Is there a pay phone around here? My cell keeps cutting out."

"You can use the manager's office." Deanna grinned. "She's my partner."

Alone in the office, Leigh tried Ally's phone and got voicemail. Jess's cell was no better. She hoped Ally and Jess got her message soon, because she would need directions to Ally's place when she got closer. She briefly thought of staying the night in Guerneville, but wanted to get there. She planned to arrive at Ally's about the same time Conn landed in Paris and wanted to talk to Conn and assure her she was safe. That way Conn would have one fewer thing to worry about.

Deanna walked out with her to check with the attendant who, as it turned out, spelled her name with a *Y*.

"No action, Leigh," Phyl said. "I've kept my eyes open and a few light-colored cars have gone by, could have been a Volvo in there. Once, I thought I was being watched, but it was probably nothing. Sometimes people just stare at me. But you still need to be alert. Is someone expecting you?"

Leigh nodded and scanned the area nervously while waiting for Phyl to pull the car around.

As she waved at Deanna and Phyl and pulled to the edge of the dark two-lane road, some of her steely resolve seeped out. *One more leg of the trip, that's all.* Then the connection to Robin and, finally, waiting. Her dinner curdled in her stomach, the thought of Conn's dangerous situation making her nauseous. She firmly shoved those thoughts away.

"Gut up, Leigh. If Conn can risk her life for Marina, the least you can do is drive the measly distance to Mendocino and stay safe for her return."

She checked her cell phone and repositioned the switchblade in her sleeve. *Remember, it's defensive. If you need to use it, slash and try to disable. And run.*

As she pulled out onto the road, the rain had stopped, so she pushed the switch for the rear camera and watched it pop to life. The roads were narrow and twisting, so it wouldn't be very reliable, but it would be on.

"Okay, let's go, Leigh. Time to finish this trip." Eva Cassidy cued up on her iPod, and it was sing-along time.

She headed for the coast at a moderate pace. The roads were still wet and the curves a bit intense, but when she thought about it, she was glad to be driving up the coast at night. Being on the inside lane of the highway would help, though by far the biggest plus was not being able to see the sudden drops into the Pacific Ocean on her left. Even though it was dark, she knew they were there. As it was, just anticipating their presence made her palms clammy.

Suddenly a set of bright headlights in her rearview mirror tore her from her thoughts. "Asshole. Turn your damned lights down."

The tiny hairs on the back of her neck stood up. The car was closing the distance between them rapidly, so she sped up and glanced at the rear detection device. If it was a new signature she would be happy to have the car pass. If not…

Leigh sighed in relief to see the readout as a sport truck, new signature. She slowed and pulled as far over as she could to allow the jerk his manly freedom. The truck sped past and she resumed her normal speed.

After a few quiet minutes, a loud, insistent beep sounded from the device. Leigh glanced down to see the screen flashing red and the sign reading, Warning! Take Evasive Action! Checking her rearview mirror, she saw a car gaining on her, and as she sped up, she glanced at the readout. '84 Volvo. Light colored. Number of detections: four.

"Fuck!" Leigh hit the gas and the car shot forward so fast she almost lost control as she barely negotiated the next turn. At least she'd gained some breathing room. She needed to settle down.

The Volvo was closing again. *Think, Leigh. That car is a lot older; it doesn't have the traction control you do. Increase your distance on the turns and find a place to disappear.*

The gray car was almost on her when they came to a hard curve. They both slowed to negotiate it, but Leigh accelerated through and again put distance between them. She saw the older car fishtail behind her and slow down.

"Ha! Take that, you bastard!"

She tried to remember the road, but it looked so different at night.

A sign appeared to indicate a road going to the right. *It must parallel Highway 1, but I don't know where it actually goes. Better to stay on the main road.*

The distance was great enough that she was out of sight for a few seconds when she whizzed through some of the turns, then came to a straightaway that bisected a hamlet called Duncans Mills, just before Jenner and the coast highway. The rain had started again and fog was settling in as she quickly whipped into a common parking area that served several restaurants and retail stores, slid between two other cars, and killed the engine and lights, ducking down and praying.

The Volvo roared past the lot. Popping her head up, she waited until the taillights disappeared into the fog and thought about running into a restaurant, but inspecting it more closely she realized it was closed. She thought of calling Ally and Jess, but they were an hour away and hadn't answered the phone earlier. She stared down the road and saw nothing. The Volvo was probably on Highway 1 by this time. She tried to call 911, but the hills around made her cell still useless. Maybe if she ran and banged on the restaurant door someone would be there, but she couldn't convince herself to take the chance, and she felt so vulnerable without the safety of the locked car. She started the Audi, then backtracked to the road she hoped would indeed run parallel to the coast. Too late, she remembered the Glock fastened under the seat. There was no time now to retrieve it. The sign was difficult to read in the bad weather and she missed the turn, but flipped around and made it the second time. Driving up the road, she realized that the surface was relatively new, with no center and side markings. It was narrow and twisting, without streetlights to help, and she could barely see.

She tried her high beams, only to have the fog reflect them back at her. *No good. Where's the fog-lamp switch? Damn it!* Forced to slow to a crawl, she discovered she was gripping the steering wheel so tightly her hands hurt, and she had to consciously relax them.

The road was deserted, so she drove down the middle, feeling her way along. If there were turnouts, she couldn't see them. Even driveways seemed to disappear into a void. Though she felt so nauseated that she was afraid she would have to stop and heave her dinner out the door, she managed to literally swallow the feeling and keep creeping up the road.

Something caught her eye in the rearview mirror. Headlights. She couldn't even pull over to let them pass. What if it was the Volvo? She quickly checked the readout, but the fog and rain made it useless. The car eased closer, moving slowly and steadily gaining.

The alarm sounded just as she felt a solid jolt from behind as the other car rammed her rear bumper. It had its high beams on, flooding the Audi with light. The Volvo kept moving, shoving her toward the edge of the road. She screamed and hit the brakes, but the road was slick and the car slowed only a little. Thinking quickly, she forced herself to tap the accelerator enough to disengage and gain some control of the car.

The Volvo rammed her again, and this time she knew she couldn't get away. Time slowed as the Audi's front tires lost purchase on the slippery road and the car heaved over into a milky void. It hung, partially suspended, only its rear tires connected to ground. Hearing a car door open, she stared out the window at the man who had been following them in Tahoe, the man who had ordered the execution of her former fiancé, the man who wanted them dead.

As he stood next to her window and smiled, she looked him in the eye and pressed the accelerator, sending her over the side of the road and into the trees and forest below.

❖

Free fall for a second, then bumping and scraping, mowing down small ghostly trees and bushes. Suddenly Leigh saw a large tree trunk dead ahead and tried to steer around it. The car had been gathering speed and started sliding sideways as she worked the brakes and gas to gain traction and avoid the worst. On impact the side airbags deployed and she was enveloped in white and choked by the odor of gunpowder.

When the car stopped, Leigh's chest and stomach hurt from the seat belt's grip and she couldn't see, so she fought the fabric of the airbags to get them to deflate. Though it was dark inside the car, the headlights were still on and the engine running. *Turn off the lights. Disappear!*

She found the switch on the dashboard and was in total darkness. Then she turned off the engine, and the silence enveloped her like the fog.

The door was too heavy to open at that angle, and the passenger door rested against the tree. *The back door on the passenger side might be free.* She struggled to get her seat belt unbuckled, finding it difficult to breathe, and noticed that her left arm hurt and she had trouble gripping.

She heard voices from above, one of them familiar and female. Shouting. Flashlight beams played over the car, and she intensified her battle with the seat belt.

"There! There it is. Go!"

She heard a male voice, footsteps and thuds, swearing and loud noises getting closer. Finally her seat belt released and she fell, landing painfully on the gearshift before smacking into the side window. Ignoring the buzzing in her head, she attempted to climb between the bucket seats and into the back, and the car shifted.

When the flashlights arrived, the two people holding them argued about how to open the door. One final push and Leigh was in the back, making the car rock and the yelling stop. A beam played over the car, and she heard a quiet discussion outside.

Leigh was panting from exertion and painfully turned so she could see out of the side window. Pitch black. She had no way of knowing what was out there. Trying the door, she couldn't get it to unlock and realized she must have locked it centrally from the master control switch. If she did get it open and dropped out, the car might roll on top of her if it came off its perch. She could drop two feet or twenty feet, although she was relatively sure she was poised over a valley, not a cliff. Relatively sure.

Loud banging sounds got her attention. A hand holding a gun, butt first, was repeatedly hitting the driver's side window. The safety glass was holding its own, but for how long? Grabbing the seat in front of her, she pulled back with her weight, and the banging stopped as the car rocked again.

When a beam of light shone in her eyes, she stopped the rocking and sat back.

"Stop it! Stop moving in the car. We're going to get you out. We're going to help you."

*What? Are these different people? Are they going to rescue me?* Suddenly hope replaced fear and she tried to find her voice.

"Who are you? Show me your faces!"

A slight pause, then, "Lady, we don't have time for this. Just unlock the doors so we can help you out."

The slight German accent helped clear her head, and bile started to rise in Leigh's throat. "No! Show me your faces."

Light raked over the car again. The beam rested on Leigh's face, and she raised her hand to shield her eyes. Then the light left her face and shone outside, settling on a gun being held about a foot from the window and aimed directly at her. The Glock flashed through her mind but Leigh knew she'd be dead before she could even reach it.

"Carefully. Lean up and unlock the car. There's no one coming to rescue you, Miss Grove. Only us. You are better off taking your chances with us than being crushed to death if the car falls."

*Dieter.*

"And you need me to get back in good graces with your bosses, am I right?"

Leigh heard a woman's harsh laugh come from the direction of the gun and knew where she had heard it before.

"Hello, Georgia. Having fun?"

Dieter's voice cut in. "Very astute, Miss Grove. However, you need me, too. I can keep you safe until we deliver you and your tall friend to my employers. Once that is done, you can negotiate for your safe release. So cooperate now, please."

*They want Conn. Of course. Dieter doesn't know where she is. And if I go with them and they find out...*

"Georgia has a gun on me. Why should I trust you?"

"She won't hurt you. She takes orders from me."

She heard a snort and the gun moved slightly. She fought the panic that was starting in her stomach and knew she had few choices now. To go with them was certain death, so she had to take her chances in the dark—and no matter what happened, she had to unlock the doors.

The car groaned against the tree, tilting farther into it. If the tree gave way, the car might flip on the way down. *Give yourself as many options as possible.*

"Okay! I have to reach the driver's door to unlock it. Wait a minute and back off!"

She saw the hand from the other direction grab the door handle.

"I said back off, unless you want to go down with it. I'm also trying to roll down some windows in case the door is jammed. Got it? Dieter, call off your bitch!"

There was some angry discussion, but the hand came off the handle.

Every second counted. Leigh inched her way forward, holding on to the back of the seat and using her legs to power her body toward the lock panel on the driver's side of the car. She fumbled around, trying to buy time to steel herself for what was next. *First, the right side windows, then the door lock.*

"Hurry up!"

"I'm trying!" She could barely control the trembling in her hand.

Feeling the control panel, she hit a button, and the rear window behind the driver slid down. *Shit. Other side*. She tried another. Nothing. *Must be broken.* Now she didn't know where the buttons were, and the car was starting to rock again. She tried to counterweight it by leaning forward, then pushed another button and the driver's side window started down.

After noticing a flashlight shift and come closer, she resisted the urge to jump away, pressing every button she could find. When she finally heard the central lock release, she felt a hand grab her arm and pull as the car leaned in the other direction.

Her fear sent her into overdrive. She vomited on the hand, and Dieter cursed and lessened his grip enough for her to slide away and land in the backseat. The force of her landing caused the car to tip too far to return, and it slowly reared up and began to sink into the black void, like a mortally wounded passenger ship sliding into the depths. Leigh could only pray the void wouldn't mean her death.

## Chapter Sixteen

Leigh came to as someone was dragging her by her arms through dense undergrowth and brush. She stifled a groan, instinctively realizing that it was in her best interest to stay dead weight. Pain shot through her reinjured left shoulder, but as far as she could tell, everything else seemed to be intact, though the rocks and underbrush were scratching and bruising her.

She slitted her eyes and tried to get her bearings, but she couldn't see a thing. She heard the labored breathing of the two dragging her uphill in the rain, and the few words they said to each other weren't friendly. They were arguing, and though some of the words were German, she knew the subject of the argument.

Leigh thought about options. If they got her into their car she would be dead, but not before they tried to use her to get to Conn. The hill was getting steeper, and from the grunting and huffing coming from her captors, she guessed they would have to rest soon. That would be her chance. She tried to feel if the switchblade was still in place, but couldn't tell. It didn't matter; she was going to make her stand.

When they pulled her over a sharp outcropping on the hill, she involuntarily yelped and twisted in pain. They stopped, and she added what she hoped was an unconscious moan before going limp again. She was dropped roughly, the back of her head smacking the hard ground. Yanked to her feet by the front of her jacket, she came face-to-face with Georgia Johnson.

"You think this is a joke? You ruined everything! You bitch!" Georgia pulled back to slap her, but Dieter grabbed her arm.

"No! We need her awake. You hit her now and we'll have to drag her again. Come on. Someone is bound to have heard the crash. We won't be alone forever."

Georgia glared at her, then ground out, "You're going to think Hatch was a choirboy by the time I'm through with you. Now get moving."

Shoved roughly in the direction of the hill, Leigh fell on her injured shoulder and screamed, and Dieter clapped his hand over her mouth as he hauled her upright.

The rain was running down their faces, and he spat as he growled at her through clenched teeth. "Shut up. Move!"

Slowly she started up the hill. The pain from her shoulder and her brain buzz had disoriented her, and she was beginning to feel sticky warmth down her neck and back. In the distance she registered sirens and wondered if they were for her.

Her legs felt heavy and she stumbled often, needing her good arm to reach out and steady herself. The fog and rain continued but the sirens seemed closer. She looked up the hill, able to see only alternating shades of light and dark gray. If she could get closer, maybe she could yell and make a break for the lights.

As if reading her mind, Dieter shoved the barrel of a gun into her back. With one arm wrapped tightly around her neck, he forced her chin up and toward him. Even with the wind and rain, she could smell her vomit on his arm.

"If you try to run, I'll shoot you in the spine. Then you won't be able to feel anything, but you'll still be able to tell me what I want, so be a good girl. Keep going." He pushed her up and away from the flashing lights, and as she tripped over a rock and thrust her hand out for balance she registered the switchblade, still in its place.

After two more steps she went down on her knees, doubling over with her forehead touching the ground. Clumsily using her injured side, she was able to free the weapon and slide it into her good hand. With the feel of it came the image of Conn and the courage of familiarity, so she coughed loudly and popped the blade into place. It was now or never.

Georgia grabbed the back of her jacket and hauled her upright, but as Leigh settled onto her feet, she slashed Georgia's thigh. Releasing her as if nothing had happened, Georgia let go of Leigh's jacket and looked down, so Leigh made her break, taking advantage of the distraction. Georgia grabbed her hair and tried to yank her back, but she twisted away, slicing at her hand, and Georgia yelped and lost her footing, falling backward.

Dieter was farther downhill and stood there, probably trying to figure out what had just happened. As Leigh started running down and away, he shouted for her to stop, but she kept going, ducking and weaving, more in an attempt to keep her feet under her than to perform any skilled evasive maneuver. She hoped that if he shot at her, the noise would at least attract attention. The ground was uneven and slippery, making her fall a lot, and each time she went down, pain shot through her shoulder. The first time she fell she lost the knife. *Damn it!* Feeling around, she located it, folded it quickly, and shoved it into her pocket. Sweat mingled with rain ran down her face.

"Keepmovingkeepmovingkeepmoving."

After a few minutes the ground evened out and it was easier to keep her balance. Stopping to listen, she heard distant shouts and sounds of machinery and longed to head up to the rescue workers, but feared running into her pursuers. She heard footfalls closing on her and took off.

Entering a more forested part of the valley, she slowed to avoid running headlong into a tree trunk. The trees here were tall and thin, not much to hide behind, and the undergrowth was thick, so her progress was noisy. She stopped again. Dieter and Georgia were still some distance behind her, so she picked up her pace, ignoring the sounds and looking for a house or car or a place to hide.

Conn had taught her how to not go in a circle, so she checked the compass on her watch and headed north, sweeping her good arm in front of her to avoid collisions. She saw some darker shadows that she guessed were shacks or unoccupied homes, and she thought to break in and hide, but the idea of being trapped made her change her mind.

She stopped again and listened. They were getting closer. She took off, gathering speed and concentrating on distance because she seemed to have found a stretch that was empty of trees. She was making progress right up until the moment she plowed into a large fallen tree trunk, pitching forward at a speed that knocked her senseless when she landed.

Head spinning, she had no idea how long she'd been lying there. Suddenly she was completely alert. They were close, almost on her. Lifting her head up out of the deep loam and leaves that surrounded the rotting tree trunk, she discovered she was buried in the mixture. If she moved they would have her, so she quietly laid her head back down and concentrated on making herself invisible.

Dieter and Georgia, who seemed to be right on the other side of the tree trunk, were arguing again.

"I need a doctor. I'm going back to get the car. We'll find her later." Georgia sounded close to hysteria.

"No! She's here. I can feel her. If we don't get her now we'll be out of time."

Georgia laughed derisively. "You mean *you* will be out of time. I'd probably be better off distancing myself from you. For all we know, they already have her friend."

Leigh stopped breathing altogether.

Someone sat down heavily on the tree trunk. "She cut my leg, too. I'm bleeding a lot. Let's get out of here."

Leigh heard a small click. She tensed and had to use all of her will not to buck and run. *Relax. Relax. Invisible.*

Georgia's voice was incredulous. "What are you doing? Are you crazy? After all I've done for you? I could have left you, but I stayed. I love you!"

Dieter's voice sent a chill through Leigh. She could tell he was smiling.

"You have become a liability, my dear. How am I to explain you to a doctor? You whine and carry on because of a little blood. What am I to do?"

She heard leaves rustling and imagined him pacing. "I should have dealt with you back in San Francisco. My heart is just too generous. You leave me little choice but to dispose of you here. It's dark and deserted, and you won't be found before the forest creatures have had their way with you. Good-bye, my—"

Leigh heard a scream coming from just above her, then gunshots so close they almost deafened her. She felt more than heard a struggle going on, but all she could do was hope she wasn't discovered or hit.

A shot zinged to the ground not three inches from her head, and someone howled. Then silence. The tree trunk groaned as something landed heavily on it; then Leigh heard one more shot. A whoosh of air stirred the decaying leaves around her as dead weight landed on her legs, pinning her where she was. Keeping her face buried, she bit her tongue and tried to ignore the sounds of dying.

"You stupid bastard. Look what you made me do!" Georgia

sounded out of breath but satisfied. Suddenly she shouted, "I'll be back for you, cunt! I'll make you pay for stabbing me, and then I'll collect the money I should have made in the first place. I need a doctor. Now, which way should I go?"

Leigh heard the click of a flashlight and froze, aware Georgia was looking at her fresh kill.

"And you. I'm sure the newspaper accounts of your death will be enough to earn me a fee. That is, if they find you before too many animals have had dinner." The flashlight clicked off, and footsteps receded. Georgia was actually chuckling.

Leigh stayed still for a few minutes, afraid to move. When she could no longer hear Georgia, she raised her head, took a few breaths, and made herself look over her shoulder at the weight that kept her fastened to the ground.

Dieter lay splayed across her legs, arms thrown carelessly to his sides. Bubbles and hisses were still coming from him, but she knew that he was quite dead, so she focused on extricating her legs from under the body. The adrenaline that had been pumping for the last few hours, and particularly the last few minutes, was ebbing away, leaving her weak.

Managing to crawl a small distance from Dieter, overwhelmed by the stench of blood and body fluids that had soaked her legs, Leigh retched, having nothing in her stomach to bring up. Her head was swimming and her shoulder throbbed, but she was alive.

She struggled to her feet and took a minute to pick a direction. *Away from Georgia.* In what little light she could detect she saw the fallen tree and the body beside it, legs still draped across the trunk. She could just make out the trail of disturbed detritus Georgia had left behind.

She checked the compass again. *Okay. She went that way. West. Good. I want north. This way.*

After she slowly crossed the flat part of the forest, she realized she was climbing again and thought maybe she could find a road like the one she had been on before all hell had broken loose. Her legs felt heavy, and she couldn't concentrate. She was again on grassy land, but the fog was so complete she couldn't see her hand in front of her. Suddenly the surface changed and she staggered to avoid losing her balance.

"A road! I'm on a road! Civilization!"

She heard an engine in the distance, but the fog muffled and distorted the sound so she couldn't tell from which direction it was coming. Then it was on her, lights blazing, barreling down the road.

She leapt out of the way as it sped past, barely missing her, and her legs kept churning until she crashed, headlong, into a chain-link fence and fell backward, unable to break her fall. She lay there, staring up into nothing, and began to sob quietly. *That's it. No more. I can't do this anymore.*

Finally sitting up, she sniffled and wiped her nose with her sleeve, then heard a soft snort in the bushes to her left. When she raised her eyes she saw a white dog—*or wolf?*—crouching and staring at her.

"Lobo?"

## Chapter Seventeen

Conn sat in the comfortable lounge chair of the airplane and stared out the window into darkness. She had tried to sleep, but her mind was in overdrive. She thought about her mission to rescue Marina, her aunt Jen, her childhood, her training, her career, and her life. Mostly, though, she thought about Leigh.

Her mind looped around every detail of her lover: Leigh's eyes and the sound of her laughter, the texture of her skin, the passion between them, the kindness in her soul. Thinking about Leigh was the only thing that gave her peace, but she was having trouble concentrating. Something was interfering with—

"Conn? Conn?"

Maggie's voice pulled her from her thoughts. "Hmm? What is it?"

"We'll be landing in about twenty minutes and meet with Jen a half hour after that. You should be able to call Leigh then." Maggie had an amused grin.

"What makes you think I'd do that first thing?" But she couldn't deny it. She just wanted to talk about Leigh, hear her name spoken. She couldn't even hide a smile. Shameless.

"My dear, you might as well have a sign on your forehead: I love Leigh Grove. You've got it bad, don't you?"

Conn warily searched Maggie's eyes for judgment and found none, then lowered her own. "I've never felt this way before, Maggie. I've never been in love. Leaving her was the hardest thing I've ever done. I miss her terribly."

Maggie's eyes warmed, though she looked surprised, probably because Conn rarely shared personal feelings. Conn suspected that

Maggie's years of carefully shielding her own feelings and reactions allowed her to understand.

"She's certainly special, Conn. And, from what I could see, she returns your love. She let me know, in no uncertain terms, that I was to deliver you back to her in one piece, and soon."

"She did? When did she do that?"

"The night we met, at the pier. Just after I got out of your car. Remember?"

Conn recalled that Leigh had quickly jumped out of the car to follow Maggie. She hadn't thought much of it at the time, except when she and Leigh were driving back to their cabin Leigh had made a puzzling remark: "Maggie seems okay. I hope she keeps her promises."

Within an hour they were at the hotel where Jen was waiting. Actually, it was a four-story building that the State Department owned for such purposes. It had six huge suites, two on each of the second through fourth floors, and though the ground floor looked like the lobby of a small residential hotel, the security was state of the art. Conn hugged Jen tightly, happy at being with her again, and Maggie left them alone in the living room and went to get an update from the staff.

"Oh, Conn! It's so good to see you and so awful for the reason why," Jen said. "I still want you to reconsider your decision. You're like our daughter, and I know Marina wouldn't hear of it either."

Conn took her hand and they sat down on the couch. "I'm the only bargaining chip they want. Money doesn't mean anything to them, so I'm afraid we don't have a choice, Aunt Jen. We have a plan to get me back as soon as Marina is safe. Leigh and I talked it over and decided it's our only hope."

At the mention of Leigh's name, Jen looked closely at her and quietly asked, "Why didn't you bring Leigh? She could have stayed with me."

Conn firmly shook her head. "Having you two together would be too dangerous, because terrorists would be willing to risk more to capture both of you at once. I wanted at least one of us to be safe at home. Now, I wish she were here. I—Aunt Jen, I'm so much in love with her. I feel like my life is just beginning."

"And I know she loves you, too." Jen squeezed her hand. "I could see it in her eyes from the first day you met. I'm really glad for you, sweetheart. Marina was excited, too, and then this…"

The tears Jen had probably been trying to hold back began to flow, and Conn held her close.

"It's all right, Aunt Jen. We'll get her back and we'll all be in Bolinas by next week. I'm going to call Leigh now and tell her I made it here, and you can talk to her. Then we'll go over the plan and get this show on the road."

Conn pulled out her cell, punched in the numbers, and the phone rang long enough to flip to voicemail. Conn hung up and called again, this time tapping in a few more numbers to override voicemail and keep ringing. It rang for a long time, pulling Conn's attention away from Jen.

After what seemed like an eon the phone was answered, much to Conn's relief. She winked at Jen and smiled into the receiver. "Leigh? Leigh? Where are you, love?"

Maggie was hurrying into the room, but stopped when she saw Conn's face. Conn had dropped the phone, and Maggie quickly picked it up and spoke into it. "Who is this?" She glanced at the two women sitting on the couch.

The gruff voice at the other end responded impatiently. "I said, this is the Sonoma County sheriff. Now, who are you?"

"Why are you answering my friend's phone?"

"It was found at the scene of an accident. The plates came back registered to a Constantina Stryker. Is that who owns this phone? Help me out here, ma'am."

Maggie took a breath, her eyes flicking to the window. "The phone belongs to a woman named Leigh Grove. She was driving the car to Mendocino at Dr. Stryker's request. Is she injured?"

"To tell you the truth, we don't know. We haven't found her. There was some blood and what looks like vomit on the inside of the vehicle, but there wasn't anybody inside. There's another car up on top, abandoned. Nobody's around. Do you—hello?"

Conn reached for the phone when Maggie mouthed "can't find Leigh," and her voice was completely controlled. "This is Dr. Stryker. Are you saying you cannot find Ms. Grove? Where was the accident?"

She listened as he described the location and condition of the Audi, and her stomach turned to acid when he told her about the other car, an older gray Volvo. "Listen carefully, Deputy…what is your name?"

"Deputy Leonard Wicks."

"Deputy Wicks. Ms. Grove is an important witness in a criminal case, and attempts have recently been made on her life. The car you describe as abandoned has been observed following her. It is imperative that you treat this as a crime scene and find her immediately. I don't care who you have to call, but do it!"

"Lady—er, Dr. Stryker, I don't have the authority to pull out all my men just from our talking here. We'll do the best we can, but—"

Maggie, evidently seeing Conn's self-control had begun to shred, pulled the phone away from her. "Deputy Wicks. You will have a complete forensic team from the FBI there within two hours. Within twenty minutes you will receive your authorization call. I suggest you carefully preserve the scene and start making calls to bring in your search-and-rescue units. Ms. Grove is probably in grave danger. Are we clear?"

"Yes, ma'am!"

"Good. I'll be calling for a report every few hours, Deputy. Keep the phone with you."

"Say, what's your name, anyway?"

"Colonel Margaret Cunningham. Good-bye."

The silence in the room was deafening.

Finally, Jen spoke. "You have to get back there, honey. When they find her she'll need you."

Conn didn't reply and Maggie was silent. Conn fought for rational thought.

"Not yet. If the worst has—then there's no point in losing both of them. We'll proceed here and let the authorities do their job. Maggie, call Jess and see if they've heard from Leigh. Tell Jess that I want my car picked up after the forensics team is through with it. Ask her to have Robin's crew do it. She'll handle it from there. If she's up to it, I want her coordinating and being our liaison." Conn reached for another phone.

"Done. Who are you calling?"

"Pat Hideo. He's Leigh's best friend and will want to know. And I want someone from Stryker there in case we can help."

The air was thick with unspoken fear and emotion as they made their respective calls, and Jen went into the kitchen to cook something and probably to have something to do.

Half an hour later, as they picked at French toast, Maggie gave an update.

"Jess said that Ally got a voicemail from Leigh at ten last night. She tried to call, but it kept rolling over. Given the terrain, they didn't think much of it. Then the power was out due to the storm, and they assumed they missed her next call. Leigh said she'd stopped to eat in Guerneville and was heading up to spend the night with them. They thought that she'd decided to stay in Guerneville because of the weather and were just starting to panic when I phoned. Jess is still on crutches, but Ally is driving her down and will contact Robin about the Audi. Who's Robin?"

Conn's gaze slid away from Maggie. "A friend of Ally's who's repairing the motorcycle. She and her crew can handle the car. They have a flatbed tow."

Maggie seemed to know there was more to it but didn't push her, and Conn was grateful.

"I talked to Pat, and he's on his way from D.C. We'll help the investigators and searchers any way we can, including food and drink stations and the latest and best telecommunication."

They continued to push what was probably a delicious meal around on their plates in silence.

"What time is it?" Conn asked. "Can we call?"

Maggie glanced at her watch. "It's only been an hour. Give them a bit more time to get set up and for Jess to arrive. They're moving as fast as they can, Conn."

"But what if she's hurt and out there with—" The fork clanged on the plate as she abruptly stood up and left the table, heading for the bathroom.

By the time Conn lay down and tried to rest, she heard Maggie come in and say that Jess and Ally had arrived at the site. They would be in hourly contact and coordinate the operation. Forensics had just arrived with more search-and-rescue units.

Conn lay on the bed with her eyes open, trying to breathe evenly. Eventually she dozed, only to be jolted awake screaming. She had dreamed that Leigh was calling for her and she couldn't reach her. She was sweating and panting, tears rolling down her face as Jen rushed into the room.

She allowed Jen to hold her and try to provide some comfort, whispering, "I should have brought her with me. She should have come to stay with you. I did this. My God, I did this." She shuddered as pain ripped through her.

Jen held her tightly to her chest. "Honey, you did what you thought was right. Don't you dare second-guess yourself. Leigh wouldn't have it. We need to stay clearheaded and calm."

Conn stayed in her aunt's arms, trembling with the effort to settle down until she managed to ask, "How long was I asleep?"

"About two hours, sweetie. Can I get you something?"

"No. I'm going to shower and change. If any news comes in—"

"The moment we hear anything, you will. Promise."

Regular reports revealed nothing for the next four hours, during which time they busied themselves with plans for getting Marina back.

The exchange was supposed to happen in Karachi, Pakistan. Her captors had wanted a more remote location but agreed to the crowded city because Conn insisted. The more deserted the area, the bigger the kidnappers' advantage. She would take her chances in the city, with at least some hope of rescue.

The phone rang, though a report wasn't expected for another half hour. They watched as Maggie hustled to answer it.

"Hello. Yes…oh…what time? How…do you have a name? Get pictures that you can identify and get the crime team cracking. Anything…? Call back as soon as…yes. I'll tell her." She hung up and looked at them.

"They've discovered a body. A male body."

Jen and Conn slumped back on the couch, and Conn asked, "Identification?"

"Not yet. About five-ten, graying hair. Several gunshots to the chest and one to the head. Jess couldn't be there because of her leg so they're taking digital pictures to her, which she will e-mail to me. She just heard via walkie-talkie."

"Dieter Reinhold. Maybe Georgia Johnson wasn't with him. Maybe Leigh shot him."

"My thoughts, too. They mentioned something else. It looks like tracks leading away from the body go in two different directions and are of two different sizes. One smaller and lighter, the other could also be female and looks like a foot is dragging a bit, and there's blood on both of the trails. Jess knew you'd want the information right away. She was excited."

Conn felt a flicker of hope, and a small smile played at the corners of her mouth. "Smaller and lighter. Georgia Johnson was probably with him. Maybe Leigh nailed her with her switchblade. If anyone could get away…she's smarter than they are, that's for sure."

*You can do it, darling. Never give up.*

"I'm sure they'll find her soon," Maggie said. "If she's hurt…they said the weather is lifting a bit, so that should help the searchers."

It was only twenty-four hours before the exchange was to take place, and transport was picking them up soon. Conn prayed for an answer before she left, prayed for Leigh's safety. If Leigh was dead, Conn hoped that Marina would return safely, but she knew she wouldn't care if she herself came back or not.

❖

Time dragged, spent in small conversations, trying to sleep or eat, going over the exchange scenario, and trying to imagine all the possible ways it could screw up.

The trade was supposed to occur on an ancient stone bridge over a crowded area of one of the poorer sections of Karachi. Each group would stay on its side, and the two women would walk toward each other, pass, and keep going. No weapons would be visible, although Conn had no doubt that both sides would have snipers in place and be heavily armed.

Conn was hoping they weren't both cut down as they stood, counting on the captors needing her alive. The kidnappers had agreed to the exchange site, which indicated that either they needed to be rid of Marina or wanted Conn more. Probably both were true. Public sentiment around the world opposed them taking Marina but was probably less concerned about a businesswoman from America. Her captors, on the other hand, were no doubt looking forward to trying to extract information from Conn.

A female physician arrived and placed a signaling device the size of a grain of rice under her skin, on the inside of her left thigh, where it barely left a mark. It would emit a signal undetectable to everything but the most sophisticated scanner; however, it had a limited range and, once activated, would probably last for only seventy-two hours. They were hoping not to need it.

Conn went through the planning and procedures automatically, having a hard time focusing. She was packing her small duffel and laying out the clothes she would wear when the phone rang. Glancing at her watch, she realized it was time for an update.

Everyone gathered in the living room and waited for Maggie to finish the call. It took a bit longer than the others, which gave Conn hope of at least some fresh information. Maggie kept her face neutral, so she knew they hadn't found Leigh, or at least found her alive.

Maggie rang off and turned to Jen and Conn. The other staff members had quietly filtered in, too, which had begun happening a few calls back. Their caring comforted Conn, though it vaguely surprised her.

"Jess said that they have lost both trails." Conn gulped as Maggie went on, "But in different ways. The prints with the foot dragging ended on the road a few miles away. Looks like she was picked up. The sheriff is setting up roadblocks. The other set of prints just ended."

"What do you mean, 'just ended'?"

"Well, as it was explained to me, the search dogs tracked her to a place on the other side of the same road where they lost the first tracks."

Conn fought for control. What if Georgia had been able to capture Leigh again?

Maggie quickly added, "It looks like the second tracks were at least a half-mile before the others, and the car picking up the first one was aimed in the opposite direction, away from the second. Anyway, the trackers don't think a car picked her up."

"What the hell *do* they think?"

Maggie sighed. "They don't know. There's a tall fence about ten feet from the road. The dogs traced the tracks there and found some blood. Then—and this is what I was told, Conn—then the dogs got very excited and started running around in circles and seemed confused."

"What does that mean? What about the place that's fenced?"

"Well, it's a religious monastery. Very cloistered and private and completely surrounded by the fence. No one knows what happened from that point. The dogs aren't tracking. Period. The agents are trying to contact the monastery to see if anyone saw anything from that end."

"What kind of monastery is it?" Jen asked.

"Jess asked some of the locals who are helping with the search and said most of them didn't know anything." Maggie shrugged. "However, one of the search-and-rescue dog handlers, a woman Jess described as about six-two and strong as an ox, with a very funny sense of humor, provided a lot of information."

Conn nodded, realizing that was Jess's way of saying that some of Robin's crew were on the job, searching. She recognized the description of the six-two dog handler as one of the women at the bar a week ago. *A lifetime ago.*

"They say it's Buddhist," Maggie continued. "Up on a bluff, on what was for years considered uninhabitable land owned by an Indian tribe. They bought it, put up the fences, and basically just became quiet neighbors."

"But they're trying to question them, right?"

"Yes. The searchers said it's not easy access, but there is a number to call, and they'll keep us informed."

Conn sat with her forearms resting on her knees, staring into space. "I guess that's good news. Are we sure it's Leigh and not Georgia?" Maybe Leigh was safe somewhere else and this was Georgia.

"Yes. They spot-tested the blood. Two different types, and this one is B positive, Leigh's."

"Was there a lot of it?" Conn could barely ask, but she had to know.

"No. Just some that the dogs discovered. We'll find her soon, Conn."

She was exhausted. With some effort she rose to go into the bedroom and finish preparing. She knew Jen and Maggie were watching her, but they thankfully left her alone.

As the car waited to take her to the military base for transport, Conn used the bathroom and washed her hands, finally letting her gaze rest on the image in the mirror. The haunted eyes and the dark circles under them spoke volumes about her state of mind. She felt lost and alone, with no real news about Leigh. *Where are you, baby? Are you okay?*

On the way to the plane, Maggie said, "Conn, listen to me. We *will* find her. She'll be safe, but she'll need you. She's feeling the same as you are right now. You have to come back to her or you'll break her heart. Do you understand?"

*How could she know?* Conn thought bitterly. But the words sank in. She willed herself to believe they were true. If Leigh was alive, she *would* need her. Conn had to get back soon. Her faith that Leigh was alive was all she had to cling to.

## CHAPTER EIGHTEEN

"Where am I?" Everything seemed out of focus as Leigh looked around the room, trying to make sense of what she was seeing.

A tall, slender woman regarded her. "You are at a monastery and you are safe, but injured. My name is Elaine. Please, try to stay still. A nurse will be here to help care for you. You might need a hospital."

"No! Ow…no, please." Leigh closed her eyes again and drifted, exhausted by the effort it had taken to protest. The soft voice with its slight accent beckoned her back to the room.

"Try not to worry. I think you have a fever and a cut to the back of your head. We might have no choice. The Ghost Dog brought you to us."

Leigh smiled. "Lobo." She settled down and closed her eyes. She was safe.

After a few seconds she heard, "Lobo. It's nice to know his name. Now if we just knew yours." Leigh was too tired to answer.

She next heard a soft knock on the door and the woman said, "Ah, good morning, my friend. I'm so glad to see you. We found a young woman on the property this morning, injured. We need your help."

Leigh watched through a haze as the nurse stepped up into the room, the floorboards creaking as she came closer. "Of course. Let's see what we ha—oh my." She clasped her hands in front of her and stared at Leigh, who thought she seemed familiar but couldn't concentrate.

After the nurse quickly checked her bandages and shoulder and took her vital signs, she turned to Elaine and requested some additional blankets. Leigh dozed.

Roused again by the door opening, she listened to the nurse ask, "Do you need for her to leave the property?"

"The Lama said we could care for her as long as she was in no medical danger."

Leigh thought that the nurse seemed somewhat surprised, but she barely paid attention, trying instead to remember how she knew her. "Well, her shoulder is badly bruised. She may have torn something. She doesn't appear to have a concussion, but I'll need to stitch the cut on her head. That's fairly simple. She has a slight fever and might have pneumonia or an infection, so I'll draw some blood and start her on antibiotics. If she doesn't respond quickly we'll have to take her to the hospital in Mendocino. As it is, I might ask Doc to come and look at her."

Elaine nodded as if she was familiar with the doctor.

Leigh tried to focus on the surroundings and, concentrating on the nurse, finally said, "Tuck? Is that you?"

Tuck smiled at her and said, "It sure is, sweetie. Long time no see," then leaned back. "Elaine, may I present Leigh Grove. Leigh, this is Elaine Richmond. She found you and called for me."

Though Leigh tried to reach to shake Elaine's hand, she didn't get far. Elaine quickly took her hand and gently squeezed it. "Welcome, my dear. You should rest now."

Leigh started coughing, so Tuck held a glass of water for her to sip. As the water cooled her throat, a thought made her head pound.

"Tuck, you have to get word to Conn. Tell her I'm okay."

"Where is she? I'll call her right away."

Leigh's worry increased as she tried to scan the room. "My cell phone, I need my cell phone."

"Elaine?" Tuck asked.

Elaine bent closer to Leigh. "We didn't find anything on your person except a knife and your watch. There was no phone. It wouldn't matter anyway, because cell phones don't work up here."

"Oh, God. How will I reach her? I have to let her know I'm okay. She'll be worried." She struggled to get out of the bed, only to have Tuck gently but firmly place a hand on her chest and settle her back down. She was too weak to fight. Tears rolled down her face.

"Tuck! She's out of the country! She needs to know right away. Please, find Ally and Jess. Jess can reach her. Please, please."

"Take it easy, honey. I'll get in touch with her, don't worry. I promise. I'll get word to Conn. Now, rest or I'll have to take you to the hospital. I mean that."

"No, no hospital. Too dangerous. I…find Conn. Tell her I'm okay." Too exhausted to talk anymore, Leigh closed her eyes.

Tuck patted her hand, then stood. "Well, I've got some phone calls to make. I can leave the property or if you have a spare land line—"

"Use the line for the residents. It's usually busy, but this is an off time. Come with me." Tuck hurried after her, feeling Leigh's sense of urgency.

Tuck called the compound and listened to the phone ring. She didn't have Robin's cell phone number with her, so she waited patiently, knowing someone would answer eventually.

Finally, someone did, sounding irritated. "Hello!"

"Hey, this is Tuck. Thanks for picking up. Where is everyone?"

The voice changed to friendly. "Oh, hi, Tuck. I really don't know. I was doing some chores and looked up to see most everyone take out of here in a hurry."

"Damn. Do you know Robin's cell phone number?"

"No, sorry. Want me to give her a message?"

Tuck let out a sigh and squeezed the bridge of her nose to try and think. "Yeah. Tell Robin…can you write this down?"

She waited while the woman searched for paper and pen.

"Ready."

"Tell Robin that I have Leigh Grove. She's okay. Tell her to get that message to Ally as soon as possible. It's really important. Say, do you know the name of the store where Ally works?"

She heard continued writing and muttering. "Really…important. Um, isn't it called the European Down Shop? Try Information. Anything else?"

"Just make sure she sees the note as soon as she gets back. Thanks."

Tuck hung up and tried to get Ally's store number. A few years ago a local operator would have answered and known what she was talking about, but the person who answered this time had a distinctly Southern accent and had no idea how to help if she didn't have the exact name and spelling. *Useless.*

After hanging up, Tuck returned to her patient to draw blood and finish cleaning and stitching her wound. Leigh barely responded. She gave Leigh a shot of antibiotics and left Elaine some pills to give her.

Tuck had to see several people who also needed her attention because of the regular doctor's absence and would drop off the blood at the lab on her way home later, after she checked on Leigh again. One of the members of Robin's community was a lab tech at the hospital and always ran the tests without reporting them.

Having done what she could, she put her curiosity about Leigh in the back of her mind as she concentrated on the rest of the day.

## CHAPTER NINETEEN

Conn and Maggie landed at a military base a short distance from Karachi, the unofficial capital and commercial heart of Pakistan. They would stay put until just before dawn, when the exchange was to take place. Even the kidnappers wouldn't risk being on the streets at night—rogue gangs with their own agendas might pirate them. There was little honor among these thieves, who were raised in hopelessness and had loyalty to few.

In some ways the rogues would be preferable to those who held Marina; at least they could be bought. Marina's captors were taking orders elsewhere and would follow them to the last man or risk death and dishonor to their families.

Conn and Maggie were driven to a small building on the base that housed American military and intelligence officers, many of whom Conn recognized, though they all kept their faces carefully neutral. When they were shown to a dingy room furnished with two cots and a sink, toilet, and mirror, Maggie left her there to go check on arrangements, and Conn took the private moment to make her final preparations.

Fifteen minutes later, Maggie was back and sat down heavily on the cot across from where Conn lay, an arm thrown over her eyes.

"Okay, Operation Rising Storm will commence at dawn. We'll leave in three hours for the exchange, with an armed escort. There's always the chance that they'll try to keep both of you, get greedy. Of course, we want both of you, too."

Conn barely heard her. "Any news?"

"No. Jess said they are following up on the monastery, but nothing so far."

Conn was silent for a few minutes; the air in the room smelled of cigarettes and sweat. "She's alive. I know she's alive, I can feel her. You have to find her, Maggie, and tell her I love her. Promise me."

"Tell her yourself. We'll get you back."

"Promise me."

"I promise. I promise, you, too. You're coming back."

Conn smiled slightly as she used her forearm to shield her eyes from the naked light bulb hanging in the room. "Hey. Just checking to make sure my bases are covered. First Marina, then me."

Maggie sighed, switched off the light. Then she plopped down on the cot across from Conn's and as she landed sent up a small puff of dust that made Conn cough.

They lay there for a time.

"Maggie?"

"Hmm?"

"I know I've never…been much of a…friend…or anything. I just want you to know that I appreciate all you've done." Conn's voice broke on the last word and she was quiet, unable to go on.

"No problem. Get some sleep, Conn."

"Thanks."

❖

"No!"

Leigh jackknifed to a sitting position, sweat pouring off her, wildly looking around at unfamiliar surroundings. It was dark and she was trapped. She had to get away. A searing pain tore through her leg, and she grabbed it and screamed.

Suddenly someone was calling her name, and gentle hands tried to calm her. She fought to escape but the person held her, and a voice called to her, tried to soothe her. She was too weak to fight any longer, her breath ragged as she told the voice she needed help.

Finally, she slumped back on the bed, crying and vaguely registering voices around her as she felt a cold, wet cloth on her forehead. The voices sounded worried, but she couldn't help them; she couldn't even help herself. She drifted into a heavy sleep, sure something was terribly wrong.

❖

"What? What the *fuck* are you saying? *God damn it!* Where is she? Do you have her on the scanner? Why not? Where's Kouros? Is she okay? Get her here *now*! And find Stryker!"

Maggie slammed the phone down, picked it up, and slammed it down again. Then she threw it across the room to shatter on the far wall.

"Fuck! Fuck! Fuck!" She leaned heavily on the desk, staring at the offending instrument. The room was completely still, the fetid air even more cloying. No one was moving; all eyes were averted.

Running her hands over her face to try and get some semblance of control, she yelled, "Get a new phone over here! Sergeant, try to pull something up on the scanner. Move!"

The room came alive with activity, and she suspected many didn't know what they were supposed to be doing but didn't want to be the target of another outburst. They looked anxiously at one man who was desperately trying to make something show up on the scanner and another who was scurrying around finding a new telecom unit.

"People! Stop!"

The room froze for the second time in two minutes.

Maggie took a breath. "We recovered Marina Kouros. She's on her way back here to be checked out. She appears to be okay."

The few exclamations of excitement quickly died on the lips of those who uttered them. Maggie hadn't finished.

"We've lost Stryker. By that I mean we can't find her. There was gunfire, and they think she was hit. Then they escaped. They goddamn got away with her!" She knew she was roaring, but the frustration was tearing at her. She had to control herself and act quickly, before it was too late.

"Start searching, check with your sources, get on the Internet, listen to rumors, monitor the news wires. I don't think Kouros's release has been announced yet. Any luck with the scanner?"

The sergeant shook his head. A female intelligence officer quietly picked up a blinking secure line, listened, then walked over to her.

"Colonel, Ms. Kouros is refusing medical attention until she talks to the officer in charge."

Maggie reached for the receiver and stood up, ready for action. "This is Colonel Cunningham. Ms. Kouros? Yes. You should be checked out by a physician in case…yes…yes. I'll meet you there in fifteen minutes." She handed the unit back to the officer.

"Get me a car and driver. We're going to the base hospital."

They were there in five minutes and watched a caravan of five trucks speed up to the entrance, where hospital workers stood by with gurneys. As they pulled up, Maggie realized there had been injuries in the exchange. They were unloading men, some wounded, several dead.

Maggie stood ramrod straight, arranging her face into neutral as the lead officer hurried out of his vehicle, his arm hastily wrapped in a field dressing but noticeably leaking blood, and made an automatic attempt to salute. She waved it away.

"Status?" She started in the direction of the waiting doctors, steering her officer toward the help he needed.

"Operation Rising Storm was partially successful. Ms. Kouros is in our custody, but we lost Dr. Stryker to them. We have it on tape. As I saw it, the women passed each other on the bridge, stopped, and said something. Couldn't have been more than five seconds, ma'am. One of the kidnappers yelled at them to keep moving, which they did. Ms. Kouros walked fast, and Dr. Stryker walked, but slow. They got more upset and started firing their guns into the air. Then they started shooting at the ground around her. When one of the rounds hit her in the leg, all hell broke loose. We tried to give Stryker cover and get Kouros out of there, and nailed more of them than they got of us, but they managed to drag her into a truck and disappear. We couldn't shoot at the truck because we might hit her. They escaped into the crowds. Shit. Excuse me, ma'am."

Maggie listened, her jaw grinding in frustration as they neared the emergency workers. "You did what you could. Get fixed up. I need to see the tape ASAP, and I want a complete report. You know the drill. How's Kouros?"

"Pissed, ma'am. She told me the doctors could go to hell until she speaks with you. I like her." He smiled shyly, sweat pouring off him, his color getting worse by the second.

Maggie shouted for a medic, watched them load the young officer on the gurney, and followed him inside to discover who was in charge.

Judging by the ruckus in one of the rooms in the emergency ward, Marina was already here. Angry shouting rang down the halls, so she followed the noise.

"Get that thing away from me! Nothing will touch me until I speak with the officer in charge of getting Conn Stryker back! No blood, no pulse, and if I die right here it'll be your fault! Now find me that officer!"

Maggie had to smile. She'd never met the woman before but had heard some stories that Jen and Conn had shared in Paris attesting that the tiny woman was a fireball. Watching the doctors scurry around, Maggie didn't doubt the truth of the stories.

"Ms. Kouros, I am Colonel Margaret Cunningham, in charge of this operation. Welcome back."

The woman spun around and locked eyes on Maggie. "Do you have Conn?"

"No. We need to talk. Why don't you let these doctors check you out, and then we can debrief."

"I'm fine," Marina replied coldly. "Where can we talk? Alone and without listening devices or ears. Now."

As Maggie and Marina stared at each other, Maggie could see that the journalist had lost weight and looked exhausted. But her eyes were still full of the passion that had made her famous over the years.

"Can you walk?"

When she got a nod, she told the doctor it would be a few minutes, and the man threw his hands up and stalked from the room. Looking over her shoulder at Marina, Maggie started for the hospital entrance.

Once outside, they walked away from the buildings and stood together, their backs to the hospital as Maggie cautioned, "We're probably being watched through binoculars and God knows what else."

Marina smirked. "I am a Greek speaking English. Almost impossible to lip-read. And I move around a lot and cover my mouth occasionally. It's worked in the past. Add the wind out here, and even listening devices aimed at us will be ineffectual."

"Had this problem before, have you?"

Marina shrugged. "In this business, an exclusive could make a career. It happens."

"What do you need to tell me that can't be in the debriefing report?"

"A lot of lives depend on you keeping the secrecy of what I tell you. Women's lives. I need for you to promise to keep the confidence, at least for a while longer."

Maggie stiffened. She was military and intelligence. She couldn't comply.

Marina probably observed the body language, but she kept talking. "If this comes out before Conn is rescued, Conn will be executed and the women will be hunted down. They will be tortured, raped, and put to death. And any future help from those who are left will be forever closed to us as an avenue of rescue for our people. Do you understand me? I can't risk it and neither can you."

"But all the information would be held in strictest confidence." Even as Maggie protested, she was aware of how easily information got leaked, especially if it commanded a high price. The look she got from Marina told her she knew as well.

"Okay. My word. For now. Now, what did you say to Conn?"

Marina studied her, seeming to assess her words, and finally said, "I was able to say only one word. I gave her a password."

"What did you say?"

"*Azadi.* It means 'freedom.'"

## CHAPTER TWENTY

Leigh drifted in and out of consciousness for several days, suffering nightmares and horrific visions of losing Conn, of Conn hurt and in trouble. Leigh was terrified. When the antibiotics kicked in and she started to improve, her visions of destruction faded. During the day she lay quietly, concentrating on her memories of her beautiful lover, of their last time together, and praying for her safety. The first few nights she was never alone. Elaine stayed with her, tending her until she improved.

Finally, Leigh awoke one day feeling stronger and asked Elaine to help her to the communal showers. She had to hold her arm tightly to her body to avoid jostling her shoulder, but she was going to be clean.

The effort exhausted her, and someone had to help her walk back to her room and dress in the clean sweats that Tuck had brought for her. Her hair was washed at last, albeit sticking out at odd angles. She lay down to rest, knowing Tuck would arrive soon since she visited every other day and hoping surely she would have news of Conn.

She concentrated on the quiet hum of the constantly revolving prayer wheel just outside her room, which calmed her fears, and envisioned the prayers going straight to Conn and helping her. Then she slept.

A quiet knock on the door woke her, and she opened her eyes to see Elaine smiling at her, holding a tray of tea and muffins.

"I thought you might be hungry after your excursion to the shower."

Leigh smiled. "You've been so kind. I can't thank you enough for all of your help."

"You look better. Now let's get some food in you before Tuck arrives." Elaine placed the tray on the table and helped Leigh get out of the bed and sit in one of the chairs.

They shared their meal in silence. Even in her fog, Leigh had noticed that people seldom talked at the monastery, especially during the workday. When she asked one of her helpers about it, the woman had explained that the practice was called "essential speech," adding that while some people chose to maintain silence as part of their time at the monastery, most did it because they had much to do and were merely focused on their tasks. Leigh decided that it was one of the things that made the place very peaceful and healing. She was grateful because it allowed her to concentrate on Conn.

"I really enjoyed meeting Mike yesterday, Elaine. He's one of the sweetest men I've ever talked to. You go well together."

Elaine beamed at the mention of her husband. "Thank you, I think so, too. I look forward to someday meeting your Conn."

Leigh looked at her, somewhat surprised. "Um, Elaine, how much did I say when my fever was so high?"

Elaine's smile grew larger and she seemed amused. "Nothing too specific, my dear. Enough to know that Conn is a beautiful woman and you love her with all your heart. I presume she returns that love. And I understood that she's in great danger. We are all praying for her safe return to you. I would enjoy meeting her, I'm sure."

Leigh sat back in her chair, touched and heartened by Elaine's words, and whispered, "I would love to introduce you to her. Soon."

Changing the subject, Elaine suggested that Leigh might like to walk around the grounds after Tuck cleared her to have a little exercise.

Tuck arrived a short time after Elaine left to examine Leigh's cuts and abrasions and make sure her stitches had held after the shampoo. She seemed to avoid looking at Leigh, and finally, Leigh took a hand before it reached for yet another bandage and got Tuck's attention.

"What is it?"

Tuck's eyes darted around and finally settled on Leigh's. "We saw on TV that Marina has been released. They had an interview with her on her own network. It's all over the news. I brought this for you to—"

Tuck pulled a newspaper from her bag, but Leigh stopped her.

"That's really good news. Anything else?"

"Jess told us Conn traded herself for Marina. Damn, I admire that woman."

"And? Is there any information about Conn?"

"Not in the news. Marina is being very cautious about what she says. The trade isn't common knowledge. But Jess got some information, and she wanted me to pass it to you."

Leigh felt deadly calm. "Tell me."

"The exchange fouled up." Tuck sighed. "They lost her, Leigh."

She must have seen panic on Leigh's face because she immediately added, "I mean they *literally* lost her. They don't know where she is. There was an exchange of gunfire, and they believe her leg was wounded. Other than that, there's been no news."

When Leigh heard about the gunfire, her hand immediately went to the inside of her thigh. *The dream I had when I had a fever.* She was afraid she would be ill so she took some deep breaths, knowing she couldn't make it down the long hall to the bathroom in time. Now wasn't the time to be weak. She needed time to think, to be alone.

"Thank you for telling me, Tuck. Please tell me about anything, anything good or bad. Promise me."

Tuck looked at her with compassion. "Of course. Listen, in a few days you'll be able to leave. Have you made any plans? The authorities know you're here and are itching to talk to you."

Leigh hadn't thought about it.

"It's something to consider, okay? Robin said you're welcome at the compound for as long as you wish, and Ally said you could stay with her and Jess. You don't have to decide yet." She patted Leigh's hand and stood to leave.

"Thanks, Tuck. I appreciate it. Have they heard any more about the woman who shot the man who tried to kidnap me?" Leigh's head hurt and her heart was literally aching. She hadn't paid much attention after Tuck had told her what had happened to Conn, but she needed to know if they had Georgia.

"Oh! Yeah, I meant to tell you. They found a local man murdered and dumped at a campground yesterday, probably the poor soul who picked her up that day, and his truck is missing. The cops suspect her and they're looking for the truck. If she has any brains at all, she'll be long gone."

Leigh gazed outside at the beauty of the monastery, so insulated from the terrors of the outside world. "I don't trust that she'll be long gone, Tuck. She's crazy. Tell everyone to stay on the alert." She tried to smile but knew she faltered. "Please give them my thanks for the kind offers. If you can put the police off for a few more days, I'll talk to them. See you soon."

Tuck kissed the top of Leigh's head. "Take care, hon."

❖

A short time later Elaine came by to take Leigh on a tour of the grounds, bringing a long, wide piece of cloth to fashion a sling for Leigh's arm. At least she would have one free hand.

As they strolled down long lanes lined by fruit and plant orchards and roses whose myriad colors now waned with the season, they passed outbuildings designed to hold the works always in progress, artistic and otherwise, as well as temples and a beautiful golden stupa that held many humming prayer wheels.

The magnificent structures, the abundant flora, and the people's industry amazed Leigh, but she saw everything almost through a filter of fear and longing for a part of herself that was with Conn: her heart. She struggled to be polite.

"Do you give tours? That would be a great way to raise money for your projects."

Elaine gazed into the distance. "Oh my, no. Think about it, Leigh. If anyone could pay a fee and come here, what would that do to the energy that surrounds us this very moment? Each person has his or her own kind of energy. What would that be like?"

They walked in silence for a few moments as Leigh pondered Elaine's words. "Elaine, why have I been allowed to stay? Several people have mentioned that it's unusual to allow someone who isn't able-bodied or Buddhist to remain here."

They sat on one of the granite steps of a different temple that rose five stories behind them.

"Well, to tell you the truth, I don't know. The Lama gave his permission."

"Did he say how long I could stay?"

Elaine looked at her with complete equanimity. "No. Until it's time to go, I suppose."

Leigh digested that simple philosophy.

"Did Tuck have any information about your Conn?" The pain that assaulted Leigh must have shown on her face, because Elaine touched her hand. "I'm sorry. I didn't mean to upset you."

"No, it's okay. I was going to tell you. She's missing, and they don't know where she is, or even if she's alive. But I know she is. I know it." Leigh studied Elaine for a moment, figuring if anyone might understand, it would be this woman in this setting. "Before Conn left, we had an experience that I can only describe as a union of our spirits. Since then I can feel her presence, sometimes I can hear her voice. I knew she was hurt before they told me, and in the same way I also know she is still alive."

"Good. Then she will need your love and determination even more while she finds her way back to you." Elaine pointed to her left. "You see the large oak tree in front of that temple? Many say that this is the most powerful energy field in the monastery. Your communication could be stronger there."

Leigh smiled at Elaine, gratified and relieved at the confirmation of her experience. "I want to stay here until your Lama decides it's time to go. I need to work, to be busy, but I can't do much for a while. I could do small things that would free up some of the others. Would that be okay?"

"That would be very okay, but why don't you start tomorrow? You've had enough exercise for today."

As they walked back to the main temple where the residences were, they passed a wiry older man busily shoveling topsoil from the back of an old truck.

Elaine stopped. "Bill, this is Leigh. She'd like to help with the gardening as best she can while her shoulder heals. Can you find something for her to do?"

Bill smiled warmly and nodded. "I sure can. Why don't you find me tomorrow morning and I'll set you up. Do you know how to deadhead roses?"

"Yes, trained at my mother's knee. Anything else that I can do one-handed, I'd be happy to try."

"Good. We'll keep you busy. See you tomorrow."

Returning to the main temple where the residents lived and the guest rooms were located, Leigh looked forward to working; perhaps she could somewhat repay these people for their kindness. Strangely, she felt that staying here was the best way she could help Conn. Their fate was in other hands now. She gazed out her window and found the large oak tree she was certain Elaine was telling her about.

❖

Conn moaned and tried to turn over, a sharp pain in her thigh taking her breath away. She couldn't see anything—because there were no windows, she hoped. Either that or she was blind. As she tried to assess the damage by lifting her hands to her face, she realized she was shackled, hands together, feet together, connected by a chain. When she raised her hands, her feet moved, painfully reminding her of her injury.

She lay back as best she could and tried to clear her mind. *What the hell happened? Oh, yeah. Operation Rising Fucking Storm screwed up.* She fervently hoped Marina had made it to safety before all the shooting had started.

Her leg was throbbing and she touched the area, feeling some wet, sticky cloth wrapped around it. Evidently someone had attempted to stop the blood flow, because although it hurt, the wound wasn't bleeding. They probably hadn't hit an artery. Good. She pushed the idea of infection aside for the moment.

Closing her eyes allowed her to concentrate on her other senses. The odor of rancid cooking oil nearby, and the acrid smell of unwashed bodies, but not urine or feces in the room itself. They provided a bathroom somewhere. Perhaps a chance to escape.

She thought she was alone. Tentatively, and with some effort, she stretched her hands out in front of her and after a short distance ran into a wall. She couldn't extend her arms fully, so she tried to sit up and put her legs flat in front of her. Painful. And the room wasn't large enough to allow even that much movement. *So it's some sort of closet. Is this where Marina was held? God, I hope not. What a stench!* She sniffed the air again, searching for some scent of her other mother, however remote. She was sorry she tried.

Wondering how long she'd been there, she felt for her watch. Gone. She guessed less than twelve hours. Combined with the nine-hour time difference from California to France and an additional four hours to Karachi, she was even unsure what day it was.

Heaviness settled around her heart when she thought of being so far away from Leigh. A wave of nausea hit her as she realized she didn't even know if Leigh was alive or dead. *Alive, I know she's alive. And she has to know I am. I have to get out of here and get home. I have to find her.*

Her thoughts drifted to the homing device the physician had inserted before she left Paris. *Maybe they're on their way right now.* She tried to touch the spot where the device had been placed, but ran into pain and bandages.

*Shit. The shooter took it out. I don't fucking believe it.* She wanted to laugh out loud at the ludicrousness of the situation. *Those assholes couldn't hit the broad side of a barn with those old rifles, but they nailed a homing device the size of a grain of rice. If it wasn't so funny I'd be impressed. Damn it, what else can go wrong? Never mind, I don't need to find out.*

Just then she heard heavy boots—several pairs—and some lighter footsteps, tromping up the stairs. The conversation was terse; instructions were being given in Urdu, the primary language of the country. Whoever was on the receiving end of the instructions wasn't saying much, and Conn wondered if the words were about her. Since they were getting closer she arranged herself the way she'd been when she woke up and tried to look unconscious.

Someone jerked the door open and switched on a light. The males seemed to be at the door, peering in, and the door creaked as it opened wider. She could hear one pair of heavy boots march closer, and she screamed in pain and cursed the man who'd kicked her, unable to see anything but the old Russian-issue army boots he wore. A flashlight beamed in her eyes.

Laughter erupted from the group at the door, followed by some movement outside the doorway and a softer voice. A small woman dressed in a burqa appeared in Conn's already blurred vision and spoke rapidly, taking the flashlight and shining it on the injured leg. The men left, but not before the one who had kicked her demanded something and pointed at Conn's feet. Then they were alone.

The woman took the cloth off the wound and cut back the khaki material of Conn's pants, then examined the wound and washed it in some tepid soapy water. Conn could see only her hands, which appeared young but moved without hesitation. The woman pulled out some kind of powder, which she sprinkled on the cleaned wound. It didn't hurt. *Antibiotic, perhaps?* She wrapped the leg in fresh cloth and sat back, seeming to study her.

Conn had borne the painful process of wound cleaning and dressing without a whimper, but she was sweating profusely from the effort of controlling her reaction to the pain. The woman extracted a piece of flat bread from the folds of her garment and handed it to Conn, who took it with a grateful nod, suspecting that someone was just outside the door so she and the woman couldn't converse. She knew few words of Urdu anyway, but she let her eyes show she was grateful for the gentle treatment.

The attendant then untied Conn's boots and removed them. When Conn reached down to stop her, the woman held up her hand and gestured to the door and to the boots again. Evidently the man who'd kicked her had been telling the woman he wanted Conn's boots.

It made perfect sense. They were about the same height, and Conn's were new and Western made. And she would be much less able to do anyone any damage in bare feet, or so they thought.

Exhausted, she didn't resist the removal of the boots. Taking the offered bread, she tucked it inside her shirt and behind her to keep the guards from spotting it and prepared for total darkness again.

The woman finished her task and gathered her supplies to leave, but just before she did, she leaned closer to Conn's face and murmured something, then quickly straightened and knocked on the door. The guard opened it and laughed when he saw the boots, shaking his head in obvious approval of the woman's work. After he slammed the door and locked it, Conn heard his footsteps fade.

She crumpled back and pulled the flat bread out, chewing slowly and deliberately to try to make her body use the calories completely. Who knew when the next meal would come? She thought about the woman and the word she had spoken.

"*Azadi.*"

That was the word Marina had whispered in her ear when they stopped briefly on the bridge. Realizing it was some sort of identifying password, Conn smiled into the darkness. She was going to get out, and soon.

After finishing half of the bread, she hid the rest in her shirt for another meal, lay back on the foul-smelling rags that made up her bed, and concentrated on visions of Leigh. Holding hands and walking on the beach, laughing over a private joke, her face as she looked at Conn with unconditional love and acceptance. Their marriage. She prayed that Leigh was okay and told her to be patient and wait, she would find her soon. Then she slept.

# CHAPTER TWENTY-ONE

Leigh was up at dawn the next day, dressed in borrowed jeans and a T-shirt and holding a large flannel overshirt that Mike had lent her to keep her warm until the sun was higher in the sky. Elaine brought tea and muffins and helped her wrap her arm tightly to her shoulder and secure the flannel shirt over it.

Then Elaine took her to meet Bill at the gardening shed, and he provided her with gloves, pruning shears, and a bucket.

She worked for three hours, stopping only to remove the shirt when it became too warm. The prayer flags that lined the walkways whipped in the steady ocean breeze, every whip sending prayers into the cosmos. Leigh knew exactly where her prayers were going.

Her back and shoulder were starting to protest as Elaine approached and offered her a cup of water. Stretching carefully, she accepted the water and drank all of it in a few gulps.

"My goodness, I've been at it for three hours and haven't made a dent! I must be slower than I thought. How many roses do you have up here?"

Elaine laughed. "Hundreds of bushes, perhaps over a thousand. Many varieties, too. You look a little tired, so why don't we say enough for today and go eat something? Since you're still on antibiotics, limiting time in the sun is probably a good idea. Tuck will be here soon."

"I think you're right. I'd probably do more harm than good right now."

Walking to her room after lunch, Leigh heard her name called, and Tuck lumbered over and hugged her carefully.

"I have some news. Let's go inside." She was smiling, and Leigh's heart started pounding.

"What is it? Have they found her? Is she okay?" She was so distracted she could barely get her shoes off before entering her room.

"Calm down, and I'll tell you everything I know." Tuck sat on the twin bed opposite Leigh. "Jess contacted us and said they've heard from the kidnappers. They claim to have Conn and have made demands."

Leigh leapt up and immediately sat back down, her shoulder reminding her to not make sudden movements. "Oof. That hurt. What are the demands? Can I go there?"

Tuck looked a little concerned. "Well, here's what Jess said. They agreed to the money, but they're asking for the release of some jailed terrorists, and that's the sticking point."

The wind left Leigh's sails. She knew very well that the U.S. never allowed prisoner exchanges, and several people had been executed because of this policy.

"Besides, they haven't provided videotape evidence that she's with them and alive," Tuck continued. "That's where it stands now. We're demanding videotape and trying to negotiate them down to just accepting money. Jess wasn't supposed to tell us that much, but she did."

"Has the media picked up on the kidnapping yet?"

Tuck's eyes brightened. "Yeah. Marina finally talked about it and made Conn out to be a hero. Because of who Conn is and what she looks like, they're pouncing on it. I'll bring some papers, or if you like, you could maybe come out for a day, meet with Jess and Ally, watch the news?"

Leigh looked at her warily. The idea of leaving this haven disquieted her, though she wasn't sure why.

"Besides, Jess has been helping us put the sheriff off, but they really want to talk with you," Tuck said rapidly. "They're starting to make noises about coming to the monastery."

"I don't want that. It would upset the whole place."

"Yeah, I know," Tuck said softly. "Think about it, okay?"

"Could I come back?"

Tuck shrugged. "You could ask."

"I will. I need to go into town anyway and buy some clothes. These people are very generous, but they need what they have. Perhaps someone could give me a lift?" A thought struck her. "What happened to the Audi?"

Tuck grinned. "Robin and the crew retrieved it, per Conn's instructions, and are triaging it as we speak. Jess has been helping."

Tuck gave Leigh a full checkup and removed the stitches in her head. Then she gave her Jess's cell phone number, just in case, and left to attend to her other charges.

Leigh lay down on the bed, completely exhausted. "Conn, where are you? I hope you're okay, sweetie. I love you."

She awoke from a dream of being wrapped securely in Conn's arms and held it for as long as she could before the reality of the single bed became undeniable. She stared outside for a while, thinking. Her mind made up, she walked out on the property to find Elaine, explained what she needed to do, and asked if she could return after several days.

"Of course. The Lama told me you would need to be gone a bit. He said you could return."

Leigh just looked at her, but knew better than to ask, so she left Elaine to find the phone and call Jess.

The next day, with the sun shining brilliantly on the monastery grounds, Leigh walked to the service gate with Elaine, who stepped outside and studied the country road. No one was in sight. "I'll wait until you're safely inside the car."

Grateful for her thoughtfulness, Leigh hugged her. "I can never thank you enough for all you've done for me."

"Nonsense. I have a new friend, a kind and gentle one. And the roses are looking better all the time. Hurry back, my dear. And be careful. Sometimes the outside world can be a bit jarring at first."

Though Leigh wanted to ask her what she meant, just then Ally and Jess drove up and immediately jumped out of the car to hug her. She looked around to introduce them, but found Elaine gone and the gate secured.

Jess was using a cane, but she and Ally looked wonderful and in love. Leigh was happy for them, even though seeing them together made her heart ache for Conn and wish the four of them could be as they had been just a couple of weeks earlier.

Once they were buckled up and on their way, Jess started talking. "So, what do you want to do? Let's make the most of our days. We have to get you to the sheriff's office, and a number of people have said they'd like to see you, but other than talking to the sheriff, you don't have to do anything you don't feel up to."

"I want to know everything you do about Conn. Tuck mentioned videotaping news shows. I just need everything, Jess. I also need to shop for some clothes. I'd like to go see Robin and check on the car and motorcycle, although the bike will have to wait for Conn."

Silence fell over the car. From the backseat, Leigh could see Ally's eyes suddenly glued to the road in front of her.

"What is it? Has something happened? Tell me!"

"Nothing definite has happened," Jess said quickly. "We just haven't heard from the kidnappers after the first contact and our response."

"Which was 'no release of political prisoners.' Am I right?"

"Right. But we're working on other angles, provided by Marina."

That got Leigh's attention. "What angles?"

Jess hesitated, but got an encouraging look from Ally. She shrugged and laughed. "God. If anyone, especially Maggie, finds out how much I've told you two, I'll be busted down to my sports bra."

"Conn is my lover and my soul mate. Tell me what you know." It wasn't a request.

"Marina told Maggie that she survived because several women took care of her. The men didn't want to be bothered, and their culture frowns on men tending to women's needs. Marina said that even most of the women were gruff and full of anger and resentment at having to care for a Western infidel, but they do as they're told. One in particular was younger and very kind, and gradually they started communicating.

"The woman spoke English, and over time, Marina learned that the girl was part of a group of, I don't know, rebels. Female, all of them. Marina got the impression that these women had been through horrific atrocities and had somehow survived and formed a network to quietly fight back and help others. They were planning an escape for Marina when the exchange took place, and Marina is hoping they can use their plan for Conn instead."

Leigh's heart was pounding so hard she was surprised the others couldn't hear it.

"There's only one problem," Jess said.

Her heart stopped.

"The plan involved Marina wearing a burqa and slipping out.

Because she's Greek and small, she could pull it off. Conn is six feet tall and, in case no one has noticed, has rather startling blue eyes. And we think she's wounded."

Leigh closed her eyes and fell back on the seat, then heard Jess turn to face her. When she looked, Jess had a sly smile on her face. "Conn is very resourceful, Leigh. She plans for fuckups."

She almost jumped into the front seat. "What?"

"I've known Conn for several years and during several missions. She always has a plan, and she always carries a disguise." She ticked off the items on her fingers. "Antibiotics, in case she's wounded. Brown contact lenses to hide the color of her eyes, and a mustache."

"A mustache?" Leigh croaked. "She's going to be a man?"

"Yup. She figured if she was captured, she would need to escape. No way could she make it in a burqa, but at least some of the men are her height. With the clothing they wear and the head coverings, she could pull it off, especially if she can get her hands on a weapon. When most people see a gun, they don't want to see the face attached. It's safer that way."

Leigh frowned. "In this plan, how was she going to get out?"

"Well, that was the problem. She could try to make it to the authorities, but that would be risky, to say the least. Who knows where their loyalties lie? They settled on her attempting to deal with some of the street gangs that control the drug trade. Money talks. It was the best they could do. Now, maybe there's an underground railway of sorts. That's what we're hoping."

The news was more than Leigh had expected. The prayers she had whispered while she still tossed with fever, the ones that she hummed along with the prayer wheel, that she sent heavenward with every flap of the prayer flags and every day and night as she lay in bed recuperating, and with every petal of every rose she plucked—it seemed that all of these pleas and promises were being answered. Her spirits higher than at any time since Conn had left her side, she almost broke down in tears of relief. Almost. When she held Conn in her arms, she could cry. But then she noticed Jess's profile, her jaw muscles tensing.

"Is there something else?"

The car bounced along the country road. "The unknown is her injury. We had implanted a homing device on her, but it never activated. We have to wait for something to break."

As they headed down a hill, Leigh's stomach lurched slightly, and she looked out of the car to notice that although it was sunny where they were, the coast was socked in by fog. She thought of Conn, holding her with tenderness and love, then sent her message out into the universe to reach her mate.

# Chapter Twenty-two

Conn guessed that several days had passed since she'd seen the woman who had spoken the password. Although they all wore burqas, most of the women were rounder and had much older hands, and they were mean. They seemed to resent changing the bandages and roughly pushed and shoved to finish their duties as soon as possible, making no attempt to keep the wound clean. They had to accompany Conn to the bathroom and seemed disgusted with her. She was passive most of the time, but when they got too obnoxious, she stared at them and growled, having discovered that they cowed rather easily.

The men who held her captive seemed fascinated with both her height and the color of her hair and eyes. She was taller than most of them, and that fact appeared to intimidate them. She realized they had probably not seen many blue-eyed people, except perhaps on television.

Something else was happening, too. Her leg was infected. She knew she was running a fever and needed antibiotics probably not easily gotten in this part of the world, but she couldn't get to her stash with her constant, hostile guards.

Finally, the first woman returned, recognizable by her hands and her gentle touch. Conn had started talking to all of her captors, trying to desensitize them to the sound of her voice and see who among them spoke English. She told jokes, talked about the weather, insulted them with a smile on her face. She realized that most of them didn't understand, but a few most definitely did. If she wasn't sure, she assumed they did. They were the ones to watch out for. They were more clever than the others.

That day she was sure her guard didn't speak English, and she wondered if the young woman did. The burqa revealed nothing, but Conn talked—told her about herself, what part of the United States she was from, made a few sly comments about some of the guards. After a few moments she noticed the woman was shaking and had placed a hand to her mouth to keep from laughing out loud. *Gotcha.*

Through the gauzy fabric of the burqa she could make out white teeth and a smile. The woman held up a finger in front of her mouth to silence Conn.

Conn stopped and smiled at her. She whispered *azadi* and lay back on the rags, suddenly tired and in pain.

As the woman gently removed the bandages and shone the flashlight on the wound, Conn heard a sharp intake of breath that confirmed what she already knew. She had to get to the antibiotics.

"What is your name and can you take me to the bathroom?"

The woman leaned back on her heels and stood to help Conn to her feet, and Conn rose awkwardly and balanced on one leg. She tried to drape one arm over the woman's shoulders for support, but the shackles stopped her. The woman knocked on the door for the guard to open up.

The guard glanced at the wound and looked ill. When the woman instructed him to remove the shackles so she could help Conn to the bathroom, he quickly did so and motioned for them to precede him into the bathroom, telling them to close the door. They awkwardly hobbled to the small room that by American standards was filthy, but wasn't bad considering their location.

Turning her back on Conn, the woman busied herself with trying to coax some warm water out of the faucet while Conn used the toilet, then removed something the size of a tampon from inside herself. Just as she was pulling her pants up, the smaller woman turned and stopped, a cloth dripping in her hands.

Conn knew she was taking a huge risk, but she had no choice. Quickly unscrewing the container, she dumped the contents into the palm of her hand and held it out so the woman could see pills lined up in a row, as well as another container.

As the woman moved closer and tried to examine the contents through the gauze of the garment in which she was shrouded, Conn murmured, "Antibiotics. I must have them. Please don't tell."

The woman pointed to the other container.

*Oh, well.* "Brown contact lenses and a fake mustache."

Her head jerked up and she stared at Conn with a question in her eyes.

"For my escape."

The woman immediately raised herself on tiptoe and whispered, "Take the pill quickly and save a few more out to hide for later. Put the rest away. Be patient."

Her English was excellent, with a British or Indian accent. Conn nodded and rapidly did as she was told, then kept up a monologue while the small woman quickly, if painfully, cleaned her wound and dressed it as best she could. She actually overacted a bit to assure the guard outside the door that she was being properly tortured, winking at her helper to let her know she was putting on a show. The sweat was real enough.

Just as they were reaching for the doorknob to go back to what Conn thought of as her cell, a different guard, one of the smarter, meaner ones, jerked the door open.

"Silence!" he screamed. "No more talking. You have nothing to say!"

*Well, he speaks English.* "Okay, okay! Sorry. Sheesh, a girl tries to make a little conversa—"

He stood back and lifted the rifle, taking aim at her heart, and she held up her hands and shut up, hobbling faster to the room.

As she was settling down, the man threw the shackles at her and pointed for the woman to put them on her again. She complied, and he watched closely to see she did it correctly, yanking the keys away and checking the locks as he motioned the woman out of the room. As she was leaving, the guard's attention was momentarily drawn to the window, and the woman leaned closer to Conn.

"Zehra. My name is Zehra."

The door slammed shut and Conn lay back on the makeshift bed, already feeling the antibiotics working. She whispered to the blackness of the closet, "Zehra. Get me out of here, Zehra. Get me home to my girl. Hurry."

❖

Conn thought about her need to return to Leigh. Did she not trust that Leigh would wait for her? Or fear that she would meet someone else? No, she was almost surprised to realize that jealousy no longer had anything to do with it. Since that time before she left for Pakistan, that magical moment, her jealousy had disappeared. She wanted to return to her love, the wonderful other half of her.

She thought constantly of Leigh, and at times she could almost hear Leigh speaking to her, reassuring her that they would be together soon. Conn realized that others might say that she'd been in that cell too long, but she was certain Leigh was truly with her.

"Leigh, I need you now. I need your strength," Conn murmured, and just thinking about Leigh brought her closer. *I can smell her fragrance.* Conn used some deep-breathing techniques for relaxation. With all of her well-trained intention she focused on Leigh. "I want to embrace you, Leigh. Can you hear me?" Conn drifted into a deeper relaxation, stepping out of time and onto the shoreline of slumber.

❖

Leigh sat on the ground with her back nestled against the large oak tree. Elaine had told her that a peaceful stillness would appear if Leigh practiced an ancient meditation technique. Eyes closed, she concentrated only on her breath as it entered and left her body. In her mind's eye, only Conn existed. Breathing in, down to her belly, she saw her. As she exhaled, she focused completely on Conn. Then she heard it, the faint promise of a voice.

"Leigh, I need you now."

Across the horizon of no time and no space, Leigh sent her message. "I need you, too, Conn."

Leigh saw a luminous golden light in her mind's eye. There, in the canopy of the light, Conn lay asleep on a bed. "I am here, my love. Wake up." Leigh stepped into the familiar facets of the golden light and, bending over, she kissed Conn. The response sent a shudder of sparks throughout Leigh, and the kiss became an intensity of desire.

Conn's hands polished the bare skin of Leigh's backside, pulling her down. "I want to be inside you, Leigh."

"Every day, every night, you're inside me, Conn." Leigh pressed into Conn's pelvis until she felt the beat of their clits drumming together.

"I love you, Leigh."

Hotter and hotter came the promise of their love. "I feel you deep inside me. How can that be?" In that moment Leigh imagined herself inside Conn, thrusting and satisfying her.

"Leigh, Oh Leigh…faster, harder."

Their lovemaking became the whirling intensity of energy, each woman filling the other with the essence of the soul's richness, slowly rotating into the depths of each other, the silky wetness saturating each movement, pulling the other in more deeply.

"I am filling you with all that I am, Conn."

"And I am giving to you from my soul." Together they became pure heat rising and dancing until Leigh heard the sound of rapture, echoing into her heart as one with Conn.

"Leigh? Wake up, my dear. I think you're dreaming. You should be getting inside now."

Leigh was startled to open her eyes and see Elaine standing over her, a quizzical expression on her gentle features. "Oh! Oh. Yes, of course."

She felt her face warm as she stood and started walking back to the main temple with Elaine but chose to remain silent, and Elaine never asked.

The raucous sound of male laughter roused Conn from her reverie, the harshness of it jarring her back to reality. The guards were changing shift and joking with each other, and she became aware of the rancid smell of the closet that was her prison. Staring into the darkness, she smiled and whispered, "Was it good for you, my love?"

Conn reviewed a mental checklist, inventorying what she had and what she needed. Her wound was healing, thanks to the meds and the fact that, instead of the old hags, Zehra had begun coming more often to minister to her. Someday she hoped to ask how she'd pulled that off.

Since too much talking would attract the attention of the guards, they had developed a communication of sorts, which involved hand signals, a few spoken words, and something Conn could only describe as a sense of knowing. Zehra had an escape plan and assured her that within the next week it would be set in motion.

The sound of boots on the stairs roused Conn from thinking about walking on the beach with Leigh, and she noticed that the steps were a different cadence than she was used to and had arrived at a different time. She was expecting Zehra, but something definitely was amiss.

Suddenly the door flew open, the light blinding her, and she shut her eyes against it as a guard dragged her out into the living room of the small apartment and pushed her into a chair next to a square table the guards used.

Hanging her head to let her eyes adjust before squinting at the man across from her, she studied his feet under the table. Expensive European shoes. *Hmm.* She looked around at her guard, this one vaguely familiar and standing behind her, gun ready. She glanced down and saw her boots on his feet. *Ah.*

The man across from her was about her height and dressed traditionally, covering his head and wearing long, flowing robes. He spoke perfect English, and she had no doubt he was in charge. She knew she had heard his voice, perhaps the first day she was captured.

"Are you enjoying your stay with us, Dr. Stryker?" The smile on his lips was a separate entity from his dark, cold eyes. He had a sparse, graying beard that poorly hid the rough, scarred skin under it.

"I have a few suggestions for future guests, but other than that, no."

The man glared at her. "No matter. We'll be moving you soon."

Careful to reveal nothing in her eyes, she asked, "Have you reached a satisfactory price for my release? I'd like to get out of here to a bath and," tilting her head toward the guard, "a new pair of boots."

The man's eyes flashed with anger, and he slapped her across the face. Though she saw the blow coming and moved with it, defusing some of the sting, she reacted as though he'd knocked her senseless for a moment, playing for time. This was not good news.

"You Americans think money can solve everything. The arrogance of your belief is your downfall, you know that? Allah will guide us to destroy you."

Conn needed to know what they had planned for her, so she baited him. "Well, I've noticed it also takes money to do Allah's work, so have you reached a price?"

"We have decided not to negotiate with the Americans for you. We sent a note saying we wanted this and that, but now we have other plans for the illustrious Dr. Stryker."

"You sold to a higher bidder, didn't you?" She kept her voice even, but her stomach was churning. She couldn't let them take her.

A soft knock on the door signaled Zehra's arrival and the guard let her in. He motioned her to the side. The men ignored her and Conn didn't dare look.

The man seated across from her smiled again. "We sold you to a soldier of Allah, one who knows your true worth. He told me you have many secrets to divulge before he disposes of you in a most embarrassing way for your government."

Conn's mind was in overdrive. Whoever it was, they might be aware of her connections and her other life. Once she was turned over to them, she wouldn't be able to escape. "When do I leave and where am I going?"

Now he laughed. "You command me to answer. Very well. Soon and far, far away. In a place where no one will find you." He leaned forward conspiratorially and said in a soft voice obviously meant for all to hear, "I think they have other plans of a more…intimate nature for you also. I wish I could be there for that."

Conn stared at him. "I thought all you soldiers of Allah wouldn't touch a Western infidel. Won't it sully your tiny little dicks?"

His face grew dark with rage. "Ah, now you see, that shows how little you know. Because you are an infidel, violating you is almost a sacred responsibility, no matter how disgusting the task. We strike you down in a number of ways. Western women are too—"

Just then Conn heard a strangling sound coming from the guard behind her, and she twisted her head to see his eyes fly open, then dull as he fell against the wall, sliding to the floor and leaving a trail of blood.

The man at the table started to stand. "Wha—?"

Conn shoved the table up and into him and lunged. They toppled over, his head covering flying off as she grabbed his throat and squeezed as hard as she could. When she hit the ground her grip faltered momentarily because of the shackles, and he twisted away, landing a fist to her jaw that disoriented her. They wrestled for an advantage before the man managed to get on top, trying to cut off her air.

Conn knew he didn't want her dead; she was worth more alive. She also knew this was her last chance. As she managed to jack a knee up into his groin, he groaned and gave a bit, but came down harder, obviously infuriated with her and at this point not caring if he killed her.

Suddenly she heard two spitting sounds, and the side of his head exploded. He dropped on top of her, instantly limp.

"Get him off me!"

Zehra appeared and rolled him off so that he was on his back, sightlessly staring at the ceiling.

Conn scrambled to her knees but needed help standing because of the chains, and Zehra dug in the guard's pocket and found the keys, then removed the leg and arm restraints. Conn stood to her full height for the first time since she had been captured and exhaled, then cracked her back and rubbed her throat.

She surveyed the damage. "Ooh. Remind me not to piss you off."

Zehra ignored her. "We are fortunate he came today and brought his bodyguard. I haven't been able to find shoes for you. We are unfortunate in that the next guard change will be soon. We must hurry."

Conn noted the absence of emotion in the girl's voice; she'd killed before.

They got to work. Zehra had smuggled in a set of male clothing for her, complete with the head covering. Conn applied her contact lenses and mustache with the help of a shard of mirror in the small bathroom, then secured her long hair at the base of her neck and stuffed it inside the shirt she wore under the robes. After donning the head covering, she pulled it to cover the lower half of her face, then put on the dead guard's mirrored sunglasses.

Zehra, who was gathering up shell casings and wiping her knife on one of the bodies, stopped when Conn entered.

"Well? What do you think?"

Zehra looked her up and down, yanked off the sunglasses and lowered the cloth to reveal Conn's face, and examined her eyes, now brown because of the contact lenses. She stood back. "It is amazing. All you need are the boots. Let's hurry. We don't have much time."

They removed Conn's boots from the dead guard, and she silently vowed to burn them when she got to safety, but for now she was extremely grateful to have them. The streets of Karachi weren't known for their cleanliness.

She was about to say something to Zehra when they heard someone climbing the stairs. Conn quickly stood behind the door while

Zehra knelt beside the leader's body and started rocking and wailing. The steps halted outside the room, and the door crashed open, a guard standing in the doorway, weapon ready.

After a few seconds of listening to Zehra he cautiously walked in, unable to take his eyes off the body and the crying woman. He nudged her to the side with the barrel of his gun and bent over to look at the last sight he ever witnessed. Zehra put her gun to his ear, fired twice, and he fell on top of his leader. The gun disappeared in the folds of her clothes.

Conn had been ready to pounce on the man and shackle him, throw him in the closet, and lock it. She raised questioning eyebrows at Zehra, who straightened up and regarded her from under the burqa.

"We had a choice. Six hours before the next change of guards, or chance twenty minutes before he made enough noise to attract attention. Are you ready?"

"Let's get out of here."

They silently left the room and trailed down the stairs, disappearing into the busy streets of Karachi.

❖

Two days later Maggie received a note at her desk in Washington. She read it three times and sat back heavily in her chair, running her hands through her hair. She was bone tired.

The note contained a translated news release from a Karachi newspaper stating that one Nawaz Nidal had been found dead of multiple gunshot wounds in his Karachi apartment the day before. Two of his trusted associates were found with him, also dead. The article suggested murder-suicide.

"Murder-suicide, my ass."

Her intelligence had indicated Nidal was behind the kidnapping, and rumor had it that he had sold to the highest bidder, exclusive of the U.S. government. She could think of several governments and terrorist groups who would pay handsomely for Conn.

"So, either you're out there trying to get home, or someone didn't want to pay the price for you and helped themselves. Shit."

She made some phone calls, set up a strategy meeting, and put their sources in Karachi on heightened alert for any word on Conn, promising a large reward.

Staring out the window at a rain-enshrouded city, she pivoted when she heard a soft knock and looked into the dancing eyes of Jess Smith, who was assigned to desk duty until she was again cleared for fieldwork. Maggie turned back to the window. "Have we heard anything yet?"

"Not yet. But we're trying to establish a connection with the group of women Marina told us about. It won't be long, Maggie. They can't just disappear. Something will break. I just hope it's in our direction. The thought of having to give Leigh bad…worse…news isn't a pleasant one."

"Is she still at that monastery? What the hell is she doing there?"

"According to her, clipping roses and praying for Conn's safe return."

"Hmm. Well, perhaps those prayers are being answered. Actually, she's probably safer there than anywhere else, just in case the Johnson woman is around. Leigh could be a sizeable meal ticket. Anyone spotted Johnson?"

"No. Hopefully she crawled in a hole somewhere and died of her wounds."

"Yeah. One can hope. So…" Maggie turned again and looked directly into Jess's eyes. "Say hello to Ally."

"What do you mean?"

Maggie shrugged. "Just be careful not to create false hopes. Now go, take an early lunch."

Jess winked and disappeared down the hall with barely a limp.

## Chapter Twenty-three

Leigh had returned to the monastery after two days, during which she'd gone to the sheriff's office and given a statement. Shortly thereafter she had thrown away her sling and was working with some of the other women now, digging and creating flowerbeds to surround the new temple they were building. During a short break Leigh wandered over to the water container for a drink, then walked around to stretch her back and shoulders a bit, thinking about her conversation with Ally the day before, when she had called to check in.

*"What is it, Ally? You're so quiet."*

*Ally sounded embarrassed. "I feel stupid saying anything. You're dealing with much more difficult problems."*

*"Nothing's stupid if it upsets you. What is it?"*

*"Jess is seeing my dad right now. He's removing the cast."*

*"That's good news, right?"*

*She hesitated. "Yes and no. It means she'll be going back on active duty. She has to leave for Washington day after tomorrow. God, Leigh, how did you let Conn go? It's tearing my heart out."*

*Leigh didn't have an answer. She'd berated herself many times for not tying her lover up and refusing to let her go. But then she'd sobered up and admitted that Conn had no choice, and neither did she.*

*Trying to be honest, she'd said, "Why don't you ask me an easy question? It's who they are. In fact, I fell in love with her in the first place partly because she's so damned ethical and honorable."*

*Clearing her throat she quietly added, "Not to mention incredibly sexy."*

*Ally sounded better. "Yeah. There's that."*

*Leigh savored her thoughts for a moment before she added, "But I can tell you one thing. If—no, when she gets out of this and comes home safely, it's going to be a long, long time before I let her out of my sight. I don't care what she or the government says. She's going to think I've been surgically attached."*

Leigh was smiling into the sun when Elaine interrupted her thoughts.

"Hello, my friend. You look happy. Enjoying all this heavy digging and planting?" She sat down beside her with her own cup of water.

"Oh, no…I mean yes…well, I am actually enjoying it. It's so strange, Elaine. It's like I can *feel* the little flowers, how happy they are to be here and in the ground. Does that sound completely insane or what?" She laughed self-consciously.

"It's not insane at all. In a place like this you can open yourself up to all of it, absorb it."

A cloud settled in Leigh's heart.

Elaine studied her. "You wish you could share it with your Conn, don't you?"

Leigh turned to her, surprised. "You're a mind reader."

"Not really." Elaine laughed lightly. "I love sharing this place with my family and friends in my letters, and with Mike. I know how much you miss her. Why don't you share it with her?"

Leigh stared at her for a moment. "You're serious. I mean, I've been sending my love and prayers to her—" *And there was that incredible dream by the oak tree.*

"Of course I'm serious. I wouldn't joke about something so precious to you."

"But how…?"

Elaine stood and dusted herself off. "Come, it's time to return to our work. This evening after dinner I'll show you. You already have a strong connection to her, so this should be easy."

Leigh was intrigued. Although her rational mind did a silent eye roll, her spirits were absolutely soaring for the rest of the day. She almost finished one of the flowerbeds before dark by herself.

Elaine knocked on her door about an hour after dinner and came in carrying a candle, some incense, and a pear from the orchards on the grounds.

"Now, I'll show you how to do this, then every night you can tell her about your day. But we start with something simple."

Leigh shook her head slowly, somewhat disappointed. *Oh hell, might as well go with it. I don't know what I expected, a cell phone with Conn on the other end?*

They lit the candle and the incense, and Elaine told her to just look at the candle and inhale to relax. After a few minutes she told her to notice her breath, how it felt to really take the air deeply into her lungs, to fill them completely. When Leigh indicated she felt relaxed, Elaine handed her the ripe pear and asked her to take a bite of it.

Leigh obeyed and tasted the sweetness and texture. As instructed, she took another bite and concentrated on how much she enjoyed eating it, absorbing every detail.

"Now, holding in your mind the pleasure of the fruit and how much you want to share that pleasure with Conn, send her your pleasure and your love. All of the tastes and sensations. Send them…now."

Leigh concentrated on Elaine's voice and her task, sometimes taking another bite and transmitting the sensations again. Before she realized it, the pear was gone, but still she gave her love to Conn. When she finally opened her eyes, Elaine had disappeared.

"Oh, my."

She got up from the table and blew out the almost spent candle, then crawled into bed and was instantly asleep.

The next morning she was up at dawn, walking the grounds, inhaling the fresh sea air, and noticing everything around her. As she sniffed a beautiful orange and pink rose, she caught a flash of white from the corner of her eye and saw a white wolf standing perhaps six feet away.

"Lobo. How are you?" She smiled at him and took a step forward. He backed up a bit.

"Lobo? It's me. Leigh. I'm part of your pack. Remember Conn?"

He sat and cocked an ear toward her, so she knelt where she was, placed her hands in her lap, and waited for him to slowly approach her. They looked at each other for what seemed a long time, then she scratched him behind the ears, and he yawned and pawed at her, gently chomping on and licking her arm. She closed her eyes and he licked her nose.

When she heard someone coming, she looked back and saw that

Lobo had vanished, then smiled as she got up. *I swear, Conn, I could feel you there with him. Where are you, baby?*

The day passed quietly and quickly, with Leigh encouraged, enjoying the fact that the work was making her strong and full of energy. At her afternoon water break, Elaine settled down on the steps next to her.

"So, did you enjoy your pear last night?"

"To tell you the truth, I don't think I've ever enjoyed a piece of fruit the way I did that pear. It was amazing."

Elaine nodded.

"I gave all of those feelings and sensations, and all of my love, to Conn. I don't know if they reached her, but I felt better for doing it." Leigh heard her voice fade as she thought of Conn.

"Did you feel her around you today?"

Leigh started to ask just how that would happen, but stopped. "Well, actually, I saw Lobo this morning. And I swear I felt her then. Maybe he just reminds me of her."

"Ah. That would explain a lot. I've just come from speaking with the Lama, and he said to thank you for all of your work. He told me you had received a message that it was time to go."

"What? But I…didn't…I thought I could stay a while longer." Leigh's stomach tightened in anticipation. "What did he say?"

"That your destiny lies outside of this property. Beyond that, he didn't comment."

"But when? Today? Should I call someone to come and pick me up?"

Elaine smiled and squeezed her hand. "Don't worry, Leigh. You'll know. I'm sure you've observed that time is somewhat different around here. Think about what you need to do and make your preparations. There's no hurry unless you feel it. Pay attention to your ability to know, and follow it. I'll see you at dinner."

Leigh immediately went to the phone used by the community members and waited until it was her turn, then dialed Ally's number.

"Hey, Ally. It's Leigh."

"I can't believe it. We must have thought each other up. I was just trying to figure out a way to reach you."

"Why?" Leigh held her breath.

"Jess called. The person they suspected of being Conn's kidnapper was found dead, along with two of his guards. The local paper called it murder-suicide, but they think Conn got away. Leigh? Are you there?"

Leigh's heart pounded as she managed to say, "I—yes! What else? Have they heard from her?"

"No, they hadn't as of Jess's phone call, but she promised to let me know. There's more she can't talk about, I'm sure. Why did you call?"

"What? Oh! I…it's time for me to leave the monastery. Could you pick me up?"

She could hear the excitement in Ally's voice. "When do you want me there? Will you stay with me?"

Leigh grinned into the phone. "Tomorrow morning, and I'd love to stay with you. See you soon."

She hung up and went to her room, her head and spirits buzzing. After gathering her bath gear, she almost skipped down to the showers and was back within fifteen minutes. Lying in bed, she carefully reviewed the day's events.

*The game's afoot, I can feel it.* She looked around the room, mentally planning how to pack. The shelf to the right of the cold-water sink had various papers on it, mostly things the sheriff had given her. Padding over to the shelf, she picked up the envelope containing her personal possessions recovered from the Audi, then took it back to her bed. Once tucked under her covers, she broke the seal and dumped the contents onto her lap. There it was, the magic cell phone.

She tried to turn it on, but the battery was dead. *Damn.* Pawing through the other articles, she found the charger and plugged it into a wall outlet. She knew it wouldn't work at the monastery, but when Ally picked her up…

In the dark she took a pear she'd picked that day and concentrated on sending her love to Conn, then told her to be careful and come back to her. Sleep was slow to come.

## Chapter Twenty-four

The stench of garbage and raw sewage filled the narrow alley as Conn crouched between two piles of the stuff, waiting, and held her AK-47 close to her body, ready to use. A shadow eased into the alley and crept in her direction. She stood.

"Find anything interesting?" Despite the smell, Conn was hungry. They hadn't eaten much in two days, and she'd been wishing for fresh fruit. They'd been on the streets for almost a week. At first, various members of Zehra's network had housed and fed them, but now both the police and her former captors were looking for them, and they had to wait until things calmed down to try to make contact again.

After Zehra produced some bread and dried fruit, and they shared the meal, Conn stole a glance at her liberator. The tiny woman was beautiful, with large brown eyes and mocha skin. She couldn't be over twenty-five.

"Zehra? Do you mind if I ask you a question?"

Cautious eyes regarded her. "What would you like to know?"

"Why did you do it? You were relatively safe, just bringing food. Why did you risk everything for someone you don't know? Now they'll kill you if we're captured. Why?"

Zehra was quiet for a moment. "I am Kashmiri. My family was killed, and I was raped and left for dead when I was twelve. I wandered for days, stealing food from starving or dead people. One day I happened upon a soldier who had grabbed a girl a few years older than me. I knew what he had planned for her. He had a knife in his belt, so when the soldier became occupied with her, I went up behind him and took the knife out of the belt. I pulled his head back by his hair and slit his throat. We ran away, and I've been running ever since."

"How old are you?"

"I am twenty-three. Very old for an unmarried woman, don't you think?" A small smile crept onto her face. She had beautiful, perfect teeth.

"I suppose it depends on what you think of marriage. How have you survived?"

Zehra shrugged. "At first, we almost didn't. But we made our way to larger towns, eventually to Karachi. Other women who understood our problem, mostly widows, took us in here and there, and we repaid them by foraging in soldier encampments and stealing food for them. But always we moved on, surviving by our wits and because we had each other.

"For a time, I found work as a servant for a wealthy British family stationed here. That's where I learned to speak and read English. The woman insisted I be included as she taught her own children. But they left because of the increasing violence, and we became smart in the ways of blending into a city and living without a family. We found others like us and developed a kind of group, to help each other."

"You and the girl you rescued that day," Conn asked, "what is her name? Are you still friends?"

"Her name was Shamina, and she's dead. She was caught, tortured, raped, and left to die. She waited for me to find her and died in my arms. Three years ago." Zehra hugged her knees to her body. "She was my lover."

The silence surrounded them. Finally, Conn gently touched her shoulder. "I'm so sorry. You must have loved her very much." They sat quietly for a while, with only the buzz of insistent flies to keep them company.

"Do you know who killed her?"

"Yes. I killed one of them in that room with you." She turned and looked at Conn. "So you see, I had my own reasons for rescuing you. Nidal was the one who ordered her murder, as revenge."

"Revenge for what?"

"For slitting his throat when he was trying to rape Shamina, many years ago. He wanted to finish what he had started and to find me. We have been a thorn in his side for a while. Our network has been providing information to whoever wanted to stop them, for a fee. It's how we survived. And his guards kept getting murdered for no apparent reason. When he captured Shamina, he tortured her to find out where I was, but she never told him."

"Have you killed everyone involved with her murder?"

"There is one more. Remember the guard who would leave you in the closet all day and take your food? The one who screamed at you in English one day when I was there? He's probably in charge of looking for us. He was Nidal's right-hand man for many years."

"What happens when you finally kill him?"

Shrugging, Zehra said, "I don't know. I don't really care. I want to get you out of here safely, collect the reward, and give it to my friends. Then—"

"Zehra."

"What is it?"

"When we get out of this mess, would you consider coming to America?"

Surprise registered on Zehra's face. Then she looked away, her expression thoughtful. "Shamina and I used to dream of America. We talked about how we would go to school and work at jobs that used our minds. We would make money and help our people. And we wouldn't be afraid. But it was just a dream."

"Look, your family and Shamina are gone, and you might only put your network of friends in danger by staying. Over there you could make the dream come true. Would Shamina want you to stay here and continue this life or be killed?"

A look of disbelief crossed Zehra's face. "You would do that for me? I have nothing. There is no reason for them to let me in. I am a murderer."

"Well, you do have something. You saved my life, and you have knowledge and information. Plenty of groups would sponsor you. You'd have your choice. At first it would be quite a culture shock for you, but you could help your friends from a safe place. You've earned it. Besides, I want you to meet someone."

"Who?"

"My Shamina. Her name is Leigh." Conn could see Zehra considering it. Finally, Zehra gave her a genuine smile, the first one Conn had seen from her. And in her eyes, Conn thought she saw something else: a flicker of hope.

"Perhaps. But first, we must figure a way out of here."

"Right. Let's find a place for the night. I really don't want to stay in this garbage dump much longer."

"Leigh. That is a pretty name," Zehra said as they cautiously crept out of the alley.

❖

Maggie was at her desk, leaning back in the chair. As she stared into space she thumped a pencil on her thigh, then flipped it to the desktop. She reached to her phone console and tapped in Jess's extension.

"This is Jess." The low voice sounded irritable.

"My office, now."

The voice perked up. "Yes, ma'am."

Maggie heard Jess before she saw her. "Come in. Close the door."

"Have we heard anything?"

"No, damn it! It's like they've disappeared off the face of the earth. The police are looking, but so is his organization and anyone else who wants to score a bundle of money for her capture. The problem is, she doesn't know who to trust. She probably can't get to us. I, for one, am sick of Rising Storm being half finished."

"Shit. I feel so helpless sitting here behind a stupid desk."

"Ever been to Karachi?"

Jess sat up straighter in the chair. "Yes. Several times."

"It's a dangerous place, getting worse every day. I have an idea, but it's got to be volunteer."

"Consider me volunteered. What is it?"

"Conn can't come to us, so we have to go to her. We gather up people she'll recognize and start being visible in Karachi. Outdoor cafés, bazaars, markets—anyplace they might go to blend in. I'm assuming she's still with the woman who we think helped her escape. She couldn't disappear for as long as she has without help."

"I've thought that, too. But time's running out. We need to hurry. They can't hide forever."

"We leave tonight. Phone whoever you can reach, and I'll make the arrangements for the trip. We'll work out logistics on the flight. Maybe we'll have people go to the open-air markets, places they have to go for food."

"Unless the accomplice does all the shopping," Jess said. "She wouldn't know the people."

They were quiet for a minute, then Jess suddenly snapped her fingers. "Maggie, what about Marina? She and Jen are still in Paris, and she's on the phone to me at least twice a day. What if she goes back to Karachi and does a live telecast? Lots of publicity, interviews with officials, put it on all the TV stations. Marina comes back!"

Maggie considered the plan. "That might be the best idea you've ever had. I'll call. We go to Paris first. We'll need lots of coverage and lots of eyes to try and find her in the crowd. Let's get busy. Remember, volunteers only, and no arm-twisting."

Jess almost tipped the chair over on her way to the door.

❖

As they drove away from the monastery, Ally announced, "Leigh, Jess is gone."

Leigh whipped her head around. "What do you mean, gone?"

"She left me a short message that she had some business to attend to and would be out of touch for a few days. She said she loved me, and that was it." Ally's voice was filled with anxiety and something else. Abruptly she slammed her hand on the steering wheel. "Damn it to hell! I feel so fucking helpless! You know this business has to do with Conn. It'll be dangerous, and I have to just sit here and wait like some idiot."

"Maybe not." Leigh reached into the backseat, pulled the small duffel bag into her lap, and rummaged until she found the cell phone.

"The magic phone. It's encrypted and programmed with all sorts of secure numbers. Now we play Dialing for Dollars and try to get some information. Keep driving until I get a strong signal."

Ally jammed on the gas until Leigh said, "Pull over, this is good."

Leigh tried Conn's number, and when a message said she would be out of touch for a few days, she ended the call abruptly.

"Shit. That was a mistake." Leigh couldn't keep her voice from shaking. "It was Conn's voice."

"Keep trying," Ally gently urged.

Next was Maggie. Same message. Then Pat. Same.

"They're all in on whatever this is. It's got to be about Conn."

They sat staring out the windshield for a few more minutes until Ally mumbled, "Any more numbers in that piece-of-crap phone?"

Leigh focused on it, willing it to give her something, anything.

"Well, I have one more—Jen's number when she was in Paris, waiting for Marina. But I'm sure they're gone by now. What the hell, let's try it. It's all I've got left."

After two rings someone answered. "Is Jen Stryker there? Leigh Grove." She glanced at Ally with hope. "Jen? It's Leigh. I'm fine. Are you with Marina? Where is she? No, I haven't seen anything on TV. *What?* When?"

Leigh roughly grabbed Ally's arm to look at her watch.

"How many hours from now? Just…how many hours? I'll call you soon." She flipped the phone closed and looked at Ally. "Is your passport current?"

"Well, yeah…"

"We're going to Paris. Drive."

❖

When Conn stirred in the cramped storage closet they'd managed to break into the night before, her stomach was gurgling. She tried to stretch, but ran first into the wall and then into Zehra, who was curled up next to her. Zehra sat up, immediately banging her head on a bucket hanging above her. Conn was pretty sure she swore in Urdu.

"Good morning. Lovely day today," Conn said. "I think I'll go for a run, then take a long, hot shower and eat a rather large breakfast. Or a small one, or *any* one."

The room was dark, the only light coming through slits in the wood. She found Zehra in the shadows and could tell she was smiling.

"Yes, that sounds delightful. Although I would do without the run, as you say. But a hot bath? Pure luxury. And food—now, that sounds good."

"Do we have any money left?"

"Not much. We're going to have to steal soon. Wait here and I'll go." She started to get up, but Conn held her back.

"I have got to get out of here. I need to feel the sun, for just a bit. These brown lenses won't be good for more than another day, so let me come with you. Please, I can't stand it."

Zehra slowly nodded, then gave strict orders. "We go to the market. You stand on the periphery with your gun ready, so people are afraid to look at you. Keep the sunglasses on and the cloth pulled around your face. Look in the windows of the shops. Only for a short while, then back in here until night. And *don't* talk to anyone."

Conn cringed as she recalled the near disaster she'd caused several days ago by trying to use a few words of Urdu and thereby immediately identifying herself as a Westerner. They'd managed to disappear into the crowd before soldiers closed in on the screaming shopkeeper on the other side of the city.

"Trust me, I won't make a sound."

They carefully approached an outdoor market place, and Zehra stopped to bargain with one of the vendors. Conn let her eyes wander to the wall of televisions in a shop on the periphery of the market, all tuned to the same station. A picture flashed on the screen.

Suddenly Conn was riveted to the monitors. A file photo of Marina appeared, then cut to an interview. She was talking and looking at the camera. Then an old photo of Conn flashed on the screen. *Holy shit! What are they saying?*

Someone touched her arm and she spun, almost knocking Zehra down. Zehra grabbed her arm and righted herself, then indicated they should leave immediately.

Conn followed her back to their tiny closet, ecstatic. "I saw Marina on TV, and they put up a photo of me, too. We have to find out what they were saying."

Zehra pulled off the burqa and smiled excitedly at her. "No need. These flyers were all over the place." She handed Conn a piece of paper with Marina's picture on it.

"What does it say?"

"She will do a live broadcast from the central marketplace tomorrow at noon. She wants to come back to Pakistan and show the people she's not afraid. There will be interviews with politicians and such. She's taking a grave risk."

"This is it! They're looking for us, and this is how we get out safely. In front of the world. Yes!" She took her contact lenses out and threw them on the floor. Her eyes felt gritty, but she was relieved. "We're getting out of here!"

Zehra apparently didn't share her enthusiasm.

"What's wrong? We're going home."

"They don't know me. I'll probably be shot and no one will notice." Zehra looked resigned to her fate. "I'll take you there and then leave. That's the best way."

"No. You're coming with me to America. I promised, and I always keep my promises. I want you to meet some friends of mine, and I want you to meet Leigh. Besides, you can't stay here."

Zehra sighed, evidently still doubtful. "I look forward to meeting Leigh. So, then, tomorrow we go?"

"Tomorrow we go."

❖

As it had been through most of the night, at the break of dawn the square where the interview was to be televised was a mass of activity. Marina's network had agreed to feed the images to major networks from all over the world. It wasn't a hard sell; they could smell blood.

Jess held a clipboard and wore a headset, ostensibly working as a sound technician. She was connected not only to the broadcast but, with the flip of a switch, to the other members of her team. She constantly scanned the audience of curious people who had been gathering since the setup began.

Aside from the uniformed guards ringing the set, armed volunteers—people whom Conn might recognize—were interspersed with the real reporters, some of whom had interviewed her in the past.

The sun rose in the sky as the activity picked up. Marina arrived under heavy guard at about ten o'clock and went into another trailer to have makeup applied and review the script. She met with the man who would be interviewing her, a colleague she'd known for years. They were both aware of the dangers and possibilities of the broadcast, and both wore Kevlar vests. They knew they'd be lucky to be shot where the vest was. Assassins aimed for the head. Permanent and dramatic.

"How are you doing, Marina?" her colleague asked her. "I'd be terribly nervous coming back here after all you've been through."

Marina chided him good-naturedly. "Sounds like the interview has already started, Aslam."

"Once a journalist, always a journalist, I guess." He shrugged. "But I really don't know if I could do what you are doing today."

"Between us? I'm terrified. I don't know if I would have done it if it weren't for the possibility of recovering Conn. She's like my daughter, Aslam."

"I didn't realize, but it certainly explains your willingness to come back here. I must thank you, though. Regardless of your reasons, it means a lot to the people that you don't show fear of these worthless individuals."

"I know. I was contemplating it before, but hadn't yet made the decision. Nothing like a little motivation, eh?" She thought of Conn and how much was at stake. "You know, I could ask you the same question. This broadcast could be very dangerous for you, too. We don't know what our terrorist friends have in mind for today. Why do it? You certainly are at the top of your game, so you could just sit back and send a lesser-known reporter."

He blushed slightly. With his thick, white hair and handsome Semitic features, he had represented his network for many years. "I guess I couldn't stand not being here. Sometimes sitting in a studio gets too comfortable. Besides, I'm tired of these terrorists hiding behind Islam as a reason for their greed and hatred. They have taken my religion and made it a mockery. This is my way of saying I will not tolerate it."

"You're a good man, Aslam."

A knock on the door told them it was ten minutes to airtime. Another knock yielded Maggie, who stepped in and shook their hands.

Marina immediately asked, "Any luck spotting her?"

"Not yet." Maggie shook her head. "If she's in the area she'll be around, though. She'll know this is her chance and make her way to us. I know it. The questions-from-the-audience segment is probably our best bet. Everyone knows what to do. I just hope we get to her before they do."

Jen opened the door to the suite and hugged Leigh fiercely. "How are you doing, Leigh? I heard you were hurt. Conn was beside herself with worry."

"I'm fine, Jen. I tried to get word to her that I was okay—did she know before she left?"

Jen shook her head. "No. But she knew you'd gotten away from them, so she told me you could take care of yourself."

When Jen saw Ally in the hall she let go of Leigh to greet her. "I apologize, you must be Ally. Leigh said she was bringing Jess's special friend."

Ally shyly came in and held out her hand to Jen, who pushed it aside and hugged her, too.

"We're all in this together now. I saw Jess yesterday, when they came to pick up Marina. She told me about you. Welcome."

They moved into the living room where the television had been on since Marina left. Several of the off-duty bodyguards were seated around the room, watching intently.

Jen filled her and Ally in. "There are guards everywhere near the television event in Karachi. Friends from every part of her life have volunteered to be there. Pat Hideo chartered a plane from Stryker Software—he said the limited number of seats in the plane forced him to turn away a lot of people. And, in case something went wrong, only those who had backup were permitted to go. No one with families. They thought Conn would want it that way."

Leigh was both pleased and worried to hear about all of the arrangements. "Good old Pat, he thinks of everything."

# CHAPTER TWENTY-FIVE

Shortly before the broadcast was scheduled to begin, with practiced movements and little effort, Zehra slipped through the perimeter unnoticed and unchecked and started working her way toward the area designated for those who had questions. As she paused and looked back to make sure Conn had gained entry, she noticed that quite a few taller individuals were granted passage. More verification that they were looking for Conn. She kept moving, stopping just outside of the desired area, where she waited for Conn to join her. After a few seconds she felt a presence behind her.

Conn glanced around, amazed at what she saw. She recognized at least four people in the audience, as well as Jess and several other "reporters." One of them was indeed a journalist, but from one of the driest technical magazines she'd ever read. The closest he'd ever come to international intrigue was reading the Sunday newspaper over coffee.

As she scanned the broadcast crew she spotted the young programmer from her company who had not known who she was when she met him. He was hauling cable and looking out at the audience. *My God, where did all these people come from?*

Realizing they were here to find her, she was so astonished she just stood there, gaping. All she had to do was make contact with one of them without causing a riot. She started to take a step in Jess's direction, but the pressure of a gun barrel against her back stopped her.

"Just stay where you are, Doctor, and no one will be hurt. I have people training their weapons on the crowd at this moment, and at my signal they will aim for Miss Kouros. Now we will back out of the audience, and you will once again be in my custody."

❖

The broadcast had begun, the lights blazing on the two reporters seated on the podium. The welcome and thanks were out of the way, and Marina was giving a brief message. The questions would come soon.

In the trailer, monitors displayed what the cameras showed as they panned the crowd. Maggie watched one camera and Pat the other.

"Stop camera two," Maggie suddenly ordered. "Go back. There. The tall one with the sunglasses and the lower face obscured. Zoom in. Look. She's moving her sunglasses down on her nose. That's it! Blue eyes. Get Jess over there."

The technician relayed the information.

"Wait! She's backing up. What? Zoom out, who's that next to her? Tell Jess it looks like someone has control of her. Behind and to the right side. Extreme caution."

❖

The questions had begun. As Zehra raised her hand and turned around to locate Conn, she saw her pull her sunglasses down and glance to her right. Following her gaze, Zehra saw who was beside her. She stormed past the two men in front of her and grabbed the microphone.

"Mr. Abdullah, I want to know why these terrorists are allowed to conduct business under our noses, right here during this broadcast."

The crowd grew silent.

After a few seconds Aslam Abdullah said, "What do you mean, madam?"

"The exchange captive, Dr. Constantina Stryker, is here in this audience and is being held by a terrorist named Farooq Syed. She is right there!"

With that she pointed to Conn and Syed, and pandemonium broke out. Conn pulled the headwear and the sunglasses off, revealing her eyes and hair, and Jess, who had been quietly working her way over to where Conn was, started shouting and pushing people out of the way. Someone landed on Syed's back and jerked him toward the ground, and his gun went off. The crowd panicked, some pushing to get closer, others trying to get out of the way, and guards rushed onto the podium and surrounded Marina and Abdullah just as gunfire broke out.

The cameras, abandoned by their frightened operators, remained focused on the spot where Conn was last seen as someone shouted, "She's hit! She's hit! Get help!" The screen went dark.

❖

In a room in Paris all eyes were trained on the blank screen. No one spoke. After a few minutes, a test pattern appeared, and after another minute a very flustered announcer came on the air and spoke in hushed tones.

"Ah, ladies and gentlemen, we have lost our remote feed from Karachi, Pakistan. We are trying to reestablish it. From what we can gather, there has been a terrorist attack on the broadcast. There are reports of gunfire, almost certainly injuries, and perhaps deaths. We cannot confirm that at this time, but will provide information as soon as we have it. Please stay tuned."

Forty minutes later, Leigh went to the bathroom. She closed the door, leaned heavily on it, and wept. After a moment she splashed some water on her face and went out to watch the television again. As she walked into the room, someone was turning up the volume.

"Breaking news. We have heard from our remote broadcast crew that our broadcasters, Aslam Abdullah and Marina Kouros, are safe and unharmed. However, there are unconfirmed reports of several injuries and two deaths."

No one moved. "We have confirmed that several of the crew working on the broadcast were injured in the melee, and the alleged terrorist, Farooq Syed, is dead as a result of wounds inflicted by the crowd. And we have been told that Dr. Constantina Stryker, held captive in exchange for the release of Marina Kouros, has died as a result of injuries inflicted by Syed before his death, although that has not been confirmed. More information as it is available." As he spoke, footage showed a blood-soaked figure being carried through the crowd.

Rising from the sofa, Leigh started toward the bedroom, but collapsed before she reached the door.

Before dawn thirty-six hours later, Leigh wandered from room to room. Registering the guards still there, she vaguely wondered why they hadn't left.

She walked out on the balcony facing the Eiffel Tower and stared blindly at the twinkling city lights and the sky growing lighter behind them. Looking down as she heard vehicles approach, she noticed activity at the entrance and turned away, not caring, amazed that life went on when, for her, everything had come to a shattering halt.

Back in her room she lay on the bed, staring at the ceiling as tears rolled out of her eyes, and she did nothing to stop them. She heard some bustling in the other room, then a quiet knock on her door. With a sigh, realizing it was probably Marina coming to tell her about Conn, she faced the window. She didn't really want to see anyone, but knew she had to eventually.

"Come in." She closed her eyes.

The door opened and in a few seconds clicked shut. Someone walked over to the bed and stood beside it.

Then, quietly, "First thought…last thought…always in my heart."

Leigh bolted upright in the bed. "Conn?"

"Hi, honey, I'm home."

Leigh looked at the figure standing beside her—thinner than when they had last seen each other, but definitely Conn.

"My God! You're alive!" Leigh pulled her down and across her body so she lay beside her, then examined Conn in the half-light. She carefully felt her lover's body, testing to be sure she wasn't dreaming. Conn lay still.

Leigh was crying, tears streaming down her face.

"Would you like to count fingers and toes?"

"Oh, God! Do I need to?"

Conn chuckled softly. "No, my love, all present and accounted for."

"I thought I'd lost you, I thought you were gone. Are you okay? You were shot. You were dead. I love you so much!"

"I love you, too, darling. I thought I'd lost you, too. But we're fine, we have our future together, we're fine."

They held each other, kissing and whispering reassurances.

Finally Leigh was calm enough to ask, "What about Jess? Is she with you?"

"Yes, I imagine Ally and Jess are doing the same thing we're doing. Darling?"

Leigh pulled back so she could look in Conn's eyes, her beautiful eyes, eyes that were right there in front of her. "Yes. The answer is yes."

Conn grinned. "You always do that to me. Make me forget what I was going to ask."

After a few more seconds, each lost in the other's presence, she said, "Oh! I want you to meet someone, Zehra, the woman who saved my life. I got her out of Pakistan because she, well, she wouldn't have lasted much longer there. I'll explain later."

"Of course! Where is she? Is the poor thing standing out there by herself?"

"No. Jen and Marina took her over immediately so I could come talk to you alone. She'd already developed a bond with Marina from before the exchange, but I imagine she's wondering where I am. I'm her only real connection."

"Let's go meet her."

Conn took Leigh's hand and led her into the living room, where Marina was fussing over Zehra and Jen was happily banging around in the kitchen. The atmosphere was absolutely joyous. Even the usually stony-faced bodyguards were joking around and smiling.

When Conn brought Leigh into the room, the conversation stopped, and Zehra shyly stood and smiled.

Leigh momentarily let go of Conn's hand and went over to the young woman. *My God, she looks like a child.*

Behind her Conn said, "Leigh, this is Zehra. She rescued me and helped get me out of Karachi. Zehra, this is Leigh, my life partner."

Zehra looked awkward, not really sure what to do, but Leigh didn't hesitate. She closed the distance between them, and as she hugged Zehra gently, through the too-large army-issued clothes she could feel how painfully thin the young woman was.

"Thank you. I can never thank you enough for bringing her back to me. You're part of our family now. Welcome."

Jen, who had been watching from the doorway with shining eyes, announced, "Come on, everyone, let's eat! It's time to celebrate!"

❖

Finally, following four hours of furious activity, they all flew to the States on a military transport, then drove directly to a secured building in D.C. normally used for debriefing.

Left alone together in a waiting room, Ally and Leigh stared tiredly at each other. "Hard to believe we were in sleepy little Mendocino just a few days ago," Ally said. "Someday I'd like to go back to Paris under less stressful conditions." Then she whispered, "I can't wait to get to Jess's apartment and have her all to myself for a while. How about you?"

Leigh rolled her eyes. "Do you think it will ever happen?"

Just then Conn and Jess arrived from a meeting with Maggie, looking haggard but happy.

When Conn asked, "Will what ever happen?" Leigh smiled.

"We were just discussing how long it's been since we've had a chance to really just sit down and talk. Alone, the two of us." Leigh let her eyes feast on her love.

"Oh." Conn blushed and turned to Jess, who was grinning. "Funny you should say that. We were just arranging for a few days of, um, R and R. You know, time off before the debriefing begins and before they announce the exaggerated report of my death." She paused. "Well, 'arranging' isn't quite the word. Begging is more like it."

"Did you get it? Permission?" Leigh asked. "Because if you didn't, let me try. Really." She set her jaw.

Conn bowed her head and Leigh couldn't see her eyes. "Well, yes and no. Yes, we can have two days, but Maggie insisted on one condition."

Through clenched teeth Leigh asked, "What is the condition?"

"We can't leave the condo. Don't want to risk being seen by reporters and such. Is that okay?"

Leigh took a moment to let the words sink in and narrowed her eyes at Conn. "Can't leave? Can anyone come in?"

"No. No, we'll be on our own. The place is already stocked with food. Can't even see Maggie and Jen or Zehra. Security, you know."

"So we'll be forced to entertain ourselves."

Conn put her hands behind her back and bounced on the balls of her feet. "Yup. Entertain ourselves."

Leigh started to say something to Ally and Jess, but when she looked she saw that they had disappeared, so she turned her attention back to Conn. "When does this R and R begin?"

"As soon as we can hike ourselves over to the condo. What do you think?"

Leigh gave Conn a look. "The sooner the better. Before I embarrass us both in front of your crew."

"Oh, my. Guess we'd better get going."

"What about Zehra?"

"Not to worry, it's all taken care of. As a matter of fact, Zehra talked Maggie into the final okay and insisted on no interruptions."

Leigh was sure she and Zehra were going to be very good friends. She whispered to Conn, "I want you in my arms, naked, within thirty minutes. If not, I'll start without you," and finished her sentence with a tiny lick to her lover's ear. Then she disappeared out the door.

## Chapter Twenty-six

Twenty-six minutes later they finally dropped their luggage, closed the door, and locked it. The quiet of the condo, after all of the noise of the past few days, was borderline spooky.

"At the risk of sounding trite, alone at last," Conn said.

Leigh smiled shyly, put her arms around her lover's neck, and pulled her into a gentle kiss. Their lips and tongues explored tentatively, then with more insistence. They ended the embrace, breathless, and gazed at each other.

"Yup, still there," Leigh said. "You make my knees weak."

"And you make me lose my concentration."

"Come on, show me around. I've never been to your D.C. digs."

Conn took Leigh to every room of the condo, all of which were crowded with gadgets, computers, and telecommunication devices.

When Leigh slid her arm around Conn's waist and said, "Sweetie, if we're going to spend much time here, do you mind if I make it a little more like home and a little less like a launch site?" Conn felt a grin coming on.

"Sure! I just never…I've only used it to sleep and work. I never thought about it. You really want to be here with me?"

Leigh stared at her, unable to believe that Conn still didn't realize how much she loved her. They had been apart for over a month. Both had been pursued and almost killed. And both had experienced life-altering events. Yet they hadn't talked about any of it. And she didn't feel like talking. Not yet.

"Show me the master bedroom."

Though Leigh approved of Conn's professionally decorated bedroom, done in warm tones and featuring a king bed, she was much more interested in the master bathroom's large Jacuzzi tub. "Ah, just what I was looking for."

She immediately started running the water, then found towels and robes. "You want me to help you take your clothes off?"

Conn shook her head, unbuttoned her shirt, and dropped it on the floor. Then Leigh opened the top button of her own jeans and saw a bit of fire flicker in Conn's eyes. Conn unsnapped her bra and let it slip to the cool tile.

Leigh's breath caught. Conn was thinner, but her breasts were just as spectacular. She tore her eyes away to look at her lover's face with its sly grin.

"Two can play at that game, missy." Leigh pulled her sweater and turtleneck off in one swoop and tossed them. No bra. Although they had stolen kisses and touches during the flight home, they hadn't actually been alone at all.

Conn breathed deeply and finished unzipping her pants, then let them fall to the floor, closing her eyes when Leigh noticed her leg. Imagining revulsion on Leigh's face, when she heard a small cry she opened them to see Leigh kneeling in front of her.

"Oh, baby, what did they do to you?" Leigh softly kissed the angry scar, then stood and gazed at Conn, eyes shining with emotion. She stepped out of her jeans and panties, then eased Conn's underwear down.

After gingerly sitting in the steaming water, Conn held out her hand for Leigh and settled her between her legs, pulling her back against her chest and wrapping her arms securely around her.

"Sometimes the thought of doing just this was the only thing that kept me sane. I was locked in a closet most of the time and replayed every moment with you, then wondered if you were alive and worried that you'd changed your mind."

Leigh rested her arms on top of Conn's. "Darling? Did you really doubt my love? Think that I was dead? Really?" It wasn't an accusation.

Conn hesitated, then answered, "No. At times I could feel you with me. Maybe I was in there too long, but I knew you were alive, and it wasn't just sensory deprivation. There were moments when the certainty of your love for me was all that I focused on, all that kept me together. We even…anyway, it was all that brought me home. You probably think I'm crazy."

Leigh sat forward and turned to Conn. "'Crazy' is the last word I'd ever use. You are the bravest, most wonderful woman in my world, and I believe that even more strongly now that we've been separated." After a moment, she took a large bath sponge from the side of the tub and squeezed water through it, then handed it to Conn. "Here, wash my back."

They washed and nuzzled for a while, slowly getting reacquainted with each other's bodies. When Leigh realized the water was tepid, she again turned to say something to a very quiet Conn and found her almost asleep.

Smiling, she tugged gently on a soft auburn curl. "Come on, sweetie. It's bedtime."

She hauled her out of the tub and dried her off, then wrapped a towel around herself. Leading Conn into the bedroom, she put her in the middle of the bed and covered her, then turned out the lights, crawled under the covers, and wrapped her body protectively around her lover's. A sleeping Conn snored softly and nestled into her arms. Leigh was asleep within seconds.

Conn stirred and started to turn over, only to hear a mewling protest close to her ear. She cracked an eye open, momentarily wondering if she had bumped into Zehra in their hiding spot. She sighed in relief and joy when she realized it was Leigh throwing a leg over hers. Relaxing into the closeness, she kissed Leigh's forehead. In response she got a satisfied grunt and a kiss just above her breast, then another on a familiar pulse point on her neck.

Leigh crawled on top of her, never opening her eyes. Her lips, however, kept moving, and her hands took their time exploring. Conn started to reach for Leigh only to find herself straddled and Leigh's hands holding hers down, out to her sides.

"No, mine. All mine. Wait your turn," Leigh said in a sleepy growl.

Conn gave herself over to the sensations of being touched and sucked, kneaded, and licked into a much-needed state. She felt Leigh press inside her and start moving against her thigh. Her lover was slick with passion, and Conn could tell she was close to the same explosion Conn was building to as Leigh increased the rhythmic intensity of her movements. At last, Leigh moved down to take her in her mouth and assault her every nerve fiber, and Conn exploded into a million stars, calling Leigh's name.

Leigh moved up to cradle her and give her gentle kisses, then held her tightly while Conn cried—while they both cried tears of relief and happiness.

After some time, Conn moved Leigh under her and made sweet love to her. She searched her body for favorite spots and reveled in the swollen wetness of Leigh's heat, slipping inside while she nipped and sucked on her beautiful breasts. They kissed and whispered until Leigh could talk no longer and Conn held her as she came again and again, her body completely given over to Conn's touch.

They fell asleep entwined and didn't move for several more hours, when the need for the physical reassurance of the other rose once more, and once more they claimed each other's bodies.

## Chapter Twenty-seven

Two weeks later Conn sat on the edge of the bathtub while Leigh put the finishing touches on her makeup. She groused, "If I look like I rent by the hour, I…"

Leigh handed her a mirror, and Conn appraised her image. "You know, this isn't half bad. You say you've done this before?"

Leigh ignored her. "Okay, pucker up, time for lipstick."

Conn dutifully puckered and for her efforts received a searing kiss. When they broke she caught her breath. "I thought I was puckering for lipstick! Mind you, I'm not one to complain."

"Yeah, well, once I have this on you it will be a while before I get to kiss you like that, so, you know, got to take advantage of the opportunity. Right?" There was a decided glint in her eye.

"Um, right. How long do you think this thing is going to take? I really don't like big parties."

This "thing" was a gala event in Conn's honor, sponsored by the senators from California. Once news of her escape had been announced, she had become a national hero. The press had gobbled up the story that friends from all over the world had risked their lives to try and rescue her. At first she had resolutely resisted the event intended to honor her, but once she learned the scope of the effort, she gave in, making sure that Zehra was properly recognized as a freedom fighter, a valuable commodity that guaranteed her right to stay in the States.

What had started as a small gathering to privately thank those who had risked their lives to be in Karachi at that broadcast had morphed into a hot-ticket event for politicians from both sides of the aisle. And Conn was the prize heifer.

Conn studied Leigh. "Have you talked to your parents again?"

"Well, once Mom found out exactly who you were and who would be at the gala, I've gone from being disowned to her saying that maybe they'd be there." Leigh sighed. "It's all bullshit but, hey, can't wait for you to meet them."

Conn started for the bedroom to get dressed. "I hope they come." She stopped and nailed Leigh with a scorching look. "You know, I can be quite charming when I want to. If that fails, I can be quite rich and powerful." She shrugged. "Their choice."

Leigh shook her head. "That's my girl." Gaze moving upward, she said, "Thank you, thank you, thank you."

❖

Just before they left the apartment, Conn took Leigh's hands. "Leigh? I have a present for you, and I want you to wear it tonight."

"Honey, you've already adorned me with earrings and a necklace. Isn't that enough? That must have set you back a fortune."

"Not quite. Will you?"

"You know the answer is always yes for you."

"Good." Conn fumbled in her vest pocket and produced a small box. "Here."

Leigh opened it, gasping at what she saw.

"Come on, the driver's waiting for us."

❖

The gala was in full swing when the guest of honor arrived. Cameras flashed and klieg lights shone as the limo pulled up to the entrance. Pat Hideo opened the door for Conn, who was stunning in her Armani tux and a deep purple vest with no shirt underneath. She waved and smiled dazzlingly at the crowd, then Leigh put out one long, beautiful leg and accepted Conn's hand. As she stood, her floor-length velvet gown the color of Conn's vest, the top of which gracefully covered her strategic areas, hugged her body perfectly. She wore diamond and sapphire earrings and a sapphire solitaire around her neck. And on the third finger of her left hand was a beautiful diamond and sapphire band, with a huge sapphire in the center.

"Hold on to me, it's going to be a roller coaster from now on," Conn whispered in her ear as the cameras flashed nonstop.

Leigh produced her best smile. "No problem."

She tucked her arm in Conn's, and they walked into the gala.

Leigh and Conn didn't stir until noon the next day, and that was under protest when an incessant banging on the front door made Leigh grab her pillow and cover her head.

"Who the hell is that at this hour of the morning?" Conn muttered. "What time is it?"

"Mmph."

Painfully, Conn opened her eyes and focused on the clock next to the bed. "Twelve. Noon. Shit."

The knocking persisted.

Conn croaked, "Never mind, *I'll* get it." She almost fell out of bed and was halfway to the door when she heard Leigh's muffled voice.

"Wait!"

Wincing, Conn managed, "What?"

"Naked."

Conn looked down. "Oh, yeah."

"Just a minute!" she yelled, then immediately grabbed her head.

The knocking stopped and Conn stumbled to the dresser and rummaged in the drawers for some sweats. Pulling out a second pair, she threw them at the semicomatose figure sitting up in the bed, who squeaked, "I'm so thirsty."

Conn stumbled to the door and looked through the peephole. Nothing. Then the knocking started again, which could mean only one thing.

"Good morning, Zehra," Conn said as she opened the door.

The tiny woman scampered in and made herself at home on the couch, where she promptly grabbed the remote and turned on the television. "Look, look. We're famous. Operation Rising Storm is famous. You and Leigh are famous. I'm famous. We're all over the news. Leigh! Leigh, come here and see!" She turned up the volume.

"Owowow! Turn it down, please!" Leigh appeared at the doorway at the same time that Conn came out of the kitchen with a glass of water and some aspirin.

Soon Zehra was talking animatedly to a half-dead Leigh, who was desperately trying to sit upright on the couch and appear interested, though a bit green.

Carefully shaking her head, Conn turned around and exchanged the aspirin for an aspirin-and-seltzer combination for Leigh, who looked up through bloodshot eyes and took it with thanks.

Zehra had also brought the newspapers and the latest issue of *People*, which had a picture of Conn and Leigh on the cover. The shot that seemed to be on continual loop on television showed them exiting the limo at the gala the night before. Leg and cleavage, jewelry, a look between them, big smiles said it all.

In desperation Leigh reached over and swiped the remote, muting the television. "Ah. Much better." She sighed. "Now, Zehra, since you seem to be in complete possession of your faculties, perhaps you'd briefly summarize last night's events and the media's interpretation of those events." The effort of speaking must have exhausted Leigh, because she slowly listed to the side and ended up half lying on the sofa, legs still on the floor.

"I agree," Conn said. "Somewhere around the third glass of champagne, everything got a bit fuzzy." She gently picked up her suffering lover and slid underneath her upper half, cradling her head. Now that Leigh had a pillow, she seemed better.

"Well, it was all quite exciting. I probably met half of the most powerful people in the world! I actually had senators and congressmen want to have their pictures taken with me. Amazing. And then the president came and shook my hand! I was astonished! Photo flashes were going off all of the time!"

Conn closed her eyes and smiled. She didn't want to disillusion her young friend about being the hero du jour and a photo op for most of the politicians. She'd find that out for herself later.

"But I must say, many of them seemed more interested in the photographers than me."

Or sooner.

"I most enjoyed talking to the people who wore the purple sashes. They told me stories about their association with Conn and why they volunteered. I didn't realize that the nice young man who had jumped on Farooq's back and got him to shoot in the air actually works for you. I think he has a…a…"

Leigh croaked, "Crush."

"Exactly! A *crush* on Conn. Although, I must say, Leigh was so sweet to him when she hugged him and thanked him. Perhaps the crush now includes her, too."

Leigh moaned.

Undaunted, Zehra continued. "I particularly liked Pat Hideo and his partner Ted. After I returned his wallet we had a lovely conversation. He told me all about his friendship with—"

Conn was able to crack one eye open and said, "Wait. Wait. Back up a bit. The part about 'after I returned his wallet.'" She stared at Zehra, and even Leigh managed to lift her head and aim a red eyeball at her.

Zehra glanced down at her hands. "Well, I happen to know how to pick the pocket. It was a skill I learned in Karachi and was often the difference between eating and not eating. Anyway, at the party I picked a few and always returned their wallets." Zehra seemed quite pleased at that fact.

"You picked their pockets? Oh…God." Conn let her head fall back against the sofa cushion.

"What did you do to Pat?" Leigh asked.

"Well, you see, Pat was the only one who caught me! I like him. He's smart. And not so tall, so I can talk to him without hurting my neck. So he introduced me to Ted, who *is* tall, and we sat at a table and did the chatting for a while. Ted said he would drive out and visit when I am in California with Jen and Marina. Isn't that thoughtful?"

Leigh grunted.

"Who else did you notice, Zehra?" Conn asked. *Note to self: Break Zehra of picking the pocket.*

"Well, I really liked Ally's parents, and your father seemed pleasant. Leigh's parents seemed, um, uncomfortable a bit. Leigh, your mother is quite attractive. I can certainly see where you get your beauty. She watched you two together very often, especially when there were photographers around."

"Yeah. I felt her eyes boring into us a few times." Leigh picked up her legs and rolled into a ball, turning over to bury her face in Conn's hip and belly while Conn stroked her hair.

"Actually, I think your mother liked me," Conn said. "She was almost civil the few times we chatted."

"Yeah," Leigh added. "After she did a quick appraisal of the jewelry and the attention you were getting. You're probably her new best friend, her new daughter." Conn didn't miss the sadness in her voice.

Zehra said softly, "Perhaps it just takes a bit of getting used to, Leigh. In my country, I would have been killed for openly loving another woman. When she looked at you, I didn't see coldness. I saw confusion. Give it some time. It's probably overwhelming for her."

Continuing to stroke Leigh's hair, Conn said, "I think so, too, sweetie. Your mother's probably coping as best she can. You'll always be her daughter, no matter what. Maybe in time."

After a few moments of silence, Zehra announced, "Well, I must be going. We are flying to *California* today. Surfer dudes and naked women drinking beer and the like."

Conn and Leigh groaned, and Leigh, welded to the couch, said in a muffled voice, "Zehra, promise me when you get to California you'll stop watching television. Just find out for yourself about life out there. Okay? Besides, you're going to northern California. Surfer dudes and dudettes wear wet suits."

"What is this 'wet suit'?"

All she got from Leigh was a limp wave.

"You'll find out," Conn filled in. "Who's on the plane with you?"

"Let's see. Jen and Marina, of course. Ted. Ally. And those two friends of Jen's that came for the party. They told me all about Jen's house and how they helped to repair it. I'm looking forward to another plane ride, too."

"Have a safe trip, sweetie, and we'll see you soon. You can come stay with us for a while in Mendocino."

"Good. I'm looking forward to it. Well, see you guys!" She hesitated.

Leigh struggled to her feet and gave her a hug, and Conn followed suit. Zehra clung to her.

"Don't worry, Zehra. You'll be fine."

A single tear rolled down the young woman's face. "Sometimes, it gets to be so much. It feels a little lonely."

Gently hugging her, Conn said, "I know. Once you're with Jen and Marina out in California, things will settle down and you can take a look at your choices. It's a huge transition. Give yourself some time. Let me walk you back to Marina's apartment. Come on." She kept her arm protectively around Zehra's shoulders and walked her down the hall.

Leigh watched the two friends until she was distracted by the phone ringing. It was Marina, looking for Zehra.

"She and Conn are on their way to the apartment. I think she's a bit apprehensive."

"I'm not surprised," Marina answered. "She's been distracted with the newness of everything, but Conn has always been there. This is different."

"Marina? Should I be worried? I mean, Conn has been very wrapped up in making Zehra comfortable. I feel like a fool complaining, but other than the few days we had to ourselves after the rescue, we've pretty much been with Zehra. I mean, I love Zehra. She's wonderful. It's just…even when we're alone Conn's been…distant. I don't know what to do. God, I'm sorry to bother you with this."

"No, no, Jen and I were wondering how you were dealing with it. I think Conn just feels terribly responsible for bringing Zehra to America. She's trying to make it work for her. And she may be having a bit of a reentry problem herself. Give her time, sweetie. You're her one and only, trust me. I know the look. It's genetic."

Leigh smiled at Marina's reference to Jen. "Thanks, Marina. I love you. See you soon in California. Have a safe trip."

"I love you, too, honey. Don't worry. She'll come around."

"Yeah, I guess I'm being silly. Bye."

Fifteen minutes later, Leigh was in the kitchen listlessly cleaning the counter when Conn's arms slid around her and a kiss landed on her neck. Soft lips grazed her ear, and Conn murmured, "I understand I've been neglecting my love."

Leigh hung her head and knew she was blushing. "Oh. I didn't realize Marina would talk to you about it."

Turning Leigh around, Conn tilted her chin up. "Why didn't you say something to me?"

"I…understand. If the situation were reversed, I'd do the same thing. It's just…Conn, it was so hard to be away from you. So hard not knowing if you were even alive. I—"

Conn hugged her tightly and said, "There were times I could feel you with me. I knew you were there. It kept me going, Leigh. I would wake up feeling you around me. I can't explain it, I just knew in my heart."

Leigh gasped. *Of course*. She hugged Conn tightly for another moment, then pulled away, saying softly, "I'm going to get cleaned up. Then you. I have a gift for you." She kissed Conn lightly on the lips and disappeared into the bathroom.

Conn stared after her. "I wonder what she's up to now? And why I wasn't invited to the shower?" She busied herself in the bedroom, and soon Leigh reappeared in her robe, smelling fresh and smiling mysteriously at her.

"Now you. Hurry up! Chop-chop."

Needing only a friendly shove, Conn aimed for the bathroom.

Twenty minutes later she emerged clean and dry. The bedroom was dark, the blinds drawn, a few candles lit, and the delicate smell of incense in the air.

"Leigh? Where are you?"

"I'm here, behind you."

Conn turned to see Leigh, her robe loosely tied, revealing the right amount of everything.

"Get in bed, darling."

Conn shed her towel and climbed in.

"Lie down and close your eyes. Keep them closed. Promise."

"I promise." Conn lay there, tingling with anticipation, and felt Leigh get in bed next to her.

"Open your mouth."

Dutifully she did as Leigh said and felt a piece of food—fruit, being placed on her tongue.

"Taste it…slowly."

Conn closed her mouth and started to chew. "A pear. A wonderful pear. It's delicious." But there was more. Suddenly she was back in that closet in Pakistan, feeling Leigh all around her. She immediately opened her eyes. "Leigh! But how—"

"Hush. Close your eyes."

She snapped them shut again, wondering.

"Open your mouth."

This time her mouth was filled with incredible softness, still tasting of pear, but with the unmistakable feel of Leigh's skin, Leigh's nipple. Leigh.

She let her tongue taste and explore, her body move, her hands find all the right places. Leigh responded in kind, and together they healed the wounds of separation, fear, and uncertainty that had been plaguing them since their reunion.

Eventually, exhausted, candles extinguished, they lay in each other's arms.

"Welcome home, my love," Leigh said. "I've missed you."

Conn kissed one eyelid. "First thought." Then the other eyelid. "Last thought." Then Leigh's full lips. "Always in my heart."

She couldn't see the smile, but she knew it was there.

# About the Author

JLee Meyer utilizes her background in psychology and speech pathology in her work as an international communication consultant. Spending time in airports, planes, and hotel rooms allows her the opportunity to pursue two of her favorite passions: reading and writing lesbian fiction. JLee's hobbies are photography, hiking, tennis, and skiing, but she hasn't had time for any of them recently. Writing is her passion and learning this new craft has been a joy. Rising Storm is her third novel.

Visit JLee at her Web site, jleemeyer.com, or e-mail her at jlee@jleemeyer.com.

## Books Available From Bold Strokes Books

**Vulture's Kiss** by Justine Saracen. Archeologist Valerie Foret, heir to a terrifying task, returns in a powerful desert adventure set in Egypt and Jerusalem. (978-1-933110-87-5)

**Rising Storm** by JLee Meyer. The sequel to *First Instinct* takes our heroines on a dangerous journey instead of the honeymoon they'd planned. (978-1-933110-86-8)

**Not Single Enough** by Grace Lennox. A funny, sexy modern romance about two lonely women who bond over the unexpected and fall in love along the way. (978-1-933110-85-1)

**Such a Pretty Face** by Gabrielle Goldsby. A sexy, sometimes humorous, sometimes biting contemporary romance that gently exposes the damage to heart and soul when we fail to look beneath the surface for what truly matters. (978-1-933110-84-4)

**Second Season** by Ali Vali. A romance set in New Orleans amidst betrayal, Hurricane Katrina, and the new beginnings hardship and heartbreak sometimes make possible. (978-1-933110-83-7)

**Hearts Aflame** by Ronica Black. A poignant, erotic romance between a hard-driving businesswoman and a solitary vet. Packed with adventure and set in the harsh beauty of the Arizona countryside. (978-1-933110-82-0)

**Red Light** by JD Glass. Tori forges her path as an EMT in the New York City 911 system while discovering what matters most to herself and the woman she loves. (978-1-933110-81-3)

**Honor Under Siege** by Radclyffe. Secret Service agent Cameron Roberts struggles to protect her lover while searching for a traitor who just may be another woman with a claim on her heart. (978-1-933110-80-6)

**Dark Valentine** by Jennifer Fulton. Danger and desire fuel a high-stakes cat-and-mouse game when an attorney and an endangered witness team up to thwart a killer. (978-1-933110-79-0)

**Sequestered Hearts** by Erin Dutton. A popular artist suddenly goes into seclusion, a reluctant reporter wants to know why, and a heart locked away yearns to be set free. (978-1-933110-78-3)

**Erotic Interludes 5: Road Games**, ed. by Radclyffe and Stacia Seaman. Adventure, "sport," and sex on the road—hot stories of travel adventures and games of seduction. (978-1-933110-77-6)

**The Spanish Pearl** by Catherine Friend. On a trip to Spain, Kate Vincent is accidentally transported back in time—an epic saga spiced with humor, lust, and danger. (978-1-933110-76-9)

**Lady Knight** by L-J Baker. Loyalty and honor clash with love and ambition in a medieval world of magic when female knight Riannon meets Lady Eleanor. (978-1-933110-75-2)

**Dark Dreamer** by Jennifer Fulton. Best-selling horror author Rowe Devlin falls under the spell of psychic Phoebe Temple. A Dark Vista romance. (978-1-933110-74-5)

**Come and Get Me** by Julie Cannon. Elliott Foster isn't used to pursuing women, but alluring attorney Lauren Collier makes her change her mind. (978-1-933110-73-8)

**Blind Curves** by Diane and Jacob Anderson-Minshall. Private eye Yoshi Yakamota comes to the aid of her ex-lover Velvet Erickson in the first Blind Eye mystery. (978-1-933110-72-1)

**Dynasty of Rogues** by Jane Fletcher. It's hate at first sight for Ranger Riki Sadiq and her new patrol corporal, Tanya Coppelli—except for their undeniable attraction. (978-1-933110-71-4)

**Running With the Wind** by Nell Stark. Sailing instructor Corrie Marsten has signed off on love until she meets Quinn Davies—one woman she can't ignore. (978-1-933110-70-7)

**More Than Paradise** by Jennifer Fulton. Two women battle danger, risk all, and find in each other an unexpected ally and an unforgettable love. (978-1-933110-69-1)

**Flight Risk** by Kim Baldwin. For Blayne Keller, being in the wrong place at the wrong time just might turn out to be the best thing that ever happened to her. (978-1-933110-68-4)

**Rebel's Quest: Supreme Constellations Book Two** by Gun Brooke. On a world torn by war, two women discover a love that defies all boundaries. (978-1-933110-67-7)

**Punk and Zen** by JD Glass. Angst, sex, love, rock. Trace, Candace, Francesca…Samantha. Losing control—and finding the truth within. BSB Victory Editions. (1-933110-66-X)

**The Devil Unleashed** by Ali Vali. As the heat of violence rises, so does the passion. A Casey Clan crime saga. (1-933110-61-9)

**When Dreams Tremble** by Radclyffe. Two women whose lives turned out far differently than they'd once imagined discover that sometimes the shape of the future can only be found in the past. (1-933110-64-3)

**Stellium in Scorpio** by Andrews & Austin. The passionate reunion of two powerful women on the glitzy Las Vegas Strip, where everything is an illusion and love is a gamble. (1-933110-65-1)

**Burning Dreams** by Susan Smith. The chronicle of the challenges faced by a young drag king and an older woman who share a love "outside the bounds." (1-933110-62-7)

**Fresh Tracks** by Georgia Beers. Seven women, seven days. A lot can happen when old friends, lovers, and a new girl in town get together in the mountains. (1-933110-63-5)

**The Empress and the Acolyte** by Jane Fletcher. Jemeryl and Tevi fight to protect the very fabric of their world…time. Lyremouth Chronicles Book Three. (1-933110-60-0)

**First Instinct** by JLee Meyer. When high-stakes security fraud leads to murder, one woman flees for her life while another risks her heart to protect her. (1-933110-59-7)

**Erotic Interludes 4: Extreme Passions**, ed. by Radclyffe and Stacia Seaman. Thirty of today's hottest erotica writers set the pages aflame with love, lust, and steamy liaisons. (1-933110-58-9)

**Unexpected Ties** by Gina L. Dartt. With death before dessert, Kate Shannon and Nikki Harris are swept up in another tale of danger and romance. (1-933110-56-2)

**Broken Wings** by L-J Baker. When Rye Woods, a fairy, meets the beautiful dryad Flora Withe, her libido, as squashed and hidden as her wings, reawakens along with her heart. (1-933110-55-4)

**Combust the Sun** by Andrews & Austin. A Richfield and Rivers mystery set in L.A. Murder among the stars. (1-933110-52-X)

**Tristaine Rises** by Cate Culpepper. Brenna, Jesstin, and the Amazons of Tristaine face their greatest challenge for survival. (1-933110-50-3)

**Passion's Bright Fury** by Radclyffe. When a trauma surgeon and a filmmaker become reluctant allies on the battleground between life and death, passion strikes without warning. (1-933110-54-6)

**Sleep of Reason** by Rose Beecham. Nothing is as it seems when Detective Jude Devine finds herself caught up in a small-town soap opera. And her rocky relationship with forensic pathologist Dr. Mercy Westmoreland just got a lot harder. (1-933110-53-8)

**Grave Silence** by Rose Beecham. Detective Jude Devine's investigation of a series of ritual murders is complicated by her torrid affair with the golden girl of Southwestern forensic pathology, Dr. Mercy Westmoreland. (1-933110-25-2)

**Too Close to Touch** by Georgia Beers. Kylie O'Brien believes in true love and is willing to wait for it. It doesn't matter one damn bit that Gretchen, her new and off-limits boss, has a voice as rich and smooth as melted chocolate. It absolutely doesn't… (1-933110-47-3)

**Carly's Sound** by Ali Vali. Poppy Valente and Julia Johnson form a bond of friendship that lays the foundation for something more, until Poppy's past comes back to haunt her—literally. A poignant romance about love and renewal. (1-933110-45-7)

**Of Drag Kings and the Wheel of Fate** by Susan Smith. A blind date in a drag club leads to an unlikely romance. (1-933110-51-1)

**100th Generation** by Justine Saracen. Ancient curses, modern-day villains, and a most intriguing woman who keeps appearing when least expected lead archeologist Valerie Foret on the adventure of her life. (1-933110-48-1)

**The Traitor and the Chalice** by Jane Fletcher. Tevi and Jemeryl risk all in the race to uncover a traitor. The Lyremouth Chronicles Book Two. (1-933110-43-0)

**Whitewater Rendezvous** by Kim Baldwin. Two women on a wilderness kayak adventure—Chaz Herrick, a laid-back outdoorswoman, and Megan Maxwell, a workaholic news executive—discover that true love may be nothing at all like they imagined. (1-933110-38-4)

**Erotic Interludes 3: Lessons in Love**, ed. by Radclyffe and Stacia Seaman. Sign on for a class in love…the best lesbian erotica writers take us to "school." (1-9331100-39-2)

**Punk Like Me** by JD Glass. Twenty-one-year-old Nina writes lyrics and plays guitar in the rock band Adam's Rib, and she doesn't always play by the rules. And oh yeah—she has a way with the girls. (1-933110-40-6)

**Forever Found** by JLee Meyer. Can time, tragedy, and shattered trust destroy a love that seemed destined? When chance reunites two childhood friends separated by tragedy, the past resurfaces to determine the shape of their future. (1-933110-37-6)

**Sword of the Guardian** by Merry Shannon. Princess Shasta's bold new bodyguard has a secret that could change both of their lives. *He* is actually a *she*. A passionate romance filled with courtly intrigue, chivalry, and devotion. (1-933110-36-8)

**Sweet Creek** by Lee Lynch. A celebration of the enduring nature of love, friendship, and community in the quirky, heart-warming lesbian community of Waterfall Falls. (1-933110-29-5)

**Wild Abandon** by Ronica Black. From their first tumultuous meeting, Dr. Chandler Brogan and Officer Sarah Monroe are drawn together by their common obsessions—sex, speed, and danger. (1-933110-35-X)

**The Devil Inside** by Ali Vali. Derby Cain Casey, head of a New Orleans crime organization, runs the family business with guts and grit, and no one crosses her. No one, that is, until Emma Verde claims her heart and turns her world upside down. (1-933110-30-9)

**Chance** by Grace Lennox. At twenty-six, Chance Delaney decides her life isn't working, so she swaps it for a different one. What follows is the sexy, funny, touching story of two women who, in finding themselves, also find one another. (1-933110-31-7)

**Erotic Interludes 2: Stolen Moments**, ed. by Stacia Seaman and Radclyffe. Love on the run, in the office, in the shadows…Fast, furious, and almost too hot to handle. (1-933110-16-3)

**Turn Back Time** by Radclyffe. Pearce Rifkin and Wynter Thompson have nothing in common but a shared passion for surgery. They clash at every opportunity, especially when matters of the heart are suddenly at stake. (1-933110-34-1)

**Promising Hearts** by Radclyffe. Dr. Vance Phelps lost everything in the War Between the States and arrives in New Hope, Montana, with no hope of happiness and no desire for anything except forgetting—until she meets Mae, a frontier madam. (1-933110-44-9)

**Innocent Hearts** by Radclyffe. In a wild and unforgiving land, two women learn about love, passion, and the wonders of the heart. (1-933110-21-X)

**Protector of the Realm: Supreme Constellations Book One** by Gun Brooke. A space adventure filled with suspense and a daring intergalactic romance featuring Commodore Rae Jacelon and a stunning, but decidedly lethal Kellen O'Dal. (1-933110-26-0)

**Course of Action** by Gun Brooke. Actress Carolyn Black desperately wants the starring role in an upcoming film produced by Annelie Peterson. Just how far will she go for the dream part of a lifetime? (1-933110-22-8)

**Coffee Sonata** by Gun Brooke. Four women whose lives unexpectedly intersect in a small town by the sea have one thing in common—they all have secrets. (1-933110-41-4)

**The Temple at Landfall** by Jane Fletcher. An imprinter, one of Celaeno's most revered servants of the Goddess, is also a prisoner to the faith—until a Ranger frees her by claiming her heart. (1-933110-27-9)

**Rangers at Roadsend** by Jane Fletcher. Sergeant Chip Coppelli has learned to spot trouble coming, and that is exactly what she sees in her new recruit, Katryn Nagata. The Celaeno series. (1-933110-28-7)

**The Walls of Westernfort** by Jane Fletcher. All Temple Guard Natasha Ionadis wants is to serve the Goddess—until she falls in love with one of the rebels she is sworn to destroy. The Celaeno series. (1-933110-24-4)

**The Exile and the Sorcerer** by Jane Fletcher. First in the Lyremouth Chronicles. Tevi and a shy young sorcerer face monsters, magic, and the challenge of loving. (1-933110-32-5)

**Force of Nature** by Kim Baldwin. From tornados to forest fires, the forces of nature conspire to bring Gable McCoy and Erin Richards close to danger, and closer to each other. (1-933110-23-6)

**In Too Deep** by Ronica Black. Undercover homicide cop Erin McKenzie tracks a femme fatale who just might be a real killer…with love and danger hot on her heels. (1-933110-17-1)

**Hunter's Pursuit** by Kim Baldwin. A raging blizzard, a mountain hideaway, and a killer-for-hire set a scene for disaster—or desire—when Katarzyna Demetrious rescues a beautiful stranger. (1-933110-09-0)

**Erotic Interludes: Change of Pace** by Radclyffe. Twenty-five hot-wired encounters guaranteed to spark more than just your imagination. Erotica as you've always dreamed of it. (1-933110-07-4)

**Justice Served** by Radclyffe. Lieutenant Rebecca Frye and her lover, Dr. Catherine Rawlings, embark on a deadly game of hide-and-seek with an underworld kingpin who traffics in human souls. (1-933110-15-5)

**Justice in the Shadows** by Radclyffe. In a shadow world of secrets and lies, Detective Sergeant Rebecca Frye and her lover, Dr. Catherine Rawlings, join forces in the elusive search for justice. (1-933110-03-1)

**A Matter of Trust** by Radclyffe. JT Sloan is a cybersleuth who doesn't like attachments. Michael Lassiter is leaving her husband, and she needs Sloan's expertise to safeguard her company. It should just be business—but it turns into much more. (1-933110-33-3)

**Fated Love** by Radclyffe. Amidst the chaos and drama of a busy emergency room, two women must contend not only with the fragile nature of life, but also with the irresistible forces of fate. (1-933110-05-8)

**Storms of Change** by Radclyffe. In the continuing saga of the Provincetown Tales, duty and love are at odds as Reese and Tory face their greatest challenge. (1-933110-57-0)

**Distant Shores, Silent Thunder** by Radclyffe. Dr. Tory King—along with the women who love her—is forced to examine the boundaries of love, friendship, and the ties that transcend time. (1-933110-08-2)

**Beyond the Breakwater** by Radclyffe. One Provincetown summer, three women learn the true meaning of love, friendship, and family. (1-933110-06-6)

**Safe Harbor** by Radclyffe. A mysterious newcomer, a reclusive doctor, and a troubled gay teenager learn about love, friendship, and trust during one tumultuous summer in Provincetown. (1-933110-13-9)

**shadowland** by Radclyffe. In a world on the far edge of desire, two women are drawn together by power, passion, and dark pleasures. An erotic romance. (1-933110-11-2)

**Love's Masquerade** by Radclyffe. Plunged into the indistinguishable realms of fiction, fantasy, and hidden desires, Auden Frost is forced to question all she believes about the nature of love. (1-933110-14-7)

**Honor Reclaimed** by Radclyffe. In the aftermath of 9/11, Secret Service Agent Cameron Roberts and Blair Powell close ranks with a trusted few to find the would-be assassins who nearly claimed Blair's life. (1-933110-18-X)

**Honor Guards** by Radclyffe. In a wild flight for their lives, the president's daughter and those who are sworn to protect her wage a desperate struggle for survival. (1-933110-01-5)

**Love & Honor** by Radclyffe. The president's daughter and her lover are faced with difficult choices as they battle a tangled web of Washington intrigue for...love and honor. (1-933110-10-4)

**Honor Bound** by Radclyffe. Secret Service Agent Cameron Roberts and Blair Powell face political intrigue, a clandestine threat to Blair's safety, and the seemingly irreconcilable personal differences that force them ever farther apart. (1-933110-20-1)

**Above All, Honor** by Radclyffe. Secret Service Agent Cameron Roberts fights her desire for the one woman she can't have—Blair Powell, the daughter of the president of the United States. (1-933110-04-X)

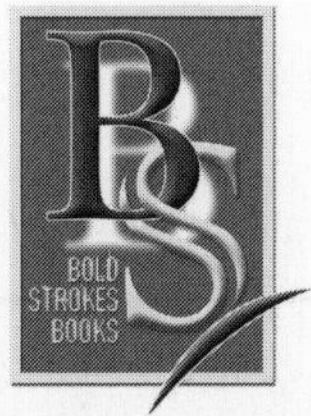